EXILES
ALIEN CADETS
BOOK 1

CORNELIA CLARK

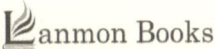anmon Books

Exiles/ Cornelia Clark

ISBN 979-8-88914-009-2 (paperback)

ISBN 979-8-88914-010-8 (hardback)

 Formatted with Vellum

To Lissa and Becca for inspiring my heroes
And Nathan for choosing my villains

"Then Daniel said to the king, "O king, live forever! My God sent his angel and shut the lions' mouths, and they have not harmed me, because I was found blameless before him; and also before you, O king, I have done no harm."

—DANIEL 6:21-22

SAM STOOD on the stage of the Crystal Cathedral in Los Angeles. Sweat trickled down his back as the front rows of the cathedral filled with members of the press. The ceiling held ten thousand panels of glass (he'd been told), and he felt as if he stood at the center of a giant electron microscope, every secret thought exposed. The reporters waited to hear him speak. They would want to pump the returning cadets for answers, but it wasn't to the press he felt most exposed. He felt as if the sun itself was a giant peering down at him, examining him for contamination. He hadn't been on Earth in over six years. Did he still belong here?

Sam shifted his weight as another crowd of reporters entered the rear doors and flooded down the aisles of the cathedral. They exclaimed and pointed and even called out to the cadets who stood at attention behind Sam. No one answered. Sam kept his face forward, neutral. He forced himself to breathe deeply, ignoring the anxious itch developing from his tension and his new uniform.

This homecoming press conference was important, and he was afraid it was already off to a bad start. The Spo liked the grand architecture of the Crystal Cathedral, and they didn't know, or maybe didn't care, that it had all the wrong overtones as their regional headquarters. On each wall the Spo had placed huge portraits, at least eight feet tall, of the cadets. Sam's face stared back at him from the second spot on the right, and the tattoo on his cheek looked horrible at that size. The posters had a distinctly fascist feel to them and Sam cringed as he saw a photographer snapping shots while he waited for the press conference to begin. One of Sam's tasks was to try and make the Spo more acceptable to humans, to begin to close the breach made by years of occupation, and they sure weren't making it easy.

"The posters?" Sam asked his mentor, Greg, when he jumped up on stage. "Where did those come from?"

Greg, whose real name was much harder to pronounce, was a typical Spo alien. He looked like the spawn of a praying mantis and a basketball player: tall, with lots of knees. Greg's face was as still as ever, but Sam knew he was concerned about this press conference. "They came from the printer located at 266 La Valente—"

"I mean, why? We didn't say anything about huge, ugly—"

"It is time to start," Greg interrupted. "You may continue later."

Cameramen were set up in the aisles and journalists filled the front rows. Greg crouched in front of the microphone, and his rubbery skin glistened in the sunlight. The Spo were not built like terrestrial insects, but their four legs and two arms gave them that regrettable similarity to a praying mantis. The eyestalks were particularly hard to get used to. They were twitchy and expressive and might have been cute on a cartoon alien.

"I can smell your excitement," Greg said to the reporters, in his tolerable English, "so I will not prison you in suspense. You will welcome the first cadets to return to Earth."

Sam sighed. Greg always spoke in commands when he felt uncertain. The aliens had actually asked Sam's advice on this press conference—The Return of the Cadets, etc.—but clearly his advice had not sunk in.

"This is Sam, one of the top cadets from Los Angeles. You will listen to him next. You may ask questions."

With this permission, the reporters immediately began shouting and Sam's stomach clenched tighter.

"Have you been allowed to contact your family?"

"What do your tattoos mean?"

"Did the Spo brainwash you?"

"Did they hurt you?"

Greg flexed his legs, shifting his weight off his front feet. Sam flicked two fingers at him, meaning, give me a second. The Spo allowed human newscasters a lot of freedom, since nothing they could do would give humanity enough of an edge to overthrow the Spo government. But, and this was a big but, Greg really wanted these press conferences for the cadets to go well. He was still Spo enough to attack someone who got belligerent, not realizing what horrible press that would be.

"Hang on. Hold your horses!" Sam said to the reporters, forcing a laugh. "I gotta say my stuff first. I am so glad to be back!" He waved to the cameras. "We all are. It's been a fascinating six years, but there's no place like home, right? The other cadet groups will return in the next few weeks. We said goodbye to them last month, and they can't wait to be home."

Sam turned back to the other forty cadets on stage. They stood in ranks, looking stiff and awkward. Greg should have released footage of the cadets stepping off the spaceship at LAX or settling into their dorm, Sam realized suddenly. This formal press conference was probably doomed from the start.

"Come on, guys, wave! We're home," Sam said.

They took a few seconds to break from ranks, but then the energy of the moment swept them along. They began waving and then smiling, stepping out of line to get a better look at the crowd.

Lights flashed as cameramen got digital shots, and the red lights of live video feeds rippled to life. Another frenzy of shouting rose from the crowd, but with a better tone. Less brainwashing talk. Sam smiled. He was performing now, and with a little luck, he could handle this crowd.

"One more thing!" Sam said, raising his hands for silence. "I still ought to say hi to my family—I think they live in Cloudcroft now. Hi Mom! Claudia!"

"What do you want to say to the world?" a reporter said.

"What was the planet like?"

"Why do you all look green?"

"Take it easy!" Sam said with a smile. "How about you?" He pointed to a short woman in the third row who'd shouted something simple.

"What do your tattoos mean?" she asked.

"Ah," he stroked the tattoo on his cheek like it was the best thing ever. "These identify us as leadership students of the Spo nation. Pretty cool, though I know my mom would never let me get a tattoo." He gave a sheepish smile. "Sorry, Mom."

There was a ripple of laughter, and then Sam pointed at another reporter. "You, purple tie."

"Are all of the children accounted for? We only count forty-one here."

"Oh, that's space travel. If you get seasick, you'll get spacesick, too. Nobody wanted to hurl on stage, so a few of them are still in the bathroom."

"No one was left on the Spo planet?" the reporter said.

Sam grimaced, he'd planned to avoid that question, but he'd walked right into it. "Unfortunately, one cadet died from an allergic reaction about a year ago. It was a tragic accident. I can't release his name until we contact his family. Other than that, we are all here and in the best shape of our lives."

"What is the Spo planet like?" another asked.

"Hot. Melting is a real cause of death there for the Spo. And dry as heck. Parts of it are habitable for humans. Sort of like Nevada."

"Can you speak their language now?" the same reporter asked.

"Ha! Can I?" Sam cleared his throat and then grated out a sentence in the Spo language. It buzzed in his nose and scraped at his throat.

"Learning the language was part of the reason we were taken," Sam explained. "You want to hear a joke? 'What's the difference between a Spo and a cricket?'"

Sam paused.

"Hairstyle."

More uncertain laughter.

Sam shrugged. "It's funnier in their language, I promise."

A tall lady in the back row raised her hand. Sam pointed at her.

"Why did they take you?" she said simply. There was silence after that question. This was the main one.

Sam looked right at the lady as he spoke, maintaining eye contact across the crowd. Sincerity.

"I know all the rumors that have gone around, but I promise you they weren't using us as hostages. They didn't lie about that. They didn't brainwash us to hate Earth or humanity, either. They taught us their language and culture, and introduced us to other alien cultures, also.

"For instance, if Earth joins the Galactic Council and hosts the Merith, we better keep them away from the cities, because they *hate* asphalt. The stuff makes them break out like poison ivy does to us." Sam shuddered for effect.

"Or then there's our use of makeup. The Spo flipped out when some of the girls started using lipstick sent in a food shipment. They thought it was a suicide rite. Oh, and they thought blonde women were infertile, can you imagine? We only cleared that one up a few weeks ago, because they didn't want to mention it." Sam laughed and the press laughed with him.

"There's a crowded galaxy out there, and now at least a few of us humans know about it. For the moment, our job is to improve communication between humanity and Spo. Eventually, when the Spo are done here, we hope to be liaisons with the rest of the galaxy."

If, Sam thought, we win Earth's trial first. You better hope we win or the Spo will be the least of our problems. Sam glanced back at Jonathan, a few feet away on the stage. Jonathan was going to be a primary witness in humanity's trial, and Sam didn't envy him the job.

Many of the reporters nodded slightly, receptive, but one guy raised a hand, thrusting his way forward in the aisle, not waiting for Sam to call on him.

"So what? You make a few jokes and we trade the Spooks for you, their pets?" he said.

"No—"

"Don't we get to choose? The Spo ruined our planet," the aggressive guy shouted, coming closer to the stage.

Sam felt impatient. When the aliens invaded, northern Europe had just been wiped off the map by a horrible terrorist attack on the Large Hadron Collider in Switzerland. The Spo had cleaned up that mess, and yes, killed some rebellious people in the process, but they hadn't done nearly as much damage as humans had.

"If you—" Sam said.

"I don't trust anybody that trusts them," the guy said. "Go back to Spo!"

Greg shifted from four feet to two, readiness stance.

Sam shook his head slightly. Stared at the guy.

"Are you done?" Sam demanded.

For a moment he thought the man would climb onto the stage.

"I'm done," he said finally.

"Fine. I'll lay it out for you," Sam said. "It was humans that killed nearly a billion Europeans in the Hadron explosion, wasn't it? Not the Spo. Trusting them or trusting me isn't simple; I'm not saying it is. But we cadets have a working knowledge of the galaxy and Earth's place in it. We want to help, and that can only be a good thing for Earth."

The questions started up again. Aggressive guy had poisoned the crowd.

"You are brainwashed!"

"What about the families they slaughtered?"

"You no longer believe in humanity?"

"What does it mean to believe in humanity?" Sam repeated, spreading his hands. "I believe that we exist. And I darn well hope we continue to exist, despite the state of our planet. I hope that you'll support us as we get reacquainted with Earth. We're your children; we're on your side."

Greg dipped his head forward, Sam's cue.

"Thank you. You'll be seeing a lot more of us in the future," Sam said. He stepped back, but not into formation.

Back on the chartered bus, Sam slumped into a seat while adrenaline faded from his system. The bus's tinted windows shielded him from the thronging reporters and growing crowd surging through the parking lot. They all shouted. Some had makeshift signs.

"SPO GO HOME!"

"Clear the Zone! Leave us alone!"

A rhyming chant rose erratically, "Spo. Go. Spo. Go." Others had questions.

"What did they do to you?"

"Where is Spo?"

"Can you help us?"

Some were offering help.

"They can't hurt you here!"

"You're home, come out!"

Maybe they expected one of the cadets to clamber out a window and fling themselves into the crowd.

Sam grimaced. He'd talk to Greg about getting a different set of security guys. This was Los Angeles. If any city should have security that knew how to handle celebrity situations, it was this one.

As Nat filed by him, Sam reached out to snag her hand.

"Sit with me," he said. "We're home."

Nat didn't make eye contact, just glanced out his window. "Good job out there," she said, brushing past him.

Sam sighed and leaned his head back. She hadn't changed her mind yet. She would though; they had years and years ahead of them. He'd imagined introducing her to his mother, his sister. She was proof that his life hadn't been intolerable while he was gone. Even that had fallen a part in the last year.

Would his mother even recognize him?

The last time Sam saw her, she was screaming at the aliens who had come to collect him. His dad had been at work—the Spo made infrastructure jobs mandatory even in the midst of their takeover—and his sister had been frozen on the couch in their living room. She'd been home from college the summer of the cataclysm, so she'd been stuck there the following months. And Sam had cowered before the terrifying Spo aliens, who ever so calmly held an energy weapon on his mom while they removed him to an armored car.

The Spo had needed to collect the children firmly, of course. None of the cadets' parents could have understood what a great chance this was until it was too late; all they saw were scary aliens with four legs and an exoskeleton. Someday, Sam hoped to explain to his mom that the Spo were quite reasonable, once you got to know them. But he wasn't sure when that would happen.

Greg clambered awkwardly up the bus steps, and the bus driver closed the door behind him. They slowly inched out of the parking lot, the yells of the crowd eventually fading behind them.

The cadets would live on a Spo campus in Los Angeles their first year back and Sam was secretly relieved to avoid an immediate reunion. The thought of seeing his mom, or his sister, gave him a feeling close to panic. It was one thing to wave at cameras and say hello, that was acting. What would his family really think of him?

Sam closed his eyes and let the sun beat on his closed eyelids. He'd exposed enough of his soul today.

SHARA PAUSED in the mall food court to watch the cadets on the news. She couldn't see her target until the one known as Greg moved away from the microphone. For a moment he stood center screen, but then the camera started panning the length of the stage, and he was gone again. She could rank all the cadets by age, importance, and vulnerability, but she was a little curious how they would act on TV.

The cadets wore new uniforms, Shara noted, but they were terrible. Like prison jumpsuits in baby pastels, and they looked awful on TV.

Shara stroked her emerald green sweater. She'd only been human for a few weeks, and she loved their sense of texture. The Crosspoint and the Merith both had more sensitive eyes than humans, for seeing heat gradients in darkness—but she was willing to bet that nobody saw or felt better colors. And she never had to give it up. Her species could only transfer bodies once, and she'd done it. Her new body was cute and small and she got to keep it.

When Sam and Greg wrapped up the press conference, Shara went to the next store on her list. She needed a wine bottle to make a bomb. Or no, not a bomb, a Molotov cocktail the humans called it. She just needed it to splash and burn, should be fairly simple.

She'd only been looking for two and half minutes when a store clerk approached her.

"Can I help you find something in particular?" he said.

He was hot; Shara liked his curly brown hair and squinty, little eyes. Maybe she could... Focus! Shara told herself. The hormones in her body kept distracting her.

"Can you help me find a bottle that'll break easily, with good alcohol inside?"

"Um. For a wedding or something? Is that why you need it to break?" he asked.

Shara smiled. "I want to fill it with gasoline and throw it at someone."

His cute little eyes shifted uncomfortably. "I don't think..."

"Just kidding!" Shara said. "It's for a celebration. It'd be great if it tasted good, and if it burns well that'd be even better. It's a Vegan holiday thing." Shara's superior had drilled her in convenient cultural knowledge.

The guy laughed. "Uh, okay. That's weird, but I can probably help you. Some of the champagnes come in thin bottles, and they should have enough alcohol content to do what you need."

He steered her down another aisle, and even took her back to the front for a few free samples when she couldn't make up her mind. Eventually she left with a Blanc de Noir and a pleasant buzz. She stopped at a gas station on the way back to her apartment and filled up a gas can.

Now all she had to do was pick a shirt to sacrifice as a wick. Her buzz started to slip away as she faced her closet. Maybe the tan V-neck... if it wasn't so nubby and wonderful. Shara ran her delicate fingers over her clothes slowly. Someday when her assignment was done, after humanity lost their trial and her people lived here, she would treat herself to a whole new wardrobe.

2

SAM'S CALVES burned as he and the other cadets jogged down the lawn at Pepperdine University. He could see the ocean, half a mile away, across the highway. The sky was a cloudless green, the water grayish blue with ash.

When terrorists sabotaged the Hadron collider and caused the cataclysm that had killed so many people, all those irradiated particles dispersed into the atmosphere and the ocean. Spo technology mostly scrubbed the atmosphere, but the colors were different.

He hoped Greg wouldn't jog them down by the beach today, though. They weren't up to it. Armen lurched along next to him, his head dipping with each jarring step. Melanie was just in front of them. She was usually the chipmunk of the group, but the transition to Earth's atmosphere was weighing her down. Sam tried to remind them how to breathe correctly, to avoid over-oxygenation, but Armen shook his head, still sucking air like an asthmatic.

Greg brought them diagonally across the grounds to the corner of Malibu Canyon Road and the Pacific Coast Highway, PCH. The light turned red as they approached and Greg halted on the sidewalk.

Melanie grabbed Sam's arm as they stopped, doubled over and

panting. Her brown hair was coming out of its ponytail; strands of it stuck to her face and fell past the tattoo on her cheek.

"Physical strength, important to survival," Greg said to them. "Survival is sanity!"

"Survival is sanity," chanted Sam.

"Survival is sanity!" Greg shouted.

"Survival is sanity!" they repeated. Sam could hear Armen, Melanie, Nat, Downy, and all the others yelling with him.

Greg nodded, and began running as the crossing sign changed to WALK.

A yellow Mustang squealed to a halt at the intersection. The driver's mouth hung open as he watched Greg bound in front of him, and he groped for his phone, holding it up to snap a picture of Greg in the street. The Mustang guy must be a tourist, Sam thought. There were still a few of those, even though LA plummeted in popularity when the Spo made it their global headquarters.

The driver took a picture of Sam and his friends, too. The tattoo on each of their cheeks displayed what they were. Spo cadets. The newscasters had already dubbed Pepperdine the 'alien academy.'

"Don't quit, Sam," his friend Armen muttered. "Remember, Snickers are sanity."

"Right. Idiot."

Greg jogged them through a huge parking lot on the other side of the highway toward the water. It was one of those gargantuan parking lots for beach visitors, with section labels so people would remember where they parked. There were only a few cars in it now, although July was perfect beach weather.

A general moan trickled through the group when Greg left the asphalt and they started across the sand.

Half an hour later they started back up the hill to Pepperdine. Sam was getting a bit of a runner's high now, but he ran at the rear of the group with Armen, who clearly wasn't on a high. Greg headed straight towards their dorm, but Sam saw Nat veer off to run past the tower at the front of campus.

Sam grunted to Armen and followed her. By the time he caught up, she'd stopped. Sam pounded to a stop next to her, in front of the Theme Tower. She was standing off the path, staring at the tower with her arms wrapped around herself. The tower had no purpose now; it was several stories high and about six foot square, sporting a huge, empty cross on the front. It could be lit from within, making the cross visible for miles around. Pepperdine's had been a Christian university.

But Nat wasn't looking at the cross.

The base of the tower was defaced. A huge yin yang, in red paint, was swirled on the wall. Sam remembered his sister wearing the symbol on bracelets and stuff. Asian, meant peace or tranquility or something? He couldn't remember. He did know they were black and white. This yin yang, in red paint that was drying brown, looked messy. Long drips and smears made the circle appear to be melting, dripping onto the ground. Nat rubbed her mouth, and then spat. Sam saw with surprise that she'd thrown up on the ground nearby.

Sam stood next to her for a moment, and then put his arm around her. She looked cold, after all. From this angle he could see that the next wall said, "Die, now," in the same dark red.

"That's nasty," Sam said. "Somebody else angry with the Spo, I guess. We knew it would be a problem."

Nat shook her head. "Go around," she said.

Sam frowned. He took his arm away from her and circled the tower. The yin yang was on his left. "Die, now," was scrawled on the next wall. The wall after that held a sketchy picture that might have been a Spo killing a person. Or maybe it was a Spo and a human making out. Sam squinted at it. Maybe a human cutting off a Spo's head. The figures were strangely drawn. Sam was no criminal profiler, but it disturbed him. The details were unclear but still managed to scream violence and passion. Whoever painted them didn't see the world the same way Sam did.

Sam forced himself to complete the circle. On the back wall of the tower, facing campus, were two slaughtered sheep. Not just slaughtered, but dismembered. And skinned. Parts of them were scattered on the ground before the tower, and their pelts, clotted wool and skin, were taped on the wall with duct tape. Some of the wool was stained with blood. The perpetrator must have used the wool to paint the other sides of the tower.

Sam didn't throw up, but he turned away and stared back toward the ocean for a few minutes. He breathed deeply of the fresh sea air and let his stomach settle. And his mind. He didn't blame Nat for throwing up. The sheep slaughter was disgusting on a deep level. Sam ate meat, he didn't think it was wrong to slaughter animals for food, but something about this wrenched his gut.

Pull it together, Sam, he told himself. You've been trained for analysis. Why exactly is this scary? He walked away from the dead sheep, back to Nat. He didn't speak to her, but just looked at the yin yang symbol for a while. Then he circled and looked at the other three walls again.

The violence in the killing was a rational reason to be upset. But some reptile part of his brain was telling him that he and Nat should run. Get under cover, out of the open.

Sam started to tabulate the parts that disturbed him. The sheep, of course, and particularly the chaos of the dismemberment. The wacko who did this should have placed them in an orderly arrangement. Or placed a piece at each corner of the tower. Or something.

If he didn't want to do anything with the pieces, why did he cut them apart? He didn't have to do it to skin the sheep.

The yin yang. It was a fairly benign symbol. Not a swastika or an upside down cross or anything that your average American would find intimidating. Heck, a McDonald's M might have conveyed more.

"Die now." That was just boring. It was trite and didn't fit the visual creativity used for the rest of it. It didn't even have an exclamation point, just a period. That had to be weird.

Nat started circling with him.

"We should go talk to Greg. This isn't a normal hate message."

Sam started to rub the small of Nat's back, but she moved away from him.

"Don't do that, Sam."

"I wasn't—sorry, Nat. I miss you. You're not going to let Greg's stupid plan get in the way forever are you?"

"No, but... how can I not? They've controlled everything in our lives Sam. Everything. I can't let them control this too."

She shivered and backed up a step. "I need to get cleaned up. Will you tell Greg about this?"

THAT AFTERNOON SAM showered off in the dorm. Grey sand ran down his legs and made silt lines around the drain. Greg had called the local police to report the graffiti/animal blood on the tower, and now some unlucky grounds crew guys were cleaning it up. Greg took the threat seriously, but advised Sam not to be overly concerned.

"The Spo fascination with sheep has been widely publicized. I'll get a Spo investigator to look into it, but I suspect the rage is aimed at the Spo, not the cadets."

Armen and Downy were already showered off, but they lingered in the large bathroom. Armen put on deodorant, and Downy crouched near the sinks rubbing engine oil in his joint crevices and chattering. Downy was small for a Spo at about six feet tall. His skin was slick like a McDonald's toy and he smelled like a tire shop, which the engine oil only enhanced.

Spo faces, when relaxed, looked like they were smiling. It didn't mean they were happy, but gave them a cheerful animal look—like a dolphin. Of course, when one of them threatened you with death for noncompliance that same half smile became extremely creepy.

"You know what guys?" Downy said. "I want to go to a petting zoo in La Brea tomorrow. It sounds very great. Goats, pigs, chickens, even an emo." He rubbed the thick oil into his second pair of knees.

"I think you mean emu," Sam said. "At least I hope you do. And if you get that oil on my clothes I'll put sand in your bed."

Downy flicked a hand, spattering drops of oil toward Sam, who jumped backward.

"Hold still," Downy said, "It would only improve your smell."

Sam grabbed his clothes off the counter. "If we're going to talk about smell—what did you eat this morning? I almost puked during Greg's debriefing."

"I drank root beer," Downy said simply. "It is fantastic."

Sam groaned while he brushed his teeth. "Please, please Downy. Stick to Spo food. You're my roommate, you owe me."

Armen laughed. "That's why none of us would take him. It's your own fault, Sam."

Sam and Downy went down the hall to their room, where Downy dropped to his mattress on the floor. Downy wasn't a bad roommate, really. Just smelly. When Sam was fully dressed, Downy hoisted himself off the mattress and walked with him down to Greg's office for a meeting.

"So, what do you think? Did I pass at the Cathedral?" Sam asked.

"I hope, dud. Dud, is that right?" Downy asked.

"Dude—friend, cool buddy."

"Ah. I think so, dude. Your species is very aggressive. I was told so, but it is different to see it."

"You should talk. Your species owns half the galaxy."

"It is our winning personalities," Downy said, turning green with pleasure.

Sam slapped the back of Downy's head affectionately. "Crazy alien," he said.

Downy flicked Sam with the smooth side of a claw. "Look who's talking."

Sam followed him into Greg's office, wiping his grin away.

Greg was a seasoned warrior of the Spo nation, with a long, half melted scar of battle on his face. Sam stood and Downy crouched at attention when they entered. Greg motioned for them to sit. He was pale lavender—extremely tired or disgusted.

Six years ago, when Sam and a bunch of other terrified kids were loaded onto a Spo spaceship, an alien met them in the loading bay.

"You," he said, gesturing to the first boy in line. "What is a common male name?"

The boy just looked at him, the giant four-legged alien.

"Come now," the alien said. "What is your grandfather's name?"

"Um.... Greg?"

"Acceptable. I will be Officer Greg. I will be your teacher. Please follow me."

And that was that. It was typical Greg, as they learned later. He didn't waste any time. He chose an acceptable name and went with it. Armen said if he took a last name, it would be Acceptable.

Downy was just the opposite. He'd picked their brains about their favorite names and watched hours of TV. He almost chose Cinema as his name, but then he'd seen a Downy commercial with a little teddy bear flopping around on a pile of white, fluffy towels. He fell in love with it. He was Downy from then on.

Greg turned on the lamp behind his desk.

"The police want a statement about the tower vandalism, Sam. I've already given mine. Call them this evening," Greg said.

"Why?" Sam asked.

"They don't like the timing. Our arrival, animal killing."

"Surely they don't think we did it?"

"No. I don't think so. Don't concern yourself. We need to talk about your performance at the Cathedral."

Sam grimaced. "How'd I do?"

"You did extremely well," Greg said. "You are our best manipulator, after all. That's why I've slotted you for most of the press events in the next few weeks."

"I—Manipulator? You've never called me that before."

"We've discussed your strengths many times," he said impatiently. "You read humans extremely well, you discern weaknesses—"

"You said I was a natural communicator, that I was good at steering a crowd toward a common viewpoint."

"Exactly. A manipulator. I do not see why we are having this conversation," Greg said. His eyestalks twitched.

"Just...don't call me a manipulator, okay? It has bad overtones." A cold feeling seeped up Sam's back. He knew he shouldn't take Greg's word choice too seriously, the alien didn't understand English nuances, but somehow this assessment scared him.

"The riots in the Midwest stopped," Greg added.

Sam blinked. "Riots?"

"Yes, some protestors were killed a few weeks ago, but the riots have stopped now, because of your return. They're waiting to see what happens. That's why we spaced out the cadets' return—Los Angeles, Sao Paolo, Hong Kong, Moscow... We've got a little time, probably a matter of weeks, before the rioting resumes." Greg paused. "You're part of our team now, Sam. We showed you to the world as our human spokesperson, and there is no turning back. Not for you. Not for us. From now on you will be apprised of the major obstacles in our path."

"I already was on your team," Sam said.

"I appreciate that," Greg said, turning muddy purple, "but you haven't been challenged yet. It'll be harder to support us now that you're home."

"You mean with all the accusations of brainwashing?"

"We did brainwash you, Sam," Greg said slowly.

Sam glanced at Downy. Was this some kind of test? "What—in what way?"

Downy looked as baffled as Sam.

"We took you away from your home as a child. Essentially you were a prisoner of war. We taught you from a position of complete power. That's one method of brainwashing."

"Is it—did you lie to me?"

"No. But something that is true to us is not necessarily true for humans. In their eyes, we've taught you nothing but lies."

"I guess I knew that already," Sam said.

"Yes. But you haven't felt it. You assumed that you'd be a hero, or at least a popular celebrity, but they're going to hate you, too. Their fascination and pity for you won't last long. Then they'll get angry."

"And humans are stupid," Downy added helpfully.

"Thanks," Sam said. "Any advice?"

Greg grimaced. "You'll find your way, I'm sure. You're dismissed. Downy, please stay. I have a communication from your father."

Sam rose to go. Downy's father was the Spo emperor, and Sam for sure didn't rank high enough to listen in on that.

Downy was one the emperor's younger sons and Sam had heard that Downy chose to attach himself to Greg to become an expert on humans.

Sam hesitated at the door. "Has anyone contacted Paolo's family yet, to give them his things?" he asked. "I had to tell the press that one cadet died, and all the cadet families are going to be nuts until they figure out who."

"That's taken care of," Greg said.

"I would like permission to call them. I'm sure they want to know about Paolo, the last few years before he died. Like how he loved diving in the chemical groves..."

"It is unnecessary. His family died eight months ago."

Sam felt punched in the gut. "All of them? There's not anybody?"

"They died in the firestorm that took out La Paz."

"So—what? There's no one to tell Paolo is dead?"

"At least they won't suffer his loss," Greg said. "You're dismissed."

3

CLAUDIA HEARD the TV turn on in the clinic lobby as she wheeled the sedated bulldog into an examining room.

"Could you turn that down?" she yelled to the receptionist. She hated hearing the news while she worked, particularly Monday morning, when she already felt depressed. The TV quieted, and then her receptionist was at the door.

"Claudia, did you see the footage of the Spo today?" she said. "They're showing more about..."

Claudia blew some hair out of her face. "I've got to do a colonoscopy on this bulldog before his owner gets back. Feels like he's totally blocked, or possibly an advanced edema."

"Oh my gosh, you didn't turn on the TV yesterday? The cadets from Los Angeles are back! Wasn't your brother one of those kids the aliens took?"

Claudia fumbled the syringe of painkiller for the dog, her fingers suddenly numb. She lunged and caught it before it hit the floor.

"They're back?" Claudia said. "When?"

"They just arrived yesterday. Go watch! I'll stay with the dog for a minute."

In the lobby, a small TV hung from a corner of the ceiling.

Claudia grabbed the remote off the counter, turning up the sound as she approached the screen. A young man stood confidently on the stage. He was very tall, almost as tall as the Spo next to him. A dark tattoo sprawled across his cheek, distorting the symmetry of his face. He had dark skin, sharp cheekbones, Native American... Could that be Sam?

"—learned a lot from the Spo. Their language, their culture—and we've taught them a lot about us."

Claudia squinted at the TV, trying to make the resolution higher by sheer willpower. Was that her brother? A bar of text scrolled across the bottom of the TV. "Weekend News: Children taken by Spo returned to Los Angeles. Head cadet known as "Sam" speaks of their capture. Says children have not been abused. Breaking news .....

Claudia gasped. "That's my brother," she said. "That's my brother. Oh God, that's Sam." Tears filled her eyes and she wiped them with her forearm.

"Really?" said the lady who'd brought in her Siamese cat, "The one answering questions?"

"Yeah."

He looked so different. He'd been a short thirteen year old when he was taken, hadn't hit his growth spurt yet. He was tall now, like their dad, and despite the crazy tattoo on his face, she could see traces of the little boy she remembered. Claudia had been home after her second year of college when he was taken. He wanted to play video games with her all summer, and she'd humored him a little. He was starting to get interesting, or at least not continually annoying. Then the Spo showed up, and she never saw him again.

Sam's interview was over all too soon for her, and yet not soon enough. She clenched her gloved hands into fists while he defended the Spo. At times over the years she'd obsessed about what was happening to him. She'd worked to reconcile herself to a changed Sam, should she ever see him again. But seeing it confirmed made her so angry she could hardly bear it.

Claudia took deep breaths, managing the pain of futility as she often had in the past. Deal with it, she repeated her mantra. You can't change it. Deal with it. When their father left, when Sam was taken, when her mother died a few years ago—Claudia had dealt with it. She was nothing if not resilient. She knew how to handle pain.

When the live broadcast was over, the news went back to weather coverage. "Evacuations are underway in northern China for the coming earthquake. Spo are predicting an 8.9 and complete loss of infrastructure..." Claudia muted the TV.

"They're in Los Angeles?" Claudia asked the cat lady. "Did they say at the beginning of the broadcast?"

"Yes, the first Spo said the cadets would live at Pepperdine University, in Malibu. I think it's only a few miles from their head-quarters," she said.

"Malibu..." Claudia went behind the counter and got on the computer. Tickets from Arizona to LAX weren't too expensive. Tourists didn't go to Los Angeles anymore.

"They don't want family to go yet," the lady added. "You're wanting to visit him, right? I'm sure I would too. But one of the Spo said no family yet. They want the kids to "readjust as a unit" or something. They're going to announce when the cadets' families can come visit."

Claudia gritted her teeth. Six years gone and she was supposed to just ignore the fact that her brother was home? Not so much.

SAM SAT in the back of a limousine next to Downy; Greg and Nat sat across from him. Nat leaned back in the corner and closed her eyes, her hands limp in her lap. They'd gone from press event to press event in the last forty-eight hours; Greg introducing his protégés to the world. Nat and Sam handled the press well, and Greg wanted them to start growing their face and name recognition for the future.

Jonathan was lucky, Sam thought, he got to lounge around campus until the trial, which admittedly, was enough stress to crush a Spo trounce, but at least he got to relax until then.

"I'd like you to handle this one," Greg said to Sam, as they approached the justice building. "The whole meeting is yours."

Nat lazily opened one eye.

"With the governor?" Sam asked.

"However you want to do it," Greg said.

"Huh." Sam ran his hands through his hair. "Will it sound ungrateful if I ask to go back to Spo instead?"

Greg growl-laughed. "After all the fuss you made about getting back here?"

Sam laughed. "I forgot what people were like."

Downy looked at Nat. "You weren't exactly alone."

"Nat isn't people," Sam said.

"Gee, thanks," Nat said, closing her eyes again. "Wake me when we get there."

She looked so comfortable, so relaxed. Sam wished he could sit next to her, hold her hand, and close his own eyes. He missed Nat.

When they were first taken for the exchange program, the girls, particularly the younger ones, naturally turned to her. Most of the girls were twelve or thirteen. Nat was fourteen, and old for her age. He couldn't remember how quickly it happened, but after the first year or two, she was the mom of the group.

He hadn't thought much about it until one day they were alone in the garden, and suddenly she began to cry. On Earth Sam would have backed off, but on Spo, what could he do? He remembered seeing his sister Claudia crying after school, and his mom comforting her. So Sam put his arm around Nat and when she stopped crying, they finished fertilizing the last row. Before she left, Nat asked him to talk to Greg about changing Melanie and Jia's room assignment. They were fighting and Nat thought it would be easier to move them than make them stop.

Sam did, and somehow he and Nat became a team.

The first time they left the Spo planet on a short trip to Merith, when Sam was sixteen and Nat eighteen, Sam maneuvered a spot for them in front of a wall window. Armen helped him keep the seats free, and Oh Li kept everyone in the other compartments. Sam even talked Greg into altering their jump trajectory slightly. When the ship jumped, the planet Merith leaped into the center of their window. As they watched, the sun slid around the edge of the planet, and Sam kissed her.

She'd been surprised, instinctively looking around like they might have an audience.

"It's just us," Sam said. "For once."

Nat had grinned, looking from Sam to the sunrise and back. "Very dramatic."

Sam touched her cheek, and they kissed again. She'd been happy and they'd held hands while the alien sun crept around the glowing planet.

"It sounds silly here, but, will you go out with me?" Sam said.

Nat squeezed his hand. "Yes. But you have to ask my father."

"Um."

"Just kidding," Nat said, and she'd kissed him once more before the ship began to swing into position.

Armen warned them when it was time to dock, and they joined the others. Sam kept Nat's hand while they went on their first tour of a Merith space station, even though Greg had gazed at them the better part of the day.

Sam jerked out of his reverie when the limo stopped at the curb. Nat opened her eyes and realized he was staring at her. She blinked and looked away, watched Downy climb out of the car.

Cameras flashed as they walked up the steps of the Justice Building in downtown Los Angeles. Stumps lined the pathway where trees were cut for firewood during the cold winter after the explosion. Only a few palm trees remained, too inconvenient and unpleasant to burn. Sam shook his head, he'd wasted the few minutes in the limo daydreaming instead of planning his tactics for this interview. Time to focus.

At the top of the steps, the interim governor of California awaited them. He had a kindly, serious expression pasted over gritted teeth. The man's jaw quivered as he forced himself to smoothly shake Greg's hand. This guy hated the Spo. That wouldn't help the press conference at all.

Sam placed himself between Greg and the governor as he shook hands, keeping his place when Greg would have moved him forward. Nat made her own conclusions, and greeted the mayor on his right, drawing him a step further from Greg and Downy.

He and Nat were a good team. They knew how to maneuver things to their advantage, without showing it. They learned it from the Spo, and they were good students.

The reporters still shouted, but Sam didn't respond to them. He clipped a wireless mike on his shirt. Nat made small talk with the governor, kept him turned away from the aliens.

"Will the Spo ever leave?" a man shouted.

"Tell us about the alien academy!"

"When will the Spo go home?"

"Quiet please," Sam said into the mike. He took a deep breath. "As tomorrow is the seventh anniversary of the Hadron explosion... I think it would be appropriate to have a time of prayer before we start." He saw the mayor's look of surprise but didn't wait to see if it was a good surprise or not.

Downy chuckled, but broke it off when Greg's eyestalks shifted in his direction.

Sam closed his eyes. "God in heaven..."

He kept it short. He wasn't trying to make a religious statement. Well, maybe a little. But mostly he just wanted to pray before he started.

Sam had prayed back on Spo, too. Some of the Spo thought the human cadets should be broken of their indigenous religions, but Greg disagreed. He'd argued that it was a cultural norm on Earth, and would help the cadets fit in better when they got back. Greg might be regretting that now.

"I know we've all lost extended family, good friends," Sam continued after his prayer. "This is the first anniversary I've been home for, and I'm glad to be here. It seems appropriate that this is the seventh year since the explosion. Seven has always been a number of change for humans. The ancient Greeks would fast for seven days in mourning. Creation ended after seven days. Human body chemistry changes completely every seven years. I'd like to think that this could be the beginning of a new cycle for us."

Sam paused, cleared his throat. Wow, that was good. He'd been pondering the seven-year thing last night when he fell asleep, but it hadn't gelled until just now. Maybe Greg was right about Sam's manipulation skills.

"I think..." Sam started.

A car leaped over the curb, engine shrieking. It jumped onto the sidewalk, roaring toward the front of the building. Reporters screamed, scrambling away. Sam's mind went blank, he couldn't figure out where to go.

The car swerved but didn't stop. It clipped a cameraman and spun him around. Then it went into a sharp turn, and Sam saw a hand emerge from the rear window as the car swerved back toward the street. The hand threw a bottle with a burning rag dangling from it.

The bottle arced straight into the wall next to Nat and shattered on the brick. Burning alcohol splashed out and her clothes ignited.

Sam shoved Nat off the steps and into the grass. The car sped off at an angle, throwing up clods of dirt, and bottoming out as it jumped off the curb back onto the road.

Sam fell on top of Nat. He pushed her back down as she screamed and tried to get to her feet.

"Roll!" Sam shouted. She thrashed on the ground, rubbing her burning pants in the damp grass. Sam roughly kept her down, helped her beat it all out. She must not have gotten much, Sam thought, or it would have been impossible. The bushes by the building still burned.

"Are you—" Sam said, but Greg pulled her up and grabbed Sam's arm. Her clothes were black and torn, but not burning.

"Come Downy!" Greg yelled. He pulled them both to the limo, shoving them inside. Nat fell on top of Sam. Greg jumped in over them, literally, and Downy swung in behind, his legs everywhere.

The limo zoomed forward as Nat got her knee off Sam's stomach and huddled in a seat, her breath coming in sobs.

"What about the others?" Sam said, staring out the rear window at the chaotic scene.

"Nat, you're hurt?" Greg asked.

Nat hunched over, hugging her knees. Her black eyes were big. She tried to speak, but couldn't catch her breath. She just shook her head and started shivering.

"The hospital," Greg said to the driver.

Nat shook her head again, but her painful breathing began to ease.

"It's not that bad, barely second degree maybe," she whispered. She sat up slightly. Her clothes were blackened and whole patches burned away, with red skin underneath. Downy reached a hand forward and Nat glared at him.

Greg nodded. "We have to be more careful. I didn't expect

this level of antagonism. We'll still go to the hospital. Burn ointment, at least."

"Do you think they wanted to hurt us? Or you?" Sam asked.

"Doesn't matter," Greg said. "We can't afford to let this violence escalate. Earth's trial is in two weeks, and these sort of attacks only prove humanity is unfit. The prosecutors have an easy enough job without any more evidence of human instability."

"Do you think this is related to the hate message?" Sam asked.

Greg pondered. "The style is different. The vandal worked alone. He wanted immediacy, knives, and an ambiguous message. This was at least two people. They wanted a public panic, a clear message, and distance from the crime."

Downy snorted.

"My guess, not the same."

"But the same motive," Sam said. "They hate you, and we keep getting in the way."

THE NEXT MORNING, Sam watched Nat move stiffly through the cafeteria to get breakfast. Nat's roommate carried her tray for her, as one of Nat's hands was still bandaged. The doctor at the hospital, acutely uncomfortable with Greg and Downy, had talked to Sam instead. The burns were minor, the doctor confirmed, except for one on her leg, and one on her left hand. Fortunately, the attackers didn't know enough or possibly care enough to make a serious Molotov cocktail. Unfortunately Nat was left-handed.

Sam held the doors for Nat as they went back to the dorm. Greg wanted them both in his office. He'd taken over the Resident Director's apartment on the bottom floor of the dorm. This morning Greg gestured them into his living room, and let them sit on the couch. Sam hadn't been in here since they moved in. Greg had decorated the walls with Spo melt glass, Rembrandt reprints, and empty picture frames. He'd used duct tape on the pictures.

"I've got an idea for a press event," Sam said, ignoring the empty picture frames. That conversation could take hours. "These attacks—the Molotov cocktail, the tower graffiti—they may not be related. Or they might be. Either way, these people view us as political targets. They think hurting us will hurt the Spo. I want to show them how human we are."

"How?" Greg asked.

"I want us to go to a mall, somewhere popular, famous—maybe Hollywood Square. We do some press stuff, and then we just hang out. Let the reporters get personal interviews, let them film us eating burgers and buying T-shirts."

Greg nodded, thoughtful. "I'll arrange something. It's such a human idea—shopping to avoid violence."

Sam looked at Nat's bandaged hand. "It couldn't hurt, right?"

"No. It is a good idea."

Greg paused for a moment. "However, Nat, I have something else to tell you. I learned that your family is back in Los Angeles. I thought you might want to see them."

Nat looked blank. "My family? You told me they live in Tokyo now. Plus, no family visits yet."

"They're here to get a lung transplant for your sister. The operation is tomorrow, so I've arranged for you to visit them tonight."

Sam had only twice seen Nat cry, and he didn't see it now. Her face tightened up, but she forced it to relax.

"Tonight? I guess... Yes. Okay. Are you going to take me?"

"I doubt they want to see me," Greg said, with a touch of humor. "Sam will go with you, and Leo and Mike, for security."

"I don't want Sam to come—"

"No arguments," Greg said. "Take it or leave it."

Nat shrugged with stiff shoulders. "Alright then."

SAM AND LEO leaned against a wall in the waiting room, next to a coke machine, watching Nat pace. Sam didn't blame Nat for not wanting him here. The cadets had all talked so much about seeing their families again, the first few years on Spo. Then, slowly, talk of home stopped. After a certain point, they all felt so removed from their past, nobody wanted to imagine seeing their parents.

Now the situation was thrust on Nat, ready or not, along with the fact that her sister was getting a dangerous operation.

Nat's breath came unevenly and she kept shaking her hands, like her fingers were falling asleep. When she tried to sign the visitor book at the front desk her bandaged hand shook so badly her name was illegible.

"It smells like Spo in here," Nat said, continuing to pace. "Did you notice that?"

"All the cleaning fluids," Sam said.

"Akemi has cystic fibrosis. I thought... I thought she might already be dead." Nat slowed her pacing. "I didn't want to ask. She's four years younger than me. The Spo wanted her for the exchange program—she was the one they came for. They didn't know about her disease. When they saw her, they changed their minds."

Sam knew some of this. Greg explained it to him one time. Nat was a few years older than the rest of the cadets, because they'd originally picked her sister. The way Greg told it, Nat demanded that they leave her sister alone. She volunteered to go in her place.

The door of the waiting room opened and a small Japanese man entered. He wore perfectly round glasses and a grey dress shirt buttoned to the top. For a moment Nat just stared at him.

"Suki?" he asked.

Sam had never heard that nickname. Her full name was Natsuki, but she'd always been Nat to them.

"Yes, yes, it is me... Father?" Nat bowed slightly, with a jerk.

"We never thought to see you now," Nat's father said. "We just told Akemi. She is very excited, we may need to sedate her." He stepped forward to hug Nat, and traced the tattoo on her cheek with his eyes. Nat stepped away from him.

"I don't want to make her worse. Greg told me I could come, but maybe I should go."

"I did not mean that. Her joy will do her good. Come in." He flicked a look at Sam and then Leo, who followed silently.

"I'll wait outside," Leo said, at Akemi's door. Sam wasn't sure what to do, but Nat met his eyes.

"You can come in," she said.

The hospital bed looked too big for the little girl in it. Nat told him her sister was sixteen, but she looked ten. Her black eyes were heavy, and she reached up with a weak hand to pull the oxygen line from her nose. An older Japanese lady sat on the other side of the bed, holding her hand.

"Suki?" Akemi said, her voice a whisper. "I can't believe it's you. You're back."

Nat approached the bed, but when she opened her mouth, nothing came out. She made a choking noise, and pressed her hand over her mouth.

"Are you alright?" Akemi asked, looking at the bandage covering her burned hand.

"Am I alright?" Nat gasped finally. "I'm fine! How are you? I didn't think I would ever... I'm so happy to see you!"

Nat leaned forward to give her a gentle hug.

"Hello, Mom," Nat said, reaching out to grasp her mother's hand.

"We are glad you are safe home," Nat's mom said. Her eyes were bloodshot. Nat nodded, and Sam could see her breathe deeply as she focused.

"Look at you," Nat said to Akemi, "I can't believe how big you are. How tall are you anyway?"

"Taller than you, I think. Who'd have thought it? How long can you stay?" Akemi said.

"Greg said I can stay until your surgery is...until there is news."

"And after?"

"I have to go back to Pepperdine, the alien academy, you

know. But maybe... I'm sure they'll let me see you at least once more before you go back to Japan. Let's not talk about that. Tell me about you."

Akemi made a crooked, smirky smile. "I'm gonna get my ears pierced next month. I'm a pretty good animae artist, and I have 2,000 followers on my blog. Those are the highlights."

Nat laughed. "That sounds just like you. I remember you using up my pastels, coloring the wall next to your mat."

"What about you?" Akemi asked, her eyes flashed to Sam for a moment.

"Umm."

Sam wondered what she would say. I caught a Molotov cocktail yesterday? Somebody slaughtered a sheep and smeared a hate message in it?

"Let's see. Highlights," Nat said. "I'm the best translator in my squad, in the whole group, actually. My mentor is a weird alien named Greg who likes oil paintings. My friend Sam says—Oh, this is Sam." Nat gestured at him.

Sam smiled at Akemi but didn't approach the bed. "Nice to meet you."

"You look super-hot on TV," Akemi said. "Just fyi. And you're actually as tall as you look."

Sam laughed and Nat smacked Akemi's hand.

"Straight to business, huh? I missed you, little girl."

Akemi grinned. "Hey, six years on an alien planet—there better have been some hot guys."

Their mother snorted. "I cannot believe you speak that way."

"You always were a flirt," Nat said to Akemi. "That obviously hasn't changed."

"So...can I ask why you're not green?" Akemi asked tentatively.

"Oh!' Nat stretched out her bare arm. Her skin was pale and clear, but she'd heard the news report about their strange color.

"The Spo have food we can eat. But it wasn't right, made some of us feel off. A few of us asked to grow Earth food. Tending the garden was up to us, so most of the cadets didn't bother, but a few of us did."

"Had to grow your own food..." Akemi trailed off, her nose flared with each breath.

"Here, put this back in," Nat said, handing her the oxygen tube. "And don't look so shocked. We didn't go hungry. And the others—they'll probably be back to normal in a few months."

More like a few years, Sam thought.

"Enough of that. You're getting your ears pierced next month?" Nat asked. "I distinctly recall that at fourteen I had *not* been allowed to get my ears pierced." She gestured at her unpunctured ear lobes with a smile.

Her mother smothered a sob.

"Oh Mom, I didn't mean to make you sad," Nat said, squeezing her hand.

"I wish I'd let you do more," her mom said. "I wish I had more memories with you. After your sacrifice..." she gestured helplessly. "I need a minute." She stood and went toward the door.

Akemi spoke, the oxygen line drooping over her mouth. "Take your time Mom. We've got at least a couple hours before my surgery." She looked back at her sister. "No crying now, Nat. Send Sam on an errand so we can have some girl talk."

Sam grinned. "Get her to tell you about our trip to Merith," he said. Nat grimaced and blushed, and Sam went to join Leo in the hallway.

Suddenly Sam was sixteen again, back on Spo. He had walked down the tall arched hallway to Greg's office. Nat was already been there, leaning against the wall. She'd still had her arm in a cast from falling out of an air car.

Greg started right in, as he tended to do. "The genetic testing we did last year was primarily to catch your diseases. However, it was also used to predict the best possible pairing of cadets, along with your extensive personality profiles."

"Um. What?" Sam asked.

"Pairing. Mating. Marriage. We think it would be best if many of the cadets are paired with each other. You have similar childhood experiences, and similar adult responsibilities."

Sam had been so slow to catch on. "You want the cadets to start marrying each other? What, you want us to break it to them? No way. They're still kids. Melanie just turned fourteen."

"She reached sexual maturity two years ago," Greg said.

"I know, but—I mean, I don't *know*," Sam said, looking at Nat, "but that doesn't matter. They're all too young."

"I understand your culture waits some years before mating. However, I did not mean all the cadets. I am speaking specifically of you and Nat." Greg nodded at the two of them.

Stunned silence.

"I understand that since the Merith trip you have been physically affectionate—"

"Oh wow. Stop," Sam said. "You think we're... sleeping... together, and..."

"Clearly I would not have allowed that," Greg said. "I meant pre-sexual affection. Which led us to think it was time you were mated."

Nat's face was tense and red, like it was just now in the hospital. She wouldn't meet Sam's eyes.

"That's not going to work," Nat finally said. "No way."

"Yeah, no way," Sam added, backing her up. "Absolutely not. I mean, Nat's great, but we're not—you can't *breed* us like poodles."

Greg frowned, turning a little pink with displeasure. "You and Nat are perfectly compatible for your species. Also the Asian phenotype is supposed to be acceptable to western standards. Your Native American gene type would blend with hers better than an Anglo-Saxon—"

Nat jumped to her feet. "Greg. Please, *please* don't go on and on about it. You cannot dictate who we m-mate with."

Greg looked surprised. "I thought, as you turn nineteen today, and Sam is already sixteen that you would be ready, both emotionally and physically, to begin a relationship—"

This time Sam stood abruptly. "Sorry, Greg. No. We're going. I mean, I'm going. I don't know if Nat—never mind." He strode out of the room and Nat followed him. She leaned against the wall in the hallway.

Sam paced down the hall, and then back again.

"Wow," he said. "Sometimes I almost forget he's an alien. Then—wow." He paced a little more. "I wonder if he has everybody matched up."

"Probably. That'll be awkward," Nat agreed.

"Yeah. But you and I—we don't have to be weird just because of this..." Sam stooped to look in her eyes, he'd just had a growth spurt and wasn't used to his height yet.

"No. We do not," Nat said. Sam nodded and leaned forward to kiss her, but she put up a hand. "Not... for now," she said slowly. "I need to go out. I'll see you later."

Of course, Nat had barely spoken to him after that.

Greg still hoped they would match up. He probably thought this hospital time would be a bonding experience, or perhaps he just wanted Nat's family to meet Sam. Greg was so stupid sometimes. More likely than not, Nat would be even more reluctant to talk to him after this.

ON THE RIDE HOME, Mike drove, Leo rode shotgun, and Sam and Nat sat quietly in the back of the limo. It seemed huge without two Spo taking up the space.

Nat leaned her head back against the seat and closed her eyes. "You have a sister, don't you?" she asked.

"Claudia. She's a few years older than me."

"Where does she live?"

"No idea. I grew up in Cloudcroft, New Mexico, near the Navajo reservation, moved to LA a year before the Spo came. She might have stayed, might have moved back. She was in college when I left."

Nat was silent for a minute.

"I hope you get to see her again."

5

CLAUDIA FLEW into the Long Beach airport, after getting a friend to cover for her at the animal clinic. Flying to Long Beach was cheaper than flying into LAX and only 30 miles away from Malibu, where she would find Sam. She'd bought tickets right after she saw him nearly catch on fire on the news.

Claudia stretched her hands toward the ceiling, breathing in through her nose, out through her mouth. She was an inch less than six feet and liked her height, except when she sat on a cramped airplane for three hours. Most of this flight she spent cleaning out the dried animal fluid under her fingernails, which effectively silenced the guy in 27B who kept trying to hit on her.

She'd only brought a carryon suitcase, so she went past the baggage claim without waiting. As she neared the glass doors, an uproar broke out behind her.

A huge cage was jammed in the baggage chute. It was shaped like an ordinary dog carrier, but big enough to carry a small donkey. Claudia nearly turned away but stopped when she saw a long tongue flick out of the cage. The tongue was thin, purple or dark blue, and at least a foot long.

Claudia worked with animals on a daily basis at the clinic in Santa Fe. She mostly saw pets: cats, dogs, iguanas, and the occasional snake. Once she got to treat a puma, a large cat similar to a mountain lion. She'd never seen anything like that tongue, in real life or video. She walked back to the baggage area.

An airport janitor tried to dislodge the cage with the end of a broom. She could see he was trying to be careful, so as not to send the cage careening to the floor, or to jab the broom through a hole and poke the animal.

He hooked the end gently in a hole and slowly pried the cage forward. He nearly had it out when a long, clawed finger slid out of the next hole, bent backward and sliced off the end of the broom.

Claudia gasped. A jointed finger—two, maybe three joints? The short end of the broom fell into the cage.

Quickly, with premeditated accuracy, the animal stuck the broom end through a hole in the door and used it to rotate the lock.

The janitor exclaimed and several people yelled at the sight of those fingers. The crowd fell silent, mesmerized by the brown slimy fingers, with two-inch claws like a cat, manipulating the lock. With amazing precision, the animal exerted pressure until the lock gave an audible snick.

The door swung open, and people started screaming. The crowd began to move, like a flushing toilet finally plunged and flowing out. Claudia pushed against the flow, wanting to see the animal; possibly she could help contain it.

The conveyer belt under the cage suddenly gained enough friction to slide the cage the last inch out of the hole and with a bump it slid down the short ramp and onto the oval baggage carrel. The animal leapt out of the cage with a yelping scream. It was brown and toad-like, with a fanged snout. For a moment it crouched on the edge of the moving belt. Then it launched itself onto a red suitcase and tore at it viciously.

People screamed in earnest now and threw themselves backwards, away from the creature. But those by the doors were too slow, and the toilet became plugged again. As the animal circled on the conveyor belt, devouring its red polyester prey, a tangled riot of bodies developed. People twisted and fell and scrambled away from the baggage carrel, getting stepped on by others trying to get out of the way.

"Move, move! Let me through!" a man cried from the other side of the crowd. He was tall, she could see him over the heads of the others.

He succeeded in reaching the conveyor, and she lost sight of him, but she saw a spray of blood spatter the crowd, as the beast switched targets. The screams became more terrified and finally the crowd was thinning and Claudia could see the beast again.

It crouched over the tall guy, drooling on him. Claudia took advantage of the sudden space to get closer. She grabbed the nearest brightly colored bag, a yellow one, and chucked it past the animal. As she hoped, it followed the bag, leaping on it and sliding into a row of rental kiosks with a crash. Claudia went for the guy. He huddled on the floor holding his hand against his chest, his white shirt and khaki pants stained with a moderate river of blood. His eyes were wide and he scooted up against an Avis rental car desk. At least he wasn't screaming. Probably in shock.

"Here, here, I'm a doctor," she said. "Let me see."

His gaze remained fixed for a moment, but then he blinked and made the effort to look at her.

"The bleeding..." he said. "Help me stop it."

She could see now that he was holding his wrist, not his hand, and that it was pulsing blood. The animal must have cut his radial artery, definitely the ulnar and radial veins too. She looked for the beast again. It wasn't with the yellow suitcase. She whipped her head around—didn't see it anywhere. A few people were still screaming and running around. People could be such idiots sometimes.

"Hey, you, lady!" she yelled at a flight attendant nearby, as Claudia unzipped her suitcase. The woman glanced at her, and Claudia said, "Yeah, you. Call 911 right now. Tell them to get animal control. And tell them a man is bleeding out and needs a surgeon stat." The woman nodded, but now Claudia was grabbing some athletic socks from her bag and didn't look at her.

"Thanks," the guy said, focusing on her face. "Kind of light-headed here." He laughed and then gasped. "I mean, catastrophe, pretty girl. Somebody has to faint."

Claudia gently pulled the guy's good hand away from his wrist, and inhaled sharply in fear. The animal had cut through almost his entire wrist. Only one bone and a few ligaments held his hand to his arm. She swallowed the sudden thickness at the back of her throat and gently wrapped a spare T-shirt around the wrist. With one pulse, a thick red splotch appeared. She wrapped a couple socks around it tightly. Another pulse, and the blood dripped from the bandage onto her jeans.

She held it in her hands, looking up in desperation, or perhaps for inspiration. On the rental counter stood a clear bowl full of blue plastic bracelets. The thick kind, half an inch wide and printed with the Avis logo.

Claudia slid the man down onto his back, and set his wounded arm on his chest. She unwrapped it as fast as she could. The bandage wasn't doing a lot of good anyway. A quick glance at his face told her he'd passed out. She carefully slipped one of the bracelets over his fingers, and then ever so carefully over the carnage that was his wrist. When she got it above the damage it was tight. She couldn't slip a finger under it. She looked at the counter again, and found a pen. She stuck it under the bracelet and started twisting it around. She turned it three times, as tight as she could get it. Those bracelets were good quality. She'd never noticed. It made a decent tourniquet.

Holding the pen with one hand, she awkwardly wrapped up

the wrist again, applying as much pressure as she dared. The bleeding slowed. Her tourniquet wasn't keeping all the blood from seeping out, but it was no longer gushing with each heartbeat.

His eyes fluttered open. "Tourniquet, you're right..."

Now Claudia looked around for the flight attendant, but she didn't see her. The room had almost emptied out, except for a lump of people on the other side of the conveyer belt. Must be another injury. Hopefully the people over there were taking care of it. The beast's cage still circled the baggage carrel, looking still and menacing, like an empty wasp's nest.

"I like animals," the man suddenly muttered. Claudia whipped her head around. He was looking at her, but his pupils were so dilated she couldn't see what color his eyes were.

"Well, sure you do," she said. "What wacko doesn't?"

He groaned. "It feels kinda unfair," he said, his eyes rolling down in the direction of his hand. "I mean, somebody should tell that trouncer I'm a nice guy. Oh, that burns," he groaned.

It was good that he was talking. Maybe he hadn't lost as much blood as she thought.

"Trouncer?" she said. "Is that what it is?" He looked like a nice guy. He'd probably be pretty good-looking if his lips weren't white and his face covered in shock sweat and droplets of blood.

"Yeah, Spo animal—for the biocomputers..." he trailed off and started again. "I'm not normally a whiner, but oh God. That burns."

"The paramedics should be here any minute," she said. Surely if that stewardess hadn't called 911 somebody else had by now.

Sure enough, she heard an ambulance siren approaching, one long descending note.

"I can hear the siren," she said.

"Distract me. Please," the guy said.

"Um...you met any aliens? I'm here to see my brother, he's one of those cadets. The ones the aliens took for the LA exchange program."

"I know some of the Spo. Does that mean you'll be in LA for a while?"

"You asking me out?" Claudia asked.

He fixed his eyes on her. "Please go out with me. I need a reason to live."

Claudia choked. "I don't think you're going to die."

"But when will I ever get to say that again?" he said weakly.

"True. Sure, it's a date." He was silent for a few minutes, his eyes closed again.

"What's your name?" he said, eyes still closed.

"It's Claudia. I'm staying with a friend in Glendale." He probably wouldn't remember this conversation in a few hours, but if he did, he deserved to find her. "What's your name?"

"It's Chris Tatlock. But I'm never gonna remember this, you'll have to find me."

Claudia laughed, adrenaline making her slightly hysterical. "Okay, sure."

"No, seriously. Promise?"

"I'll find you. Promise."

The paramedics were finally coming through the door, the flight attendant leading them right to her. Claudia felt marginally bad for doubting her. The tan uniforms of animal control workers headed toward the box. She hoped they had guns.

The paramedics gathered around and she showed them the tourniquet she was holding.

"I thought...If it... I'm a vet..." Claudia's words deserted her.

One of the paramedics took the pen from her, another eased her away as they stuck an oxygen mask over Chris' face. Huh, she already thought of him as Chris. They kept the tourniquet on as they unwrapped the socks from his hand and she could see the shock in their faces at the severed hand. They started working very quickly then, very carefully.

"Severed artery, tendons, nerve damage, venous discharge..." the talk swished around Claudia's head like a mop. The paramedics were applying another tourniquet.

One of them turned to her, as the other three hoisted Chris onto a gurney. "You did the right thing," he said.

She tried to wave goodbye to Chris as they wheeled him away, but his eyes were closed.

Claudia collapsed onto the tile, leaning against the wall, too drained to leave. Security officials swarmed around, but she was ignored. She watched the bags go round on the silver baggage carrel, around and around. Finally someone got their act together and turned it off.

"Don't hurt him, don't hurt him!" said an alien, bounding in from the front sliding doors. "Confused, scared, wouldn't hurt anyone!" His voice made Claudia's arches cramp—it was not loud but it buzzed—velvet over a band saw.

This was her first alien encounter. She saw them on TV, but this alien looked bigger in person and more, well, alien. One kick from one of those four sectioned legs and she'd fly into the wall like a deflated soccer ball.

The alien wore an L.A. Lakers basketball tunic. One of the security guys faced the alien. His teeth were clenched hard.

"It is my baby! My wee one—" the alien said, then took in the shock on his face and started over. "Not my real baby, of course. Good heavens! I mean, she is my pet. Like my kitty, you understand?"

"Your kitty injured three people, one critically. Why on earth would you ship an animal like that as checked baggage? Why would you even *have* an animal like that?" asked the security guy.

"My Reevse? She wouldn't hurt anyone. She is highly intelligent and highly trained. Take me to her."

The guy spoke in his radio, got a stream of curses in reply.

"Come again," he said, "Did you get it?"

"...in a pod, finally..." More cursing. "Safe now. Coming to you."

A few minutes later the entourage arrived. A huge metal box, a pod for moving people's furniture, led the way. Three men pushed it on a large dolly.

"It's locked in here," one guy said. "It got two of my friends. They're on the way to the hospital, stitches at least..."

The Lakers alien laid a hand on the box. "What did you do? She is but gentle!"

There was a grating roar and they could all hear the animal lung, teeth and claws crashing into the wall with a metallic clang.

The alien leaped away, his long legs shooting him ten yards backward. "That cannot be my Reevse! What has happened? Where is Chris?" he exclaimed.

Claudia blinked.

"Chris would know. Where is he? This must be another animal," the alien repeated.

"How many of these do you think there are? That's got to be yours," the policeman said.

"But she isn't. The roar is wrong. There is some mistake."

A radio crackled and Claudia saw one of the airport guys lift it and push the button. "Yeah, Albert, go ahead."

"We've got more reports of these animal attacks. LAX. We need to contain this. How many animals at your location?"

"Just one."

"Alright. Spo here says to take ours to Malibu."

"What?"

"I don't make the rules. Malibu. The alien academy."

"That's nuts. How many at LAX?"

"Four."

"Wow. Let me know if they figure out how to move 'em."

"Will do."

The alien turned to him, "LAX? I was routed through there. They must have Reevse. They switched him with this ravening animal. We must rectify this immediately."

"If you have any suggestions, we're listening," the officer said, "but at the moment..."

"No! You don't understand! They might harvest them at any moment for the computers. I must get Reevse immediately!"

The security guys tried to pacify the alien, but clearly he was beside himself.

Only now someone noticed Claudia sitting on the floor watching the whole thing. She was escorted out and given a voucher for a free taxi ride. Her fingers stuck together with tacky blood as she clutched the paper. So much for her clean fingernails.

6

SAM STEPPED into the hot sun outside Mann's Chinese Theater on Hollywood Boulevard. He felt more nervous than usual. As the first press event he'd planned from start to finish, he really wanted it to work. This casual event could go a long way towards humanizing the cadets.

The concrete and asphalt of downtown Hollywood radiated heat, much like the desert on Spo. There were quite a few tourists, maybe sixty people, though he'd heard that was nothing compared to the tourists that would have been here on a Saturday before the Spo invasion. Beyond the tourists were the homeless. Lining the sidewalks were cardboard boxes and filthy tarps suspended for shade. The homeless huddled under these makeshift shelters, though a few lay full length in the sun. There was a faint smell in the air, dirty humans and urine. It smelled foul to Sam, accustomed to the bleach-like smell of the Spo.

This was one of the worst places Sam had seen in LA, though he knew many places in the city were far more crowded and filthy. After the Hadron explosion, many people along the coasts were displaced by rising water. The Midwest turned into a dustbowl to rival the 1930's, and people fled to the cities. Then the Spo had come, with their energy sources and eco-scrubbers, and although they'd mostly stabilized the weather systems, they'd put a lot of people out of work.

The rest of the cadets disembarked from the chartered buses, and people started gathering around. There were a lot of Asian school kids, and a few white families. Quite a few teenage girls seemed to be trying out the latest fashions. Sam saw lots of deep V-neck shirts and big jewelry. No yin-yangs though. Some of the homeless gathered in behind the tourists, who flinched and moved away.

All the people were gawking at the cadets now, whispering to each other. Their new security team began circulating through the crowd. They were tough, most of them former Special Services. Since the Spo executed the president and most of the upper echelon of government when they invaded, a lot of Special Forces guys needed jobs. They weren't thrilled to be working for the Spo, but nobody could afford to turn down work. And the last few days more than proved the cadets needed protection.

Greg got off the bus last, climbing awkwardly down the high bus steps, and swinging himself out onto the curb. Ripples of awe ran through the crowd, and they edged backward, the people closest trying to put space between themselves and the Spo. Thousands of Spo lived on Earth, but lots of people still hadn't seen one up close.

Greg stretched his limbs in the sun, as if showing off for the humans. He probably just enjoyed the warmth. The average temperature on Spo was 105 degrees.

Sam waited for the security guys to rope off the staging area. A huge gate opened from the sidewalk into the courtyard of the theater. The gate was grey and orange stone, in the ancient Chinese fashion, apparently. The courtyard inside was covered with concrete tiles commemorating actors and directors of the last hundred years. He could see people squatting down to place their hands in the handprints of their favorite actors. The sidewalk where he stood was called the Walk of Fame. Each block had a star with the name of a performer, but he didn't know most of the names. Celine Dion, Alex Trebek?

Sam had been here once before. When he was seven years old his family came to Los Angeles on vacation. They'd done Disneyland and then Hollywood. Sam could picture his sister Claudia running into the courtyard. She climbed on the back of one of the stone lions by the door for Mom to take her picture. Sam's dad took pictures of John Travolta and Buster Keaton's squares, between business calls.

Sam stumbled, disoriented for a moment, his vision doubled between the past and the present. He took a half step, to lean against a parking meter. He hadn't pictured his family so clearly in years. His vision cleared slowly, but he still felt light headed. His feelings for his family were complicated, and none of them matched the feelings for humanity that he'd learned from Greg. Not that Greg hated humans. He didn't. Sam shook his head to clear it. He had a press conference to deal with.

The security guys had things set up, so Sam walked through the cadets to take his place next to Greg. The press noticed him.

"It's Sam!"

"Are you the cadet leader?"

"What do you think of the uprising in China?"

Sam looked at Greg for permission to speak. Received it.

"We understand their frustration, but regret that they've turned to violence. Rioting is only going to hurt them more. If they really want the best for their children they need to stop. We did the best we could in the aftermath of the earthquake, and our hearts go out to those who lost loved ones," Sam said.

"You always say, 'we'—do you consider yourself one of the Spo?"

"Sam, what is it like being back on earth?"

"It's more colorful. And... louder," Sam said, ignoring the first question.

Another group of cadets got off the second bus, and Sam backed up as the reporters turned to them. Melanie scooted around the back of the growing crowd and grabbed his hand.

"Hey, you okay?" she asked. "You look so serious. This is the most fun we've had in months. Years maybe."

Sam realized his teeth were clenched and he worked to loosen his jaw. "Yeah, I know."

"Sam! Sam!" he heard, "Is that your girlfriend?" A girl who could have been younger than him shoved a microphone in his face. Probably a Teen Vogue reporter. Sam pulled his hand away from Melanie. Who cared if he had a girlfriend? Sam instinctively looked around for Nat, and saw her looking away from him. Yeah, she'd heard that.

"Just friends!" Sam said for the reporter. "Melanie's one of my best friends."

Melanie stiffened but smiled anyway. Belatedly he realized it was kind of insulting to jerk away from her like that. But she knew about him and Nat. It wasn't her. Sam sighed.

The cadets gathered in a crowd around Greg and Sam, no rows or ranks today.

A wet cement square waited for them. Like celebrities for years had done, Greg would leave his footprints in the cement for generations of tourists to gawk at. Melanie and Jonathan were going to put their footprints in the same square. Sam chose Jonathan because he would be the witness in Earth's trial in a few weeks, and after that, would be famous. Melanie he picked almost at random, because she was the youngest cadet, only fourteen, and very outgoing.

Sam felt his vision double again as he watched Greg push his long clawed feet into the wet cement and scratch his name with a finger. A small but growing part of Sam felt that he'd engineered some disturbing symbolism here. Greg sinking his feet into the wet Earth... making an indelible impression in a quickly hardening surface. It seemed like a good idea at the time. What was he thinking?

Then it was Jonathan's turn. He took his shoes off, gave the cameras a big thumbs up, and stuck his feet in the wet cement with a flourish. The tourists cheered and Sam grinned and waved. Jonathan used a finger to scrawl his name in the cement. His footprints looked puny compared to Greg's.

Melanie was next, and she looked just as cute and young as Sam wanted. A few people made catcalls as she took off her shoes, and she laughed and threw a kiss. Her feet looked even tinier next to Greg's.

"We're going to enjoy a little R&R!" Sam told the reporters. "Feel free to hang around and get individual interviews while we enjoy Hollywood."

The cadets started to disperse and Greg reminded them, "You have three hours. You will remain within two blocks of this location and in sight of at least one security man. Report at the main doors," he gestured to the big doors between the stone lions of the theater, "at four o'clock." He nodded dismissal.

Jonathan and Melanie used the water bucket to clean their feet. Their footprints were drying quickly in the hot sun. The deep holes made by Greg's claws were black with shadow.

"You coming?" Melanie asked him, shoes in hand.

"Yeah, I guess so," Sam said. He was at a mall and had three hours to himself. Time to forget about the complexities of the universe for a few minutes.

He caught up with Melanie, ignoring the stares. She was crouched over a square.

"Matt Damon was here!" she squealed. "Awesome!"

Armen laughed. "You've been billions of miles from Earth,

you've made contact with an alien species, and Matt Damon makes you scream?"

Melanie squinted up at him. "Go ahead and be all cool and ironic—I think this is awesome."

"It's not bad," Armen said.

"Look, even Nat is getting into it!" Melanie said, pointing to Nat kneeling next to a dark grey square. Nat glanced up at her name, with a tight smile.

"Hey, guys," Nat said, "Can somebody take a picture for me?"

"Uh, sure." Sam went over and grabbed a little camera from her. She leaned over and placed her hand over Julie Andrews' print.

"You should smile or something. We're all having such fun, remember?" Sam said.

Nat grinned, surprising him. He snapped the picture quickly.

"So, Julie Andrews, huh?"

"It's for Akemi. I'm supposed to fill this up for her," Nat said, pointing to the disposable digital camera.

"But Julie Andrews? Akemi is sixteen."

"But she loved Princess Diaries."

"Sure she did, but I'm betting she's way more fond of Will Smith or Taylor Lautner these days," Sam said, pausing by his square. "Get over there."

Nat knelt again, smiling for the camera. He helped her get another good six pictures and then she gestured to the lions. "I need one of you," she said.

"Really? Why?"

"Akemi. She wants to show off that she knows you."

Sam put an elbow on the lion, looking off into the distance in his best inscrutable pose.

"Oh, that's good. She'll like that," Nat said.

Sam followed her to the escalator and into the mall.

They found Armen contemplating a Nestle Tollhouse cafe with tears in his eyes.

"We have arrived. Years of horror cannot sully this moment. This is one of the best chocolate shops in the world," Armen said.

"You're going to cry, aren't you?" Sam asked. "This is embarrassing. Crying isn't exactly the image I was hoping to project with this Hollywood thing."

Nat glanced around. "No, go ahead, cry. The reporters need some good homecoming shots. And here comes Downy."

"Well, that should be distracting," Sam said. "Do what you need to do."

"Shut up and come in here, you freaks." Armen grabbed their arms and dragged them into the café, away from the cameras.

A large mirror was mounted in the wall of the cafe, and Sam caught a look at the three of them as they entered. Their tattoos were the most striking thing about them. Sam was about a foot taller than Armen. Nat was even shorter, but her bearing made her seem taller than she was.

"What are we getting?" Sam said. "'Cause if you throw up in front of the cameras I want it to look good."

Armen sighed rapturously. "You guys do whatever you want. I'm getting a triple chocolate mocha ice cream shake with an oatmeal chocolate chip cookie on the side." He said this last bit to the woman behind the counter.

Her eyebrows had been tacked about an inch too high since they came in, but at this she smiled a little.

She grabbed the scoop and slid open the ice cream container.

"You didn't have any chocolate up there, huh?" she asked without looking at them.

Armen laughed. "Oh no, they imported food occasionally. If there had been none—well, I would have been the first suicide off planet."

"You nearly were the first suicide," Sam said, "Remember the nitrogen lake?"

"Really, Sam? You shame me in front of this nice lady?" Armen exclaimed.

The woman laughed. "Nitrogen lake? That sounds exciting."

"Not nearly as exciting as what you're doing with that little machine," Armen said in a sexy voice. She was holding the lid on the food processor as she blended his shake.

She laughed for real this time. "You've been gone a long time alright."

"Anything else for you three?" the lady asked, handing Armen his shake and a cookie in a napkin.

"Yes," said Nat, "I'll have an Original Chocolate Chip Cookie."

They asked the lady to take their picture before they left and she had them stand next to the big Nestle sign on the wall. Sam draped his arm over Nat's shoulders. She flicked his hand, but he just grinned at her. "Come on, Akemi will love it."

Nat rolled her eyes. "She doesn't need encouraging. Neither do you apparently."

Sam laughed and the waitress clicked a couple pictures.

She pulled out her phone. "Can I get one with you?"

They grouped around her and Nat snapped a picture of them with the phone.

"Cool! My friends will be so impressed."

When they came out of the café Sam saw several cadets giving interviews at different spots in the mall. Others sat by a huge fountain in the center, enjoying fast food and sun. He was satisfied. If eating burgers at a mall didn't make the cadets seem human and sympathetic, what would?

He found the flyer on the way back from the bathroom. It lay under a trashcan. Someone must have shoved it in the hole, but it slipped between the side of the bag and the can and ended up on the ground.

"Remember the dead," it said on the top, with a picture of former President Gottman. In the picture, Gottman sat with the first lady and their adult son and two grandkids. Sam remembered that campaign. Gottman had been in the White House about a year when the terrorists attacked the Hadron Collider in Switzerland. Most of Europe was suddenly gone. It caused atmosphere-poisoning, tsunamis in the Atlantic, plunging temperatures everywhere. The world fell on its face. And then the Spo came.

They weren't concerned about public opinion (not then), and swept in with brutal control. They told people they would preserve Earth, but it looked a lot like an invasion. Gottman and hundreds of other world leaders made a joint statement denouncing the aliens and their brutal methods. So the Spo killed them. All of them. The Spo killed Gottman's brothers, children, grandchildren, cousins, everybody. They did the same with the other leaders. The Spo rarely executed anybody alone. They believed in killing whole families, if they killed anyone. They felt it was merciful.

"Ruthless Killers Can't be Trusted!" was typed under Gottman's picture. "The Spo caused the Hadron Explosion! We must fight!"

No name, no phone number, no website. Stupid propagandists, Sam thought. What good did they think they were doing? Human terrorists destroyed the Hadron collider and caused Europe to go up in a cloud of radioactive froth. Of course, the Spo killed a lot of people when they came. The question was, what if they hadn't come? Humanity would be hanging on by the merest thread without Spo technology cleaning the atmosphere and predicting the worst earthquakes and fallout.

He crumpled the sheet up, prepared to drop it in the trash,

when he saw the writing on the back. In blue ink, very small, it had a phone number and, "Independence Day."

Sam memorized the number quickly, as the Spo had taught him, and threw the flyer away as Armen and Downy caught up to him.

"Oh, I feel good," Armen groaned.

"Your groan says it all," Sam said. "Did you buy another shake?"

"Diligence is the mouth of success," Armen said, quoting a Spo proverb.

"Diligence in the mouth, remorse in the stomach," Sam said.

"That's not what that means," Downy said. "And I thoroughly enjoyed my malt. It was the epitome of Earth—rich, frothy, and soft."

"A malt," Armen cried. "I resent being personified as anything but a candy bar. I feel I've earned that at least."

"I wasn't finished," Downy said. "Frothy and soft—and too expensive. Besides making my second stomach convulse."

Armen grabbed Downy's arm. "That was... sarcasm," Armen said. "Downy, buddy, you've arrived." He slapped Downy on the back. "Let me teach you irony."

"Don't totally corrupt him," Sam said. "He may never go home."

"That's right," Downy said. "I'm not going home anytime soon. I have time to learn your insulting ways."

Sam was silent as they went down the escalator to the theater courtyard.

The new tile was in place. A few camera crews filmed last shots of the scene for their news report. When the lingering reporters caught sight of Armen, coming down the escalator with his arm thrown around Downy's bony shoulders, the cameras swiveled in their direction.

"Cadet, who's your friend!?"

"How do you feel about the evacuations this week?"

"Do you feel the casualty level was high?"

"Are you readjusting to Earth?"

Armen removed his arm and waved at the press. "I just had a triple chocolate shake and a cookie. I'm readjusting just great."

"Who's your friend?"

Greg appeared behind them, nodded approval. Armen obediently stepped closer to the cameras.

"This is Downy. He's not bad, actually. Loves sheep and used to sneak me the occasional Snicker bar on Spo," Armen said.

"Downy, as in fabric softener?" a reporter asked.

"Yes, I think so. Right, Downy?" Armen said.

"That is correct. Longer lasting freshness."

There was a general laugh and another round of flashes.

7

SHARA WATCHED Greg push his claws into the wet square of cement and planned her first murder. She stood in the middle of the crowd, blending in and eyeing her target. She didn't want to draw the attention of the security guys, or even worse, Greg himself. If anyone could identify her as a Rik assassin, it was him.

Even Greg would need a lot of luck to identify her in this crowd, however. She felt relatively safe. After all, she was human now, not Rik.

When Greg was done pop-starring himself, the cadets began to scatter. The sun beat down on the pale concrete, making the courtyard blaze. Most of the tourists had on sunglasses. She should have gotten some. Sam and a few of his friends continued to speak to the press, others clumped in groups, talking among themselves. Sam and Nat were among her primary kill targets, but today was for Target One, Jonathan.

Jonathan was one of five cadets who would be primary witnesses in the Earth's trial. He was the primary for the Los Angeles group, and he was her task today. The other primaries, in the other cities, would be taken care of today also.

Shara knew his personality profile by heart. He was friendly, homely, and brilliant. He had an eidetic memory, probably part of the reason they chose him. He was also one of the few cadets who'd been disciplined for 'inappropriate behavior,' during his Spo training. Shara suspected that he'd been fooling around with one of the girl cadets. He was a good target.

He stepped away from the crowd into a tiny shop at the back of the courtyard. Shara followed him. The shop sold postcards and fake Golden Globe awards that said, "No. 1 Grandson," and things like that.

The store was two steps lower than the courtyard, and she stepped down into the dimness with a feminine sway to her hips. That's what her tutor taught her in his 'seductive technique' lesson. Jonathan was in here, all right, looking at postcards of women in small bathing suits.

Shara got close to him, a matter of a few steps, and looked at some of the postcards. They didn't appeal to her very much. The women would look better with fitted clothes and maybe some knee high boots. Shara wore a pair of fantastic velvet Capri's she'd discovered in the clothing district. Earth culture never ceased to amaze her. The sheer volume of their output was remarkable. For instance, these pants hugged her bottom just right, and she'd found some wonderful earrings at Rocks and Runes. She felt pretty and sexy, all those human hormones were fantastic. The outfit was just right for seducing and kidnapping a cadet. She might change clothes before she did the killing, though. This outfit didn't say, "Killer," to her. Something more yellow, perhaps.

She saw Jonathan glance at her, and she looked up at him with wide eyes. "Oh wow. You're one of them, huh?" She giggled. "Can I take a picture with you?"

"Uh... sure." She snuggled up and put her arm around him, pulling out her cell phone to snap a picture.

"Thanks!" she said. "How long do you get to hang out here?"

"A couple hours...'till four."

Shara held onto him. "Did you know we're right next to the Hollywood Bowl? I was gonna go check it out. Do you wanna come?"

"I'm not supposed to leave," he said, taking a step toward the door.

"Are you sure?" Shara asked. "It'd be so much fun to see it with you. See, I've had this goal." She lowered her voice, getting close to him, and whispering, "I want to make out on the stage of the Hollywood bowl. But my boyfriend dumped me last week. Can you believe it? Now I don't have anybody. What can I do?"

Jonathan turned pink. "I would come. But if I disappear, there's security—"

"Oh, I'll bring you back in time!" Shara said. "We'll just have some fun first. Don't they let you have any fun?"

Jonathan took the bait. "Why not?" he said, with an attempt at nonchalance. "What can they do to me, right?"

She laughed. "Let's get out of here."

She took him to the Hollywood Bowl. It wasn't actually right next to Grauman's Chinese Theater. It was several miles away, nestled into the Hollywood hills in a natural basin. It was closed to the public during weekdays. It wouldn't open to the hordes of concertgoers until six that evening for the Los Angeles Philharmonic. Shara was hoping to come to the performance when she finished with Jonathan.

She snuck him through a locked gate with a wide gap between the doors. They wound around the outside of the amphitheater, up the numerous stairs until they finally emerged about halfway up the bowl. It could hold 10,000 people, making it comparable to the great Colossae of Rome, which Shara had seen on TV, but it reminded her of the giant death chambers on the Merith planet.

"Wow," Jonathan said. "This place is huge. It's pretty cool."

Shara agreed. They headed down the stairs toward the stage. When a janitor came into one of the bottom sections to mark off seats with a red rope, Shara and Jonathan dropped to their hands and knees, hiding behind the stone benches. They laughed breathlessly, and Shara found it natural to kiss him, with their faces so close together.

When they got back up, he held her hand, and she swung his exuberantly.

"Aren't you glad you came?" Shara asked.

"This is great. I haven't done anything fun, on my own, in—ever."

Shara laughed. "This should be a big day for you then."

She put her free hand in her purse, fingering the small spray bottle inside. It contained sasoikeo, a very efficient neurotoxin that the Spo developed. It could be gaseous, liquid, or baked into a solid, though that was time consuming. Her bottle contained a diluted liquid version. A small amount, squirted in the face, would cause instant paralysis. Another dose, squirted up the nose, or in the mouth, or onto any open membrane of the body, would cause death.

But... she didn't feel like squirting him yet. She was enjoying him.

Somehow, two hours later, she still hadn't squirted him.

"This is... I've had a great time," Jonathan said. "But I probably should head back now. I'm sure Greg is flipping out if he's noticed I'm gone."

"Do you really want to go back?" Shara said. "I mean, they basically kidnapped you right? Why don't you just leave?"

"Oh, I would. But these—" he gestured to the tattoo on his cheek. "I'd be easy to track, wouldn't I? Plus I have some stuff to do for them. Then I'm going to take off."

Shara nodded. Time to get busy.

Back in her car, she drove onto the 101 south.

Jonathan talked about his family a little bit, about the cadets. Shara didn't really listen. He just looked so cute with his orange

T-shirt and his black spiky hair. She smiled when she caught him looking at her legs.

She had to quit it. She was going human.

"You missed the exit," Jonathan said, looking out the window now. "It was right back there."

Without giving herself pause to think, Shara grabbed the bottle from her purse and squirted him in the face. She trained for this job for two years, she couldn't blow it for one cute cadet and raging hormones.

Shara sat in the parking lot of the Malibu beach across from Pepperdine University, with Jonathan slumped in the passenger seat. Coming here had been a gut decision. Shara wasn't used to having those. The electrical nuances of her new brain would get her in trouble if she didn't get control.

On the other hand, now that she was here, she could think of several good reasons for it. She smiled.

Jonathan was perfectly still in his seat, with a bit of drool dripping onto his orange shirt. The car air conditioner blew cold and hard in his face but he didn't blink. His pupils were tiny dots, and every now and then his eyeballs twitched wildly.

"It's time for me to kill you," Shara explained. She rubbed the cold bottle of sasoikeo. "The cadets go for runs here. They'll find your body soon."

Finding his body would be good for lowering morale and building fear and frustration, which was part of her larger plan. It would undermine the whole group. Except...

"Except I don't feel like killing you," Shara told him. "And don't get me wrong, I don't mind killing." She used a Kleenex to wipe his drool. More eye twitching.

"I've killed on Rik more than once. I'm aggressive and I lack empathy—that's why I was chosen. When I landed on Earth I killed a homeless guy that was camped too close and saw my ship. I don't mind killing."

She brought the bottle close to Jonathan's mouth. Her finger quivered over the button and his unfocused eyes swirled past her.

"Ugh," she said, tapping him on the nose with the bottle, not squirting it. "I don't want to."

Jonathan wheezed.

"You might die anyway," she told him. "If I leave you here you'll die of dehydration in forty-eight hours if they don't find you. And this stuff will be eating away at your brain. You won't remember me. You probably won't remember yourself..."

Shara held it over his nose. "You don't want to live that way."

But she didn't squirt.

"I don't really need you to die. I needed to mess up the plans for the trial and give Greg and General Gustav a big problem." She bit her cheek. "That's done."

Shara sighed and stuck the bottle back in her purse. She went around and opened the passenger door and lugged Jonathan out by his armpits. She was in good shape, but he had six inches on her. It took three minutes to drag him to the edge of the parking lot and settled his head on the sand. His dark eyes twitched ceaselessly, the black irises skittering around like a Rik housefly. She carefully closed his eyelids. That was better. Now he looked like he was sleeping. Shara patted his forehead and went back to her car.

GREG TOOK the cadets on another early morning jog, but this one didn't make it past the beach parking lot. They found Jonathan's body, and for a horrified moment, Sam thought he was dead.

Jonathan lay half on the asphalt of the parking lot, half on the sand. He wheezed softly through cracked lips, and his pants were soiled. His eyes jerked around under closed lids. His skin felt rough and burned to Sam's hand. He must have been there all afternoon and all night to account for that sunburn.

Greg hoisted Jonathan in his arms and carried him back to campus, the cadets strung out behind him like mourners in a parade.

Sam caught up with Greg as he loped up the hill toward the dorm. "What's wrong with him?" Sam asked. "He doesn't look hung over or... dead... and those were my best guesses."

Greg looked grim. "He has a certain smell... I'm not certain, but I think he's been poisoned."

"Poisoned? Then why leave him for us to find? They could have dumped him in the water and let him drown."

"That's a good question," Greg said. "But if it's what I suspect, we can't do him much good anyway."

Jonathan spasmed suddenly. His limbs flailed and Greg lost control of him. Jonathan's body thumped unceremoniously on the ground, twitching at their feet. A high moan rose from behind his clenched lips.

"Should I call an ambulance?" Sam asked.

"I suppose so," Greg said. "If it's the poison I suspect, we can do nothing more."

Sam accompanied Jonathan in the back of the ambulance, because Greg was too large to fit.

The paramedics shied away from Sam, trying not to touch him or Jonathan very much.

"Do your job already," Sam said. "He's not going to hurt you."

The paramedics didn't respond.

"Dehydrated, pretty bad. Sunburn," one of them said. He quickly slid a needle in Jonathan's arm attached to an IV.

The other pulled up Jonathan's eyelids, taking in his flicking eyes and tiny pupils.

"Is his skin always that color?" he finally asked Sam. "It's hard to tell if he's oxygen deprived or just green."

"Um. He is a little darker green than usual. But that might be the sunburn. The green tone is from Spo food."

"Huh. He on something? Drugs, alcohol, alien steroid crap, anything?"

"Nothing alien. But he is readjusting to Earth food. That's made some of the cadets sick. But nothing like this. I doubt he's on drugs, though I guess he might have gotten some yesterday. He's only been missing eighteen hours."

"This might be a bad coke reaction," the other med said. "Which would explain his wandering toward the school. He was half rational until the bad part hit his brain."

When they pulled the gurney out of the ambulance, Sam hopped out behind. He followed them into the emergency room, and stood next to Jonathan while the paramedics filled out paperwork and spoke to a nurse.

"What? What?" Jonathan said. His eyes were still closed.

"Jonathan, can you hear me?" Sam asked. "Are you awake?"

"What?" Jonathan said again. "Go away!"

Sam looked at the nurse. "Do you think he hears me?"

She shrugged. "Jonathan, you're at the hospital. Do you remember what happened?"

"The aliens, they took me," Jonathan whispered, blinking his eyes open for the first time. He clamped them shut quickly, like the light hurt his eyes. "My mother was crying, and they just took me away. I'm sorry Mom, there's nothing I can do."

"That's—he's remembering what happened a long time ago," Sam said.

The nurse grimaced. "No kidding. We know what happened, you know."

"Of course," Sam said. Maybe the nurse was related to one of the cadets.

"Please," Jonathan said. "Please let me go home. My mom needs me."

"Jonathan, do you remember me? It's Sam."

Jonathan opened his eyes again. "I just want to go home." Then his head slumped back to the bed, his mouth slightly open.

"Don't worry, he's sleeping," the nurse said, feeling his pulse. "We'll put him in an observation room on the second floor."

8

CLAUDIA HAD PROMISED she would visit Chris at the hospital, but now she regretted it. She didn't know him, he didn't know her. If the doctors had amputated his hand... he needed family around and people to grieve with. Not a random stranger. She bypassed the emergency entrance and got his room number from the lobby receptionist.

On the fifth floor she paused outside his room. If he was sleeping, she would leave. If he had any one with him, she might leave too. If he... darn it, she had to do this. She looked in the room.

He was alone, awake, and reading a book. He looked better than she remembered. Most people do when their blood isn't draining out in their lap. He awkwardly turned a page with his left hand. His right arm hung from a large frame over the bed, heavily bandaged and in traction. As far as she could tell, a hand was still attached.

After a moment he sensed someone watching. He glanced up and gave her a questioning look. He was handsome, in a slightly geeky way. He would look perfect on NCIS Los Angeles. He still looked blank.

"Hi. My name is Claudia. I don't know if you remember..."

"Claudia?" he said.

"Do you remember me?" She shook her head slightly to antici-pate his no.

He closed his book and placed it on the counter. "Sadly, no."

"Oh." She was prepared for that, darn it. She was.

"But apparently I asked the first four nurses I saw if their names were Claudia," he said. "It's a bit of a joke now."

Claudia laughed.

"Yeah, you can laugh but they've nicknamed me Claudia. For three days now."

She stepped closer to his bed. "I'm so glad they were able to save your hand. Is it... how long a recovery are you looking at?"

"Ugh, six months to a year for full movement."

"Honestly, I thought it was gone."

"Oh, it should have been, but that freaking sharp claw made a clean cut." He laughed. "Small mercies, right?"

Claudia chuckled. "If you've gotta be mauled by an alien animal, it helps to look on the bright side."

Chris grinned. "I agree. They found a transplant surgeon to put me back together. This is the third time he's put someone's own hand back on."

"Wow. And no infection from the... animal?"

"The slime on a trouncer is like bleach. Antibacterial. Burned like crazy, but killed anything in the wound."

"Wow," Claudia repeated. "That's providence for you."

"No joke. So, I can't be sure," he continued, "but I'm guessing you were the one who put that tourniquet on my arm. The surgeon said you might have saved my life. So—no, please let me finish—I'm obviously eternally grateful, but what I really want to know is—did I ask you out? And more importantly, did you say yes?"

Claudia didn't answer right away, and he rushed on, "Of course, if you just loaned me a quarter at the airport or something I'm going to be really embarrassed and take it all back."

"Do you make a habit of asking out the people who save your life?" Claudia asked.

"Well, I already like you," he glanced at the clock, "after three and half minutes, so I'm guessing if you were keeping me alive and I was at all coherent, I must have asked you out."

"Yeah, you were bleeding everywhere, it was very suave."

"Hey, you're here. I bleed well."

"Well, I didn't come back only for a date," Claudia said. "I thought you might help me out with something."

"You name it. I certainly owe you."

"My brother is one of the Spo cadets who just got back. I'd really like to see him, but I've heard you need a pass to go to Pepperdine. I'd like to get one."

"And you think I can help?" Chris said.

Claudia watched him closely. "The alien at the airport asked for you. When it was trying to get its pet back."

"Ahh, did she?" Chris said.

"Yes. Wait, the alien was a she?" Claudia said.

"Yep, her—uh—husband is in charge of the western US. She gets a security detail whenever she travels."

"You're—security? For the aliens?"

Chris grimaced. "Don't sound so disgusted, it's not as bad as it sounds. I used to work for the FBI before Washington closed down. It was a natural change."

Claudia took a breath through her nose, lips clenched.

"I don't like the Spo," she said.

"Who does?" Chris said, "You just have to—"

"No, you don't get it," Claudia said. "I. Do not. Like the Spo."

Chris finally looked serious. "Okay. I get that," he said softly. "I'll try to find out about seeing your brother. How's that?"

"Thank you," Claudia said.

A nurse came in with his chart. "Time for physical therapy," she said, and noticed his guest. "Let me guess, you're Claudia?"

Claudia smiled, her face tight. "That's right. I guess I know how to make an impression."

"Oh, for real?" the nurse said. "I was kidding. You're Claudia?"

"That's my name."

"Ha. We thought you was making it up, boy," the nurse said, grinning.

"Can she come with me?" Chris asked.

"I don't really—" Claudia said.

"She's the one saved your hand?" the nurse said. "Sure. We'll say she's family."

Claudia trailed Chris and the nurse pushing his wheelchair to the physical therapy room. She didn't want to get deeper into a relationship with a guy who worked for the Spo. There was no future there. She appreciated that he might help her, but frankly, she saved his life. He owed her. She didn't want to give him hope for anything else.

Claudia leaned against the wall, at a distance from Chris and the doctor. An assortment of tables, weights, and stretching equipment littered the room. A small walking track went around it all, hugging the wall.. A little girl was using the track, slowly pushing a walker as she took each step.

The therapist laid Chris on his back and set him up with some stretches for his legs. He'd lost a lot of blood, which quickly depleted muscle strength. The girl circling the room paused next to Claudia, watching Chris pump his legs in the air.

"Your boyfriend?" she asked.

"Yikes," Claudia said. "I just met him."

"He's pretty hot," the little girl said.

Claudia snickered. "How old are you?"

The girl straightened her neck. "I'm sixteen. I just look seven."

"I was going to say ten," Claudia said diplomatically.

She groaned. "Thanks a whole lot."

She went around the room again, pausing when she got back to Claudia. "What happened to his arm?" she asked.

"Animal injury," Claudia said, "cut his wrist pretty badly."

"Ouch."

"How about you?" Claudia asked.

"Lung transplant, cystic fibrosis."

"Oh. Wow, I'm sorry." Claudia could see the heavy bandages encircling the girl's thin chest and torso.

"Eh—we'll see. What's your name?"

"Claudia."

"I'm Akemi. I—" she hesitated for the first time. "I heard your friend was sliced by an alien," she whispered, so he couldn't hear.

"An alien animal—not a Spo," Claudia said.

"Oh. He doesn't work with the aliens or anything? I was hoping he did," Akemi said.

"Why?"

"I want to get a letter to my sister. She's one of the cadets. They let her come see me before my surgery, but she hasn't come again." Akemi's dejection was clear. "I fly back to Tokyo tomorrow."

"A cadet? Small world. My brother is a cadet too." Claudia said. "His name is Sam."

Akemi lit up. "You're Sam's sister! Awesome! I just met him. My sister has a huge crush on him."

"Really?" Claudia asked. "Tell me what she said! And I'll take the letter to your sister."

SAM LEFT the hospital when Jonathan's family arrived. He knew he should stay and talk with them. He should smooth things down and get a feel for their attitude.

Instead he ran down the hall and slammed the exit door open, letting his security guy rush to catch up. There was no limo waiting for him. He hadn't told Greg when he would be done. Sam strode down the sidewalk as if he had a destination in mind. As if he had somewhere to go besides the alien academy, somewhere that belonged to him.

His security guy jogged up behind him, and then hung a few paces back as he walked.

Jonathan talked all day. Talked like a twelve year old desperately afraid and wanting his family. He talked like someone who'd just been kidnapped.

Sam remembered that feeling and it made him ill. He hadn't felt it in a long time, and he didn't want it to come back now. 'The aliens,' Jonathan kept moaning. The aliens.

Before they were Greg and Gustav and Downy and HP and Lurk, they had been *the aliens*. Sam remembered being terrified by their smell. Waking in the middle of the night, screaming, only to realize that Greg was checking on him and his scent had roused Sam from sleep. It felt traitorous to remember that now. Greg had taken care of them like a father. Certainly better than Sam's own father.

Sam's mind flicked over images of his father. He'd already left them when the aliens took Sam away. His father hadn't been at home most of the time before that either. Sam had more memories of games with Greg and time with his friends than he did of his own family, even counting the first year or so of training which he only remembered vaguely.

Sam had tried to calm Jonathan, comforting him, staying aloof from his frenzy. But the whole time, all Sam could think was, "This is my fault." He'd planned the Hollywood event, even though he knew the kind of casual afternoon he'd planned would make it hard to keep all the cadets perfectly safe. Sam had gambled that the attacker liked anonymity and would dislike acting in such a public place. The gamble failed, and Jonathan paid for it.

Sam stayed calm for Jonathan until the nurse said Jonathan's family was coming down the hall. Then his heart started pounding and a cold shock sweat broke out on his back. His composure had crumbled like moist sand and he'd hit the hall running.

His reaction was pure panic. He shouldn't be out of control like that at the mere idea of facing a cadet family. No doubt more and more of the cadets' families would be appearing in the weeks ahead. He needed to deal with this. More of the cadets might get hurt like Jonathan. He needed to deal with that too.

Sam slowed and punched a palm tree in frustration, resting his forehead against the hairy bark. Jonathan had sounded so horrified, so betrayed. Some part of that betrayal still resonated with Sam, and whatever part it was, he needed to lock it down. It would be better to get rid of those emotions all together, but Sam suspected that would take years with a psychiatrist, if it was possible at all. He didn't have that kind of time.

The fact was: the aliens had traumatized them, even though they didn't intend it that way. Breathing deeply, eyes closed, Sam brought out each emotion and aired it like a bed sheet. He fluttered his horror out—the unknown aliens with their long limbs and vicious smell, pulling him out of his house—and then he folded the sheet neatly and put it in a heavy, wooden chest. Then he took out his sorrow for his family—like a large blue comforter that was almost too heavy for one person to fold—and put it in the chest. His anger with Greg, for becoming a father to Sam and yet never really understanding him. His fear of betrayal—if the Spo had lied about everything, if they turned on him... It's not true, Sam said. Fold it up. He took out his fear that he was betraying his own people, that the Spo were brutal invaders who must be fought... Sam aired, folded, and filled the chest.

He stood a moment longer, with the chest closed and locked. Sam had a purpose. The trial was in two weeks, and now Jonathan was out of action. Somebody wanted to hurt the cadets, and probably mess up the trial. Someday, maybe, Sam would have time to open the chest and wash the sheets. But not today. Today he would go back to Pepperdine and make sure no one else disappeared.

When he finally raised his head and opened his eyes the sky was fully dark. His security guy leaned unobtrusively against a newspaper stand, doing something with his phone.

"I'm ready to go back," Sam said. "Want to call a cab?"

Downy wanted to talk when Sam got back to the dorm.

"What's with Jonathan? You think he got some dope?"

"No," Sam said.

"Maybe somebody forced it on him," Downy said.

"I don't want to talk about it." Sam moved a stack of books off his bed.

"Somebody hit the other cadet groups too."

"What?" The top book slipped off the pile and fell on Sam's foot. He swore and threw them all on the floor next to his desk. "Spit it out, Downy. What happened?"

"In a mood, aren't you? The cadet groups from Hong Kong, Moscow, New York, and Sao Paolo all lost a cadet today. Not just us."

"They've been drugged, like Jonathan?"

Downy shifted his weight, his color flickering uncertainly. "No, they're dead."

Sam collapsed on his bed. "Dead," he repeated.

"Not just any cadets, either. They got Jonathan, our primary witness for the trial, and all the others too."

Sam groaned.

"Jonathan will come back though, right?" Downy asked.

"He won't," Sam said, turning out the overhead light. "He doesn't remember anything. He's not a cadet anymore."

"Huh." Downy stayed silent for a minute. "Greg still wants to do the 4th of July celebration tomorrow. Better get your speech ready."

Sam groaned. "That's a terrible idea. We shouldn't go anywhere. Someone's targeting us."

"Not my call," Downy said, "Besides, it's your holiday. G'night."

9

Less than twenty-four hours later Sam leaned against the side of a fortune telling booth and watched Downy make a fool of himself with a sausage on a stick. It was dusk and the lights of the rides and booths were starting to shine in the darkness.

"We should definitely not be here," Sam said again. "This isn't safe, and it's not necessary either." He gave a half groan as he stretched his arms over his head and then slumped back against the booth. He'd told all this to Greg and been overruled. Sam wanted to look into who had the resources and motivation to kill five cadets scattered around the world. And who wanted so very much for Earth to lose the trial.

Instead he was at a cheap Fourth of July festival. Two mobile carnivals were sharing space in a huge, muddy field, with lots of neon-lit rides and loud motors. A tall, plywood stage stood next to the game booths, where a country music group was finishing a song. They left, probably to get beer and cool off, and their absence lowered the noise level a fraction. The other cadets seemed to be enjoying themselves, which was good, because there were press in the crowd. There were also about twice as many security people as before, and all the cadets had been fitted with GPS trackers. But Sam still didn't like it.

The Ferris wheel on his right inched along letting people on and off, while the kids at the top yelled and rocked their cars. Red, blue, and yellow lights decorated the spinning cups, while the merry-go-round shone mainly yellow. All combined, the light cast a pinkish glow over the whole place.

"We're celebrating July the fourth, that's why we're here." Downy said. "Wait, wow. What is this? What. Is. This?" Downy turned pink in wonder, almost the same color as the cotton candy swirling around in the pot next to him.

"It's cotton candy," said the man running the cart. He swirled some on a cardboard cone. His beard was long, tied in two bunches against his chest. "You want some—four bucks."

Downy pulled out a ten. "I would like two. Purple and pink."

The guy jerked his head at the sign on his cart. "Three for ten."

Downy smiled, stretching his dolphin smile and showing teeth. "That is excellent."

Downy held pink cotton candy in his left hand and purple and yellow in his right as they walked away. "Wow," he moaned. "This is wonderful. Really wonderful. If you pass the trial this should be one of your first cultural exports. It would establish your Level 7 ranking for sure."

"Our what?" Sam said, jogged out of his lethargy.

"Your level 7. I'm not surprised the Rik want to..." Downy's eyestalks twitched together, crossing his eyes in embarrassment. "Oh, sheep poop. I can't tell you that."

Sam grabbed his arm and pulled Downy into the shadow behind the Ferris wheel engine. "Downy. What's a level 7? What do the Rik have to do with this? You know Nat is the new primary witness in the trial. If you have anything, and I mean anything, useful to tell me, you better cough it up."

"Sam, it's a galactic policy. I can't tell you. No choice," Downy said.

Sam pictured the flaming bottle spinning toward Nat, the homeless people lining Hollywood Blvd.

"You absolutely have a choice," he said. "You can watch my planet self-destruct—and lose our sentiency status in the trial, whatever that would mean—or you can tell me what you know. Humans work much better with a goal in mind. Are the Rik behind Jonathan and the other killings?"

"Greg would kill me," Downy said.

"Please, Downy. You like Earth, don't you? You like the sheep and the cotton candy and the root beer. Don't you want us to win?"

A strange color swept through Downy for a moment, but Sam couldn't fix on it before it was gone.

"I'll tell you," Downy said, "if you promise not to tell."

Sam and Downy were in deep discussion when Sam suddenly felt a flash of fear. He stepped away from Downy, scanning the crowd around him. Just people—drinking beer, eating popcorn, and drinking lemonade. Just—men. Huh. Sam didn't see many kids around, and there'd been hundreds an hour ago. And only a few women, not many. It was getting quite dark now. Sam and Greg would address the crowd at nine, before the fireworks.

"There's something wrong," Sam said. "I don't know what..."

Greg came towards them between the booths and carts, a path opening in the crowd. He looked pink in the light, but that couldn't be right.

"Time to get on stage," he said.

Sam shook his head. "There's something bothering me—but I don't know what." He closed his eyes. "It's... No. I can't think." Closing his eyes made him sleepy, he really needed a good night's rest. Nightmares about Jonathan kept him up.

"Just talk to them," Greg said, pulling him onto the plywood stage. "It'll get better."

Greg took the microphone from the lead guitarist and began to speak about the Fourth of July. The rest of the cadets made their way to the stage, gathering in messy ranks behind Greg. They were tired too, but Greg thought it important the cadets make an appearance on Independence Day. The irony of the aliens holding Fourth of July celebrations was lost on Greg.

Sam struggled to focus while Greg addressed the crowd. There was something wrong.

An angry rustle went through the crowd.

"What do you know about freedom, you roach!" someone yelled.

"Are you serious?"

"You don't belong here!"

Sam jerked his head up. What just happened? There was no trigger.

A can of Dr. Pepper sailed through the air and hit Downy in the head. He was standing just behind and to the left of Greg.

Greg paused. "Violence will not be tolerated."

"You don't have the right!"

"Go *&% yourself!"

The yelling started to drown out the grinding ride engines.

A bucket of popcorn sailed forward. Then a beer bottle. It shattered against the stage, peppering the cadets with broken glass. Sam threw an arm up to protect his eyes.

Another bottle flew through the air and Greg tossed the microphone on the ground. He'd already palmed the defense device from his pocket. Greg cupped his hands and thrust them forward, like he was shoving someone away from him.

"No!" Sam shouted, but Greg didn't hear him or didn't care.

A ripple of orange went out from his hand. A thunderous clap shook the air as the kinetic force wall expanded and popped. The bottle hit the field and shattered, rebounding into the crowd. People started screaming, some because they'd been shattered with glass, some in fury.

Sam felt the scream jump from person to person, like tongues of flame igniting kindling. It rose up and engulfed the crowd. They turned from a lot of ticked individuals into an incandescent beast. They surged forward and Greg thrust his hands again. The orange plane of force slammed into the mob and threw five guys into the air and back into the crowd. They were reabsorbed into the beast. Two new surges came around the huge speakers in the middle of the stage, like a Greek monster that grew two new heads when you lopped one off.

Greg tossed another kinetic device to Downy. "Cover the right!" he said.

Greg threw his arms to the left, causing another flailing mass of bodies to shoot into the air. Downy shoved his field toward the right, but he wasn't close enough to the back ranks of cadets. He deflected part of the surge, but four of the cadets in the back were outside the range of his shield. Men swarmed toward them. Sam saw broken bottles slamming at the cadets and boots swinging.

"Get them!" Sam shouted, "We've got to get to them!"

But Greg was busy deflecting the unending surge on his side and Downy was clearly outmatched. Their kinetic devices were only for personal defense. The cadets were packed together, trapped on both sides. On the edges they tried to fight, but the mob kept coming. Sam was stuck in the middle of the group, fighting to get to the ones taken down in the back.

Downy threw wall after wall, but couldn't gain any ground.

Sam's mind was on fire. This was impossible. He'd known about the riots, but this was—monstrous. It happened so fast, Sam gasped. The note, the flyer he'd seen in Hollywood! July 4th. This wasn't a random mob, it was planned. Shoot, shoot, shoot! He'd been so distracted by Jonathan's disappearance he forgot about it.

Never mind. Sam pushed past Melanie, but she grabbed his arm.

"Sam! Sam!"

"Let go!" Sam said, shoving her off and pushing toward the rear of the stage. The stage was a plywood prefab, the back wall covered with decorations and something that looked like vomit in equal portions. But as he neared the back of the stage where he could almost reach the downed cadets, flames began licking up the back wall.

The backdrop of the stage was on fire. Sam's feet were sweating hot in his shoes, and he could see fire under the stage as well. The cadets nearest the wall were yelling and shoving forward. He could barely hear their screams over the roar of the crowd.

"Fire, fire!" Sam yelled. "Get them to—"

He broke off. The sharp popping of an automatic gun pierced the roar.

Sam froze, seeing the muzzle fire of five or six handguns fired point blank into the crowd. The security men on the stage opened fire. The beast-crowd moaned in pain but only got more aggressive, a wounded bear.

Suddenly the whole place lit up, spot lights from several helicopters roved over the crowd, temporarily blinding Sam.

"Back away! *Back away!*" blared the raspy voice of a Spo on a loudspeaker. "We will fire. BACK AWAY."

Nets fell, tangling around the seething crowd. As the voice penetrated the smoke, rope ladders snaked down from the helicopters towards the stage.

SAM SAT against the wall in the infirmary, his hands shaking. Five cadets lay on cots in front of him. Their clothes—ripped, bloody, and burned—were piled in the corner. The doctors Greg commandeered from the hospital were stitching up cuts and sterilizing burns. No one was in critical condition, though Micah had a concussion and was still throwing up.

The doctors kept glancing at Sam. He didn't meet their eyes.

Greg had ordered him out of the infirmary, but Sam refused.

The riot happened so fast. But Sam had known about it. How could he have failed to report that flyer? He didn't make mistakes like that. Did he? He'd forgotten it that day because Jonathan disappeared... and he never once remembered to tell Greg?

It was impossible. Normal people might just forget, but Sam had been trained to memorize and analyze a hundred options at once. He could look at a ship computer board and remember every detail for hours.

He had to face it. Some part of him must not have wanted to warn Greg. Now five of his friends were scarred for life. The security guys who heard him yell 'fire,' had mostly fired over the heads of the mob, but Sam knew many had been hit. He suspected there were deaths. Sam dug his hands into his hair and pulled.

When Greg ruined things with Nat, Sam had an immature desire to get back at him. What Greg saw as an interesting assignment was Sam's life. He'd done nothing about it, but since coming back to Earth, he'd felt more and more distance from Greg. Maybe on some level Sam still wanted to betray him. Maybe subconsciously he wanted to prove all the reporters wrong, he wanted to prove that he was loyal to humanity. But in betraying the Spo, Sam only got more people hurt.

Everywhere Sam looked, that same fact slapped him down. He had been innocent when he yelled 'fire,' but still it was his voice that started the shooting. It seemed any way he turned, Sam could get more people hurt. If he tried to distance the cadets from the Spo, assuming Greg would even let him, it could get even worse. At least the Spo *wanted* to protect them.

. . .

SHARA WATCHED the NBC evening news while she waited next to Gate 13 at LAX airport. The newscasters were covering the latest cadet story—the riot at the county fairgrounds.

They barely mentioned Jonathan! It was all, resistance this and insurrection that. People critically injured. Trample injuries.

Shara didn't really care since she had nothing to do with it.

In the little they *did* say about Jonathan, it appeared he didn't remember anything. Perfect. She'd suffered serious anxiety after leaving him alive. The human subconscious was a curious thing. She woke in the middle of the night, sweating and terrified. She'd dreamed of her superior, punishing her for carelessness, making small slices in her soft, human flesh.

As a Rik, Shara had dreamed plenty of times. She'd dreamed memories of the day, memories of childhood, or meaningless color-scapes. The human brain took dreaming to an amazingly dark sensory level. It created scenes she never experienced—with color, smell, and pain. She rubbed her side, still able to feel the knife touching her ribs. If humans could sell their dreams, they could take over the galaxy.

Culture was money, in the galactic community. Hard resources—minerals, oil, and water—you could get those anywhere. Culture, on the other hand... was profitable. The Crosspoint, ugly little slugs, made bundles on their phosphorescent body paint and tactile poetry scrolls. The Merith made the most on their food, Merith restaurants dotted the galaxy. But Earth—Shara had never seen a culture with so much potential. The movie industry alone would support Earth for years. Their music, the ridiculous number of languages, their art... they had everything. If they could learn a way to record dreams—the galaxy would go nuts. Earth could be the first planet to enter the council as a level 8 culture.

That was why she was here. The Rik wanted Earth. Unlike humans, the Rik had no discernible culture. They were parasites with no name. The original Rik were an ocean-dwelling people with gigantic underwater cathedrals. A few generations ago, Shara's people took over the Rik planet. They converted the Rik bodies to their own use, as Shara had done with this human girl. Now they were known as the Rik, but even their name was stolen.

Of course, the Galactic Council knew what had happened, and the Rik were generally despised. If they were discovered throwing Earth's trial—bad things would happen.

All that would change soon. When humanity lost the trial, they would be declared non-sentient. They would have no protection from a Rik invasion then.

Shara smiled as she saw her next target come towards the gate.

Akemi sat in a wheelchair with a special plastic oxygen tank hanging from the back. A thin plastic tube stretched from the tank to a clear mask over her nose and mouth.

She was a slight girl, probably 90 pounds. At need, Shara could carry her without any help. That might be useful.

Akemi was wheeled down the tunnel to the airplane before anyone else. She was allowed to pre-board before the first class passengers because she needed assistance. After her empty wheelchair was brought back out the flight attendants started boarding.

"Flight 8410 to Tokyo, flight 8410. First class passengers and AirPass members may begin boarding."

Shara waited until Section 6 was called to grab her bag and get on the plane.

On the plane, Akemi had been moved to a normal seat. The oxygen tank rested at her feet, and her mother adjusted the mask over her face. Akemi's eyes were closed, and she looked in pain.

As Shara came down the aisle, Akemi opened her eyes. She gave a slight smile as Shara stopped across the aisle from her.

"I guess this is my spot," Shara said. She pushed her backpack around a bit until it slid under the seat, and plopped down next to

Akemi. She was silent for a moment, but saw that Akemi was looking at her. Perfect.

"My name is Shara. I wanted to tell you, I love your top. Very organic yet... self-contained."

"Thanks." Akemi looked ready for a distraction. "This is one of my favorites. The neckline reminds me of an iris," she paused. "Plus, it's loose, so I can wear it over my bandages." She pulled her neckline down a few inches to show the top of the thick bandage covering her scar.

"Ouch, that looks bad."

"Well, it means I'll get better, so I can live with it. I like your boots, too."

"Thank you!" Shara glowed. "I love fashion. I'd like to start my own line someday."

"Really? Are you a designer?"

"Yes, for a few years. Just grunt work so far, but I have my first big job now. You'll never believe this...it's with the aliens," she whispered.

"The Spo? Do they like fashion?"

"Oh, they don't really care. But they want the cadets to look a certain way. I'm doing research and then I get to design a uniform for them! I'm so excited. I even suggested that while I'm at it, I could design something better for the aliens, and they said go ahead. Can you believe it?"

"That's amazing. My sister..." Akemi blinked a bit. "She's one of the cadets. Maybe you'll meet her."

"Oh, my goodness. What are the odds? Tell me *all* about her," Shara said.

10

CLAUDIA WOKE when her cell phone buzzed under the pillow. She was stretched out on her friend's couch and it took her a second to find the phone under the tangled sheet of her pallet.

"You should turn on the news," Chris said, right away.

Claudia felt around for the remote. She flicked on the TV, and changed it to 4.2. Grainy footage of a burning stage covered the screen, carousel lights flickering in the background. The voice over said, "—the riot, which some have alleged to be premeditated, erupted at 9:00p.m. last evening. The Spo fired on the crowd causing four fatalities and eight injuries. Others were burned and trampled, the total number of injuries is not known.

"This man, Robert Gravies, was there." The screen flicked to a balding, white guy.

"Uh. Yeah, the cadets all crowded around the Spo. Looked like they were protecting them. Then one of 'em said, 'Fire!' and suddenly there were bullets flying—"

Claudia muted the TV. "Was he hurt?" she said. "Do you know what happened?"

"Sam wasn't hurt, but several of his friends were. I'm betting he could use a visit from his sister. Are you ready to go to Malibu?" Chris asked.

"Will they let you leave the hospital already?"

"'Course they will," Chris said. "If you pick up my car from my apartment, you can come get me."

Claudia drove Chris westward on Highway 10. His arm was in a tight sling against his chest, the wrist in a temporary cast.

"I appreciate this," Claudia said. "I know the Spo don't want cadet families showing up yet."

"Well, not to blow my own horn," Chris said, "but I have a certain amount of influence with the Spo, or at least with all their security, which comes to the same thing. They'll let us in."

"Thanks for using your influence then," Claudia said.

"It's not a bad job."

"You want to work for them?" Claudia asked. She couldn't help it. Didn't he care who he worked for?

"The Spo aren't that bad. I know you probably hate them for taking your brother. But honestly, they're not going away. It makes more sense to work with them than not," he said.

"Like hell."

"Maybe we should talk about this later."

"I'm fine." Claudia stopped at the light on the 10 on-ramp. It turned green and she surged forward, nearly hitting the minivan in the HOV lane. She tapped the brake and got in behind the minivan, but that only made her angrier.

"You were attacked. You almost lost your hand to a Spo pet. What's the matter with you?"

"That's a fair point. Working security for the aliens is the toughest, strangest job ever. I expect to get hurt. Not their fault."

"What are those animals for anyway?"

"The trouncers? They use them in their spaceships. The Spo have some kind of advanced biocomputer technology; they use trouncer brain tissue in their jump drives. A friend of mine is a programmer and he says it's incredible. I've heard they're going to start breeding them here. They're also looking into using dolphin and gorilla brain tissue."

"So now they'll start killing the animals too? Great." Like many animal doctors, Claudia couldn't stand animal testing. She should have guessed the Spo would start experimenting on animals, too.

"It's not their fault the Earth was so messed up when they got here."

"How about randomly kidnapping children and killing people? Is that their fault?"

"The kidnapping thing—I can't argue with you. And I'm not saying this makes it okay, but they don't see it as kidnapping. Apparently cross-species training programs are common on many planets. And I've seen Sam. He looks okay. And he seems—sorry, he seems pretty loyal to the Spo."

"He. Was. Thirteen. Thirteen. His voice hadn't changed. He liked Transformers and Monster Trucks."

Chris was silent.

"He had to survive. Of course he would pretend to do what they wanted."

Silence.

"He might have been brainwashed."

"Might have."

Claudia stopped at the next light. She exhaled slowly. "I'm sorry I picked a fight. It's none of my business what you do."

Chris was silent for a few minutes as she drove. Claudia finally looked at him.

"I know you're doing me a favor, so I'm not going to yell at you any more."

The expression on his face made her smile reluctantly.

Chris chuckled. "At least you calm down as fast as you get angry. My sisters can stay mad for weeks."

He pulled a note card out of his pocket. "You should take a look at this before we get there."

They were almost to Pepperdine, driving along PCH, which ran next to the beach. Claudia pulled into a big parking lot across from the school.

The note card had a list of colors.

"This is our shorthand for Spo emotion," Chris said.

ORANGE – Disgust
    Yellow – Calm, tired
    Pink – Pleasure
    Lavender – Surprise
    Grey – Anger
    Green – Interest, arousal
    Blue – Dead

"DEAD?" Claudia asked.

"That's just our joke," Chris said. "Obviously if they're dead you don't need to know how they feel."

"Okay, that's funny," Claudia admitted.

"The main ones to remember are orange and grey—those are bad. Though for you..." Chris gave her a once over. "Watch out for green too."

Claudia didn't have to look back at the card to put that together.

"Watch it," she said.

Claudia drove them back to PCH and across to Pepperdine. A tiny gatehouse sat next to the road that led into campus. A Spo, obviously too big to fit inside it, sat on a giant purple beanbag in the middle of the road.

Claudia came to a stop in front of the Spo. A security guy,

human, was in the gatehouse and he came up to Claudia's window.

"No visitors," he said. "You need to turn around." He had a hand on a holstered gun on his belt.

"Hey, Mike," Chris said, "It's me. I need to go in."

Mike hunched over to get a better look. "Chris! The trouncer didn't get your arm, huh? Gustav was pissed about that. He wants to see you."

Chris wrinkled his nose. "I know it. I'm going to try and avoid him for a few more days. His wife loved that animal."

The Spo in the road hoisted himself off the beanbag and came around to see what was going on.

"Here's the deal," Chris said. "This is Sam's sister. She saved my hand and she needs to see her brother. I want to take her in."

Mike frowned. "Did you see the riot last night? Sam was in the thick of it."

"I know, all the more reason. From what I hear, Greg's got a lot of plans for that kid."

Mike looked uncertain, but the Spo suddenly joined in.

"I saw Sam this morning. Kid's melting. Let his sister go on in."

Mike looked relieved. "Okay. Go on in. Sam's in the Fieldhouse Dorm, room 308."

Claudia and Chris went up the stairs and found their way to room 308. The place didn't feel like a dorm. The doors should have been propped open, music blasting from one or more rooms, kids snacking and talking and avoiding homework. All the doors were closed.

They finally got to 308 and Claudia knocked, four hard raps.

An alien opened the door. Claudia pulled back. He looked surprised to see her too, turning slightly purple. Lavender, that is. Chris put his good hand on Claudia's shoulder, pulling her back slightly.

"I need to see Sam," Claudia said authoritatively, though she did take another step back. "Is he here?"

"Who is it?" Sam asked from inside.

"Someone for you," Downy said, swinging the door wide open. Claudia recognized Sam, but it was hard. Her little brother Sam was there, but drowned in this hard teenager. Sam was laying on his bed, in grey sweat pants and an orange shirt. His expression was forbidding.

"What are you doing here?" he asked. "No press is allowed on campus."

"I'm not press. Don't you recognize me?" she said, stepping into the room.

"If you were at the carnival, I don't want to talk."

"Don't be stupid, Sam," said Downy, "it's your sister."

Sam sat up slowly. "Claudia?"

She nodded.

"Downy, could you leave for a while?" Sam asked. Downy looked between the two of them, turning a little green now. Claudia was blank. Green was... shoot, it was gone. She glanced at Chris but he shook his head. To her surprise, the alien opened the door and left without arguing.

"What does green mean again?" Claudia demanded, when the door shut. There was no way to ease into this conversation. If the water is freezing, you dive in.

"Green?" Sam said

"On an alien—he turned green."

"Oh. He's curious about you. Probably because I told him you were in a 4H program and raised sheep."

Claudia pulled out his desk chair and sat down. She did it to make the situation more informal, not only because she felt shaky and nauseated.

"I'll just wait outside," Chris said. He went out and stationed himself in front of the door, but left it cracked. Claudia wasn't sure if that was so she could see him, or that he didn't trust Sam with her.

"So that alien won't cause trouble for you?" Claudia asked.

"Probably not. Or else he'll tell my mentor you're here and they'll beat me and sterilize you."

She gaped at him.

"But probably not. Why are you here, sis?" he said, weariness in his voice.

"I've missed you Sam. I wanted to know that you were still you. Or if you're not, I need to know that too."

Sam didn't look gratified. "As far as you're concerned," he said, "I don't think I am."

"Is that—Sam, what's wrong? I've seen you on TV a couple times. You never looked like this. What's going on?"

"What's going on?" he echoed. "Hell if I know. Did you hear about the riot yesterday?"

"I saw it on the news. But that's not your fault. You can't take responsibility for all their atrocities," Claudia said.

"Oh, I don't," Sam said. "Only the ones I'm part of." He ran a hand over his eyes. "I'm sorry. I've thought about seeing you and Mom... but you're so different. I'm so different. I don't think we have anything to say to each other."

"Sam, we do. They've brainwashed you. Do you know how many people they've killed in the last six years?"

"Not specifically. But what if they hadn't come? Would you rather have died from radiation or poisoned water supplies?" Sam defended them unenthusiastically.

"But that's just the thing. Did they save us from that? Or did they cause it?" Claudia couldn't help glancing at the door. She sure hoped his room wasn't wired or anything.

"What." Sam said. "You think the Spo caused the Hadron explosion and the devastation? That's ridiculous. The Gamal terrorists took credit. There's proof."

"Proof, yeah, but lots of people are asking how some tiny terrorist group had the wherewithal to do that. It's doesn't make much sense."

"No. I'll tell you what doesn't make sense. If the Spo wanted to take over Earth, they could've blasted us out of the galaxy or dumped sasoikeo in the oceans." Sam shuddered. "They didn't need to destroy Europe with the Hadron explosion."

"But wouldn't somebody have been mad? I mean, isn't there like a universal council or something?" Claudia swallowed. She knew she was on thin ice here. "This way it looks like they're the good guys."

"They're not the good guys," Sam said. "They do a lot of things, but lying about it, that's not their way. They might destroy a planet but they'd tell them the truth about it."

"Are you sure?" Claudia asked. She didn't want to leave him angry with her, but this might be her only chance to make him think. She had half an hour, versus six years of indoctrination.

Sam rubbed his eyes, blinking at her like his vision was bad. Then he closed his eyes and stood up. "You've got to go," he said. "They're not too happy with me right now, and I don't want anything to happen to you."

"Gee thanks," Claudia said. The pain of his dismissal wavered in her chest, a wave about to break. "Tell me about you, Sam, before I go."

"It's depressing," Sam said. "And I'm not supposed to talk about it."

"So? Nobody's here. Talk to me."

"I'm not supposed to."

"What? You're so loyal to them you can't even talk to your sister? Can't you talk to anybody? That's why people don't trust any of you."

Sam opened his mouth to yell at her, but noise from the hallway broke in.

"Who are you?" a gravelly voice demanded. "Get out of my way."

"Hold a minute," Chris said. "I'm Chris, one of the security—I said *hold* on."

Sam jerked the door open, and Claudia saw Chris blocking a big brown alien from entering the room.

"It's okay Greg," Sam said. "He brought my sister to see me. It's no big deal."

"No family yet," Greg said. "You agreed." His smell made Claudia's nose burn.

Chris didn't move to let Greg in. "Like I said, my name is Chris Tatlock. I'm chief of security for General Gustav and headquarters in LA." He waited until Greg looked at him. "I'd like you to let them finish their conversation." His words were polite, but his tone final.

To Claudia's surprise, Greg backed off. He looked at Chris closely, then nodded. "Fine. I'll return later."

Sam raised his eyebrows. "Unexpected."

Claudia looked at Sam. "I wish I could—I don't know. I wish there was something I could do. I thought if I could just see you—"

Sam rubbed his eyes. "I'm sorry, this is bad timing. I've made several big mistakes this week and I'm just not ready... to deal with you. Maybe in a week or two, I don't know if you can stay in LA—"

Claudia grabbed his hand. "I can wait. But I'm not leaving here without a hug. I'm not doing that again." She pulled him into a hug, but kept it short. She could feel tears building.

"Oh, a little girl asked me to get this letter to Nat. Nat's sister," Claudia said.

Sam's eyebrows went up. "You know Akemi?" he asked.

"Well, I met her at the hospital, it's kind of a long story," she gave him the letter. She moved to hug Sam again but he shifted his weight away from her.

"Sorry," she said. "Okay. I'll see you again, little dude."

As Chris escorted her back to his car she saw blood seeping through his temporary cast and the sling on his arm.

"You're bleeding! What happened?" Claudia demanded.

Chris shrugged. "That big alien got in my face a bit, bumped my arm."

"That's terrible. How bad is the pain?"

Chris smiled. "Manageable. But you better take me back to the hospital. They might need to sew me up a little tighter.

11

GREG WOKE Sam up from a nap that afternoon. He crouched in the middle of the little dorm room, almost touching both mattresses. His skin was dry and brown, a very bad sign. The Spo skin color varied during their waking hours, loosely connected to their mood. It dried out when they didn't take care of themselves, or when they were stressed. The dryness helped them blend into the deserts of their homeworld when they were pursued by a predator.

Sam rubbed crumbs out of his eyes and forced himself to sit up. His back was stiff from leaning over his friends in the infirmary yesterday.

"What?" Sam said. "Is it about my sister?"

"No. I don't mind that she was here. It's the press." Greg used a claw to flick on their small TV.

An attractive Latina woman stood in front of Pepperdine, holding a microphone. "More of the Spo children are recovering from trauma today," she said. "An inside source tells me eight of the cadets are in serious condition after the riot. Only two days ago Jonathan Ortega was taken to City of Hope hospital, suffering from dehydration and a possible drug overdose. His family has been allowed to stay with him, and they released a statement that an acute attack of amnesia has blocked out his entire six years with the Spo. Hospital officials have promised he will be given the best psychological care they can provide.

"Sadly, most of the cadets, returned only a week ago, do not have family or hospital care. None of the cadets have been allowed to seek psychological counsel or comfort from family. Several eminent psychiatrists have speculated that mental breakdowns, or fugue states, are a very real possibility for these traumatized children."

The video cut to the July 4th carnival, showing the burning stage and giving a close up of screaming cadets. Then the video changed. It showed brief clips of the cadets at the Hollywood mall. One showed a group standing still, looking at the water fountain. The next was Marissa, running her hand over a huge bear outside the Build-A-Bear store. There were more, and with melancholy music playing, the whole thing looked nostalgic and pitiful. The video cut back to the reporter.

"We can't help but wonder what other manifestations of their tragic experience will emerge in the coming months." She paused. "On a global scale, the Spo children seem to be taking the brunt of anti-Spo hatred."

A shaky video showed Sam pushing Nat, with her clothes on fire, into the grass.

"Another four cadets were killed in the last two days, from the other groups. As angry as we all may be with the Spo, we at NBC urge you to recognize that these poor children are not Spo. They are human, and let's remember that we are too."

The video cut to aerial views of the devastation in Europe, a quick shot of the flattened Eiffel Tower, an old video of the first tsunami crashing into New York City. Then it cut to Sam, in the Crystal Cathedral, his first day back. "That's the good news. We—"

Greg clicked the TV off.

Sam bit his upper lip, chapped and blistered from the fire. "I can't believe I forgot that flyer. The riot must have been planned, at least loosely."

"I see two issues with the press response," Greg said, ignoring his comment. "First, they continually refer to you as, 'the children.' Second, they generally qualify it with, 'Spo children.'"

"So they don't trust us. So what?" Sam said. "The bigger problem is that they're right. People hate you so much they're killing us."

"Many Spo are looking into the murders. We will stop them." Greg shifted his weight. "We have suspicions, but nothing I can share with you."

"Well, can't I.... I don't know. Can't I do something? I need to be involved."

"You are involved, but you need to do your job. Right now, your job is to make the other humans not pity and despise you."

Sam thought for a minute and then sighed. "Okay. You win. If we could change the child image, the psychological trauma wouldn't be such a big story. If we could change the Spo connection—that's a big *if*—people wouldn't link us so much to your invasion."

Greg nodded.

"So... you already have a plan, don't you?" Sam asked. "How bad is it?"

Greg's eyestalks drooped comically. "It is not bad at all. We are in luck. There's a volcano erupting in Malaysia."

Sam rubbed his eyes some more. "That's luck? So what then? We're going to stop a volcano—or save some people and get some hero credit?

Greg nodded, scratching his dry skin. "You can direct the process from here, and I'll tell the press."

.   .   .

PEPPERDINE HAD several good computer labs. Over the next twelve hours, Sam and two of Greg's aids, Lurk and HP, turned one of the labs into a state-of-the-art contact room. Eight screens formed a semi circle around Sam's chair. Two CPU stacks, capable of running a missile defense AI system, handled the streaming video and communications. One screen showed news footage of Mount Merapi, the volcano in Malaysia, shrouded in a cloud of ash. It had erupted less than twenty-four hours ago, and slow moving lava still crept down one side. Ash filled the sky. Another screen showed a satellite view of the area, but it wasn't very helpful, showing hundreds of miles of formless grey. Many villages were in the eruption zone, and Greg was leading several teams to help with evacuation and flow control. The teams were composed of cadets, press, and actual search and rescue personnel, who probably didn't appreciate the "help." Sam was glad he wasn't there.

Another of his screens was slaved to a camera on the front helicopter. Greg was in that helicopter, surveying the villages, and Sam could alternate between Greg's helmet microphone and several news feeds on his audio channel.

Greg's chopper circled the first village, the one closest to the volcano. The afternoon sun showed dark orange through the heavy ash in the air as the helicopter banked west. Sam's eyes burned, partly from staring at blurry screens, partly because he'd only gotten six hours of sleep last night. He rubbed his eyes, and squinted down at the small set of homes. A slow stream of lava, moving less than ten feet per minute, slowly bore down on the community. It was still 200, 300 feet away; there was time to evacuate.

"Why is no one running?" Sam asked, speaking on Greg's line. "Did they already evacuate?"

Greg coughed, a harsh hacking noise, and Sam turned down his volume. The particles irritated Spo and human lungs alike.

"No evacuation," Greg said. "There've been no refugees from here."

"They why aren't they—" Sam paused, looking at the boiling black smoke billowing around the huts on the ground. He knew why they weren't leaving. "Smoke inhalation. You've got to get on the ground—start airlifting them out. Or else get one of the ground crews to get in there fast." Sam looked at another screen. It showed the GPS position of each team. Armen's group was the nearest. Sam moved his hand to toggle the communications so he could get Armen's group to the village.

"Negative," Greg said. "They'll be dead already."

"They *might* be dead already," Sam said. "Smoke inhalation can take hours to kill. Mopik told us the children tend to sleep in small closets or under beds. They might be alive."

"Doubtful. Do not send a team there."

Sam pushed away from his chair, getting close to the screen. He looked at the liquid smoke and the fluttering plumes of ash rising from the slow lava run approaching the village.

"I don't care if you're freaking certain," Sam said. "I'm alerting Armen's team."

"You will not," Greg said, his voice harsh. "I am deploying sasoikeo."

"What? Why?"

"Most, possibly all, of the people in that village are dead. If any are still alive when the lava reaches them, they will die horribly. Mercy is to prevent suffering."

"Then send a team there to evacuate!"

"The ground teams will be more effective elsewhere. Rescue must be efficient."

"Efficient? Or do you just want to avoid bad press, if there's no one alive?"

"Both," Greg said. "Deploy sasoikeo."

"Don't deploy, don't!" Sam shouted. He heard a click, and

three of his screens went dark. Sam jerked his eyes to Lurk, who shrugged with his whole body.

"Be silent," Greg said through the earpiece. "The press is undoubtedly covering this signal. I'm cutting off your access. You will not give them this information."

"You're going to kill all those people," Sam said.

"No, I'm going to make sure that if any are still alive, they don't suffer a horrible death."

"By killing them!"

"Yes. By killing them. This is my decision."

"Or what?" Sam said. He wished he could see Greg, but there was no video inside the helicopter. What was he thinking?

"If you alert Armen's team, they will come here and die from the sasoikeo."

"Along with all these people?"

"Yes. If you cannot be efficient you are a danger to us and a danger to your planet. Decide."

"You—you—"

"Will you alert Armen's team?"

In the background Sam heard another voice, "Sasoikeo away."

From Greg's chopper camera Sam could see three other helicopters hovering low over the village. Small blue canisters fell with timed precision. Drop. Drop. Drop. Each one took about four seconds to fall to the earth, where it disappeared into the black smoke. Upon reaching the ground, each would detonate and spew a clear, heavy gas that clung to the ground. It would seep under doors, through thatched roofs, and between cracks in mud walls. It would kill anyone who might have survived the smoke. If Armen went there now, he would die too.

"I—No, I won't. I won't kill anyone else... But why? This is efficient?" Sam whispered. Greg's image was cracking in his mind, shattering into a thousand painful pieces, the same way his father's had when he left.

"That is correct. It is efficient and sufficient for now."

Sam heard another click. His screens turned back on.

"Pilot, please circle to the south toward the next village," Greg said.

Sam unclenched his fists, with dents in his palm from his nails. He knew the Spo tradition on family survival and death—that it was better for families to die together than suffer broken-ness. He'd always thought it an odd, but possibly compassionate point of view. At least that was what they thought. But Sam had never seen it employed like this. He'd never seen Greg kill for his cold-blooded tradition. From here, it looked like murder, not compassion. It looked like Greg cared more about bad press than lives.

The day became a nightmare that Sam could not escape. When Greg poisoned the third village, Sam jerked out of darkness to find HP pressing an inhaler tube over his mouth and nose. He'd had some kind of panic attack. Sam shoved HP away and pressed the power button on the screen to turn off the video. He couldn't watch anymore. He had to deal with the audio and coordinating the teams on the ground; that was his role. He didn't have to see it.

There were thirteen communities at immediate risk from the volcano, and by the end of the day, nine had been evacuated. Sam felt numb.

He'd started shivering sometime around the second village, his teeth clacking painfully, but that was over now. Whenever he wasn't speaking into the microphone, he was watching HP and Lurk, who were watching him.

Sam had never felt the aliens' presence so sinister and foreign before. Who were they? These beings who would bomb whole villages for nothing? Had they been doing this sort of thing the whole time they were here? No wonder they were hated. No wonder Sam was hated. He watched Lurk and HP and the black screen, and six years of normalcy fell away from him.

When that flash mob attacked them at the festival, this was what they were attacking.

Sam had trusted Greg. He hadn't forgotten that Greg was an alien, but he'd put it aside. And ever since Sam came back to Earth the reporters and psychologists had been asking whether Sam was loyal to the aliens or humanity. He thought he could do both. Now he knew the answer.

For years, back on the Spo planet, Sam had asked those same questions. How much could he trust the Spo? How much could he love Greg before he betrayed his mom? Greg had convinced Sam that he wanted to help humanity. Greg taught Sam that the greatest commitment Sam could make to Earth was to learn everything Greg could teach him.

Sam had just taken his last lesson from Greg.

THE NEXT MORNING, July 8th, Armen explained sadly for the news crews in Malaysia that blistering gas from the volcano had destroyed four communities. He was a natural in front of the camera, sharing his sympathy for the survivors and his pride in getting relief supplies to two countries simultaneously. He managed to humbly convey how much the Spo technology, used by Armen and his friends, had helped these crises.

Sam watched the press conference alone in his room, flipping between several news stations. He'd picked Armen to handle the conference, and he did it well. Sam made a mental note to talk to Greg about having Armen do more of the press releases.

In one of the wide shots, Sam spotted Melanie, Susan, and Al in a clump, whispering together. Melanie smiled at something Al said and Sam wanted to blot out the sight. Didn't she know what was going on?

When one camera scanned the crowd, Sam saw Nat standing at attention, listening to Armen's report. Her face was a mask, as usual these days, but something in her eyes reflected the horror in his own. She knew. He was sure of it.

Sam clicked off the TV and lay back on his bed.

The dorm felt deathly empty, silent and drained.

The cadets would be back sometime the next day, and Sam didn't know what to do. How could he look at Melanie and Armen and all the rest, knowing what the Spo had done? Worse, what Greg had done while making the cadets look like heroes?

Nat knew. Some of the others probably did too. How could Greg allow those people to be killed?

Sam knew Greg. He'd taught them about efficiency and Spo views on family death—but he'd also let Melanie throw birthday parties twice a year to celebrate everybody's birthday. He'd read the whole Old Testament, when Sam and some of the other cadets talked about Noah's ark and the flood. He'd given the cadets updates on their families, though the mentors of the other cadet groups never did.

Yet, he'd just killed hundreds of people to avoid the bad press of tragic rescues. And he'd made Sam watch. Hell, he'd practically put Sam in charge of it, organizing where the rescue teams went. How dare he do that to him? Greg took manipulation to a whole new level.

12

SAM SAT in a makeup room getting touched up for his coming TV appearance. The cadets had been back from Malaysia for three days, and Sam had managed to act somewhat normally since they returned.

A big talk show host was doing a live special on the cadets. It had been planned for weeks, and Nat and Jonathan were supposed to have been the main guests. Jonathan was obviously out, and Nat had asked Greg to excuse her. One guess as to why.

Taking advantage of the empty spots, Sam convinced Greg that he would be the best one for the interview and this morning they'd driven to Burbank, to the NBC studios.

The makeup room was bright, and mirrors lined the wall in front of him. He'd been at the studios since three in the afternoon, doing screen tests and blocking. Makeup was his last stop before the live interview at six.

"Thank heaven you're not green," the makeup lady said to him, "it would've taken hours to get you looking right."

"Is the greenness that bad?" Sam asked.

The makeup lady looked sideways at Melanie and Armen, standing in the hallway. "Not in person, but on TV? The green ones look sick and cold and a little fat. The videos from Malaysia were awful... except for the Asian chick. That's why Apple requested her. But since she's injured or something, I guess you got it."

She went back to powdering his face and neck.

"Apple?" Sam asked.

"Apple Heisman!"

"Okay?"

"Oh, right, you've been gone. Well, she and Kurt Hoenal are the biggest names in Hollywood right now. The Spo requested her to produce this."

She got out a huge compact with squares of brown and pink fitted together like a jigsaw puzzle. She took a long brush and started swiping the powder on his cheeks.

"She must be something else if the Spo noticed her." Sam eyed the blush. "That's—no offense—but that's going to make me look ridiculous."

She rolled her eyes, "Military guys are always scaredy-cats. You're way too pale. This'll make you look tanned and confident. Trust me."

On stage at last, Sam looked out at the empty seats. "No audience?" he said aloud.

A voice from off stage answered him.

"Absolutely not. We aren't fools."

A small, well-dressed woman came on stage from the shadows. Sam stepped back as she advanced on him, looking him over critically. "At least you're not green. That should help the ratings. I'm Apple Heisman."

"Ratings? You don't think people will watch?" Sam asked skeptically.

"Of course they'll watch. But will they throw trash at their screen and curse the aliens or call their mom to make sure she's watching?"

"Oh. So, no pressure?"

"Sarcasm, that's good. Very American. Now pay attention. You need to play this a certain way." Sam took a step back as she leaned toward him. No wonder the Spo liked her, she had the presence of a grizzly bear. A tiny, aggressive grizzly bear.

"I'll be fine," Sam said.

"Not if you don't listen to me. If you mess this up, the riots will get worse. More people will die. Got it?"

She had no idea. Sam stepped into her space. "Are you trying to scare me? I know the stakes and I don't get stage fright anymore. You can just back off."

No one knew better than he did how many people the Spo might kill.

She didn't back down. "Fine. I'll spare you the motivational muck. You've got to be genuine, you've got to be funny, and you've got to have some bloody good reason for humanity to like the aliens. Otherwise this whole thing is a waste of my time."

"Got it."

She looked dubious. "It's my butt on the line, kid. Are they going to let you say anything? Tell me the truth."

"I've got something to say." He sure did. This would be a live broadcast, and if Greg didn't like what Sam had to say, he'd have to pull Sam off the stage in front of the cameras.

"Fine," Apple said. "Time to get started."

The show host was an older black woman, her hair shot with grey, and her makeup subdued. She looked... nice actually, like somebody's mom or grandma. He'd expected somebody all glitz or all politics—she didn't fit either mold.

"Hi hon," she said, "I'm Rita. How ya doing?"

"I'm told to feel funny and genuine. It's not coalescing."

She laughed. "That was good. You're gonna be fine."

"How did you end up here?"

"Hosting a talk show for the alien invaders? It's a long story, mostly I owed Apple a favor."

"She's a little..."

"Steel in her backbone. Makes her darned uncomfortable unless she's pushing somebody's limits." Rita gave Apple a big grin as she bore down on them for a final check. "He's not sure about you, Apple."

"Good, he's smart." Apple helped them fix the mikes and rearranged their seating a couple times. Finally she was satisfied.

"Okay," Apple said, "Rita, think maternal. Concerned, excited, proud, curious. These are your little kids, come home at last, with a story to tell."

Apple turned to Sam. "Human. Human. Human. You're not Spo. We want to know what a human saw on their planet, what a human sees in them, why a human can trust them. Tonight you are not a freakishly dangerous alien experiment. Remember that."

"You don't have children, do you?" Sam said.

She walked away, her high-heeled shoes clicking on the hard wood stage. Sam sat in a deep purple arm chair across from Rita who was seated comfortably on one side of a purple loveseat. A small rug lay between them and a fake fire place to his left. Really, a fireside chat? He'd heard of those. It was the wrong image for the chat he planned to give, but then, no one knew what he was about to say.

The spotlights made holes in his vision as the camera men adjusted things. Sam moved his head slightly so he could see Nat, Armen, Melanie, Downy, and Greg between the spotlights. If he arranged it right, one blind spot centered over Greg and the other over Downy, and he could only see his human friends.

Then one of the crew was counting down, using his fingers to silently indicate, 3, 2, 1. He pointed at them and the red light on the center camera came on.

Rita started with some light chit chat. Establishing his name, where he was from, how old he was.

Then she turned to the camera. "But as you all know, this boy isn't captain of the basketball team or class president. He's one of the cadets who recently returned from Spo. Tell us about the planet, Sam. Is it like Earth? Hotter, colder, are there animals?"

"Spo is extremely hot, but not lush and wet, like a rain forest. Everything there is hard. The animals, the plants, the Spo most of all," Sam said with a fake smile. Rita laughed. Sam saw the red light jump to another camera that was discretely pointed at Greg and his friends in the audience, before it jumped to the camera on his right. He tried not to look at it.

"All the creatures of that planet are hard," Sam explained. "They have silica in their cells, like star fish. In their deserts, wounded animals don't die and rot. They melt into puddles. Smooth, like green glass. The puddles collect in valleys, one on top of the other, overlapping for miles."

"They just, poof, melt?"

"Small animals take about a week. The biggest ones, the size of horses, can melt for months. But sooner or later a puddle replaces the dead animal. When it gets cold, the puddles harden and each one is different, like a fingerprint.

"Some Spo collect them. They polish them and hang them in their houses. My mentor, Greg, has over a hundred at home," Sam said. "Other aliens pay big money to get one."

"Other aliens?" Rita said.

"Yeah, the Merith, Crosspoint, Rik, Tergre, Vel... they all buy culture."

"How can you buy culture?"

"You've heard the phrase, 'There's nothing new under the sun,'?"

Rita nodded.

"That's true. Unless you go to another sun. Most aliens are fascinated with new cultures. They'll pay through the nose for music, clothing, art, food—anything new. It's better than money. The Galactic Council rates planets based on the richness of their culture, and we're tentatively rated a Level 8. That's the highest level ever allotted to a planet on entry to the council. It's pretty incredible."

Greg was slowly changing color. Sam wasn't supposed to know about the Level 8. Greg glared at Downy. Clearly he knew or guessed where Sam had gotten some of his information.

Sam looked away from him, back to Rita. Greg had no idea how much worse it would get.

Rita wowed for the cameras.

"I had no idea! Will other aliens come here to trade with us?"

Sam took a deep breath. "No. We're under arrest."

Greg stood abruptly. Rita's eyes flicked to him, but she held her composure. "Arrest?"

"Humanity is accused of malignant non-sentience. Our trial is in a week."

Greg climbed over the chairs, to the edge of the stage. "You must not say this," he said. The guy at the central camera pivoted to get Greg in the shot.

Rita swallowed and cleared her throat. "Why not?"

Sam held Greg's gaze. Greg wanted Sam to be a manipulator of public opinion? He should enjoy watching this.

"The Spo don't trust humans. That's why I'm not supposed to say anything. But I do trust you. I think you all deserve to know what's happening. What's about to happen. When terrorists exploded the Hadron collider, it made the Galactic Council very nervous. That's why the Spo came. They're like our probation officers."

While Sam spoke, Greg changed color again. He'd been purple, deeper and deeper, a plum color. Now he started to fade. The purple leeched out of him, and he turned grey. The grey of the ash that fell from Mount Merapi.

This was going to be bad, but Sam didn't stop. He laid out all the information he had. The riot. Jonathan. The trial. The victims of the volcano. He explained how all the witnesses were killed or hurt. How Nat was the new witness from their group. Everything he'd learned from Downy and everything he'd learned from Greg.

Rita had stopped throwing the conversational ball, and was allowing him to speak uninterrupted. He finished with a warning.

"I know this information is shocking. I'm still reeling with it, and I don't have all the answers. But listen. Killing the Spo will do no good. It will only reaffirm our status as crazy lower life forms. I'm appealing to you as the intelligent and rational species I know you to be. The Spo think we can't handle this information. They think lies are better; that with the truth we'll riot and destroy ourselves and our chance at this trial. They're wrong. Our sentiency trial is in one week. Don't give them any more fuel. Let's give our witnesses the best chance we can. Let's win the trial and get rid of the Spo."

Sam saw Apple Heisman slash her hand across her neck, in the kill signal. The cameras drooped, the red light on the center camera slowly dimmed to black. There was silence in the studio.

"Dramatic ending," Apple said. "A little cliché, but it'll do."

Nat looked frozen in place. Downy was slightly green. Sam stared back at Greg. He half expected Greg to bound on stage and throttle him right now, but Greg stood motionless next to the stage.

The show host rose to her feet, pulling Sam up with her. She had tears in her eyes. She gave him a deep hug. She whispered in his ear, "That was brave, sweetie. You did good."

She stepped back and turned to Greg, "You should—"

Sam cut her off. Whatever she was about to say to Greg would only get her hurt. He slipped gently away from her.

"It's okay. He won't hurt me," Sam said. He hoped it was true. He knew he had taken a great risk tonight. He'd told the world everything about their situation, and it could backfire horribly. However, and this gave him courage, the Spo couldn't punish everyone, they had safety in numbers. This was the only act of loyalty Sam could think of that wouldn't have terrible repercussions for everyone involved.

On the other hand, it could have terrible repercussions for him.

It was astounding how much his relationship with Greg had changed in the last few weeks. Sam would have trusted Greg with his life on Spo. He did, in fact, trust him with his life. Now he wasn't sure that Greg wouldn't kill him and his family in the next few days. Sam felt oddly disconnected from the thought. His emotions couldn't process how dangerous things had gotten.

Sam wondered again about his training. Greg told him, that second day on Earth, that the Spo had brainwashed him. Sam had denied it, but now he knew it was true. They hadn't exactly tricked him into being their puppet, but they had scrubbed his emotions. He couldn't even feel properly, even fear.

On the upside, that would save him a lot of terror and anxiety over whether Greg would kill him.

Greg nodded slowly, still grey. "It's finished. Let's go back to Pepperdine."

The ride back to campus was quiet, under a spectacular sunset.

BACK IN HIS ROOM, Sam lay on his bed. He was sleepy now. He should be scared, but he just wanted to sleep. Downy lay on his mattress on the floor. His color was slightly pink.

Sam frowned and closed his eyes. "You seem awfully happy," he said, referring to Downy's color. "I thought you'd be furious with me for blurting all that over live television."

A knock on the door interrupted him. Greg opened the door and walked in. His scarred face wore its usual half smile, but his sickly color betrayed his real state.

"Downy, you need to go," he said.

"Actually, I'd rather not," Downy said. "Sam is my friend."

"Fine," Greg snapped out. "Sit there and be quiet. Don't think I don't know where Sam got his information."

Downy sat down, sulky.

Sam didn't sit up. Back on Spo, he would have sat up in respect. Yesterday he might have sat up to be on guard. Now, neither respect nor fear motivated him.

"What next?" Sam asked. "Am I disqualified for the trial? Nat's our witness anyway."

"You don't understand," Greg said. "You may have disqualified your whole species."

"What do you mean?" Sam asked.

"You messed up," Greg spit out. "I knew you might turn on me, but you had to do it in the worst possible way. I tried to prepare you for this. You know how we handle natural disasters. In what way did my teaching fail you?"

Sam sat up. "You lied. You said the Spo killed out of mercy, but that was just... convenience."

"You do not understand... which must be my fault as much as yours. But couldn't you see where this would lead?"

He turned to Downy. "Couldn't you see where this would lead? You know our history!"

His anger finally succeeded in rousing fright in Sam. Not for himself but for everybody else.

"What's going on?" Sam said.

"We weren't keeping this information back for our own amusement. The last time a species knew the risks they tried to act preemptively. Their desperate attack assured that they would lose their sentiency trial. And they did lose it. They were called the Rik."

"You don't know that the same thing will happen here!" Sam said. "Besides, riots were already tearing through Cairo, Buenos

Aires, Phomn Fenh, who knows where! Humanity is intelligent. Now they know *why* they need to behave. Knowing the truth will help."

"You're willing to bet your whole species for that?" Greg asked.

Sam thought for a moment. "Humans work better toward a goal. And honestly, it looks like we're heading toward losing anyway. I think if we're going to fail, we should fail with all the information."

"And it's your choice?"

"Someone has to make the choice," Sam said. "Someone human."

"Risking destruction?"

Sam was silent.

"Are you taking responsibility for your planet?" Greg asked. "That's the question."

He picked up Sam's backpack, and handed it to him. "Pack some clothes. You're under arrest."

13

DOWNY WATCHED Sam throw clothes in a backpack and wanted to leap in satisfaction. Finally, *finally*, Sam was about to be beaten. Downy had baited him with the secret information days ago at the carnival, but he'd thought Sam forgot after the riot.

Sam patted Downy on the back as he went out the door. "Sorry I got you in trouble," Sam said.

Downy kept his claws retracted with an effort; the desire to slash Sam open almost overpowered him. But that would give Downy away, surely he could wait one more day to see how Sam's arrest played out.

Downy's resistance had fluctuated in the last week. Every day he had to smell Sam's sweat and urine and skin. The smell made Downy's air sacs tighten and twist. The smell of humans reminded him of a deadly bacteria on his planet. He'd smelled the bacteria the day before he met his first human, and he could never separate the smell again. He wanted to drown the smell, pour buckets of bleach in Sam's mouth until he ran clear. A slight shudder shook Downy as Sam briefly grasped his hand, but he tried to keep his color smooth and calm as he had been taught.

After these last few weeks on Earth, Downy's control was beginning to slip. On his planet it had been relatively easy to maintain his goofy, friendly façade with the cadets. On Earth it was harder; with humans surrounding him and their smell and their noise and their disgusting soft faces...

The sheer obscenity of the humans' twitchy, mobile flesh overwhelmed him. Downy touched his own face: hard, smooth, and damp, as it should be. Not quivering and reforming like a fungus.

When he'd been alone for five minutes, Downy called Shara.

"Did you hear?" he said, whispering in the Spo language. "Sam is under arrest. If his sentencing goes according to plan, they'll execute him. I did it!"

Shara was silent.

"What?" Downy said. "You botched Jonathan; don't pretend you're not impressed."

"I didn't botch Jonathan," Shara said.

"You totally—"

"Shut up!" Shara said. "I have a real job to finish."

Downy heard a voice in the background, asking Shara, "Is that Sam and Nat? Let's go!"

"What the hell?" Downy asked Shara. "Who's listening to us?"

"One sec," Shara said. Downy heard some muffled voices, then silence.

"Okay, better," Shara said. "I've got Akemi, Nat's little sister. I'm supposed to deliver both sisters tonight. I've been trying to reach you."

"I've been a little busy getting Sam to off himself."

"Fine, but he's not the next witness, is he? We need to get rid of Nat, and now we have to hurry. Bring Nat to the beach parking lot at midnight. There's a bathroom on the south side, I'll meet you there."

"Tonight?"

"Don't whine," Shara said. "They need Nat at least a week before the trial."

"But how am I supposed to get her out there in an hour?"

"I don't care. You work for us, remember? Get Nat down to the beach by midnight, that's one hour—tell her it has something to do with her sister. I'll bet she comes easy."

"What do you want her for?"

"That's Rik business. But if you wanna say goodbye, this is your chance."

DOWNY RAPPED a claw on Nat's door at 11:15. Nat's roommate answered, sleepily rubbing the tattoo on her cheek.

"What is it, Downy?" Jia said.

"I need to talk to Nat, could you tell her?"

"She's not here," Jia said. "Go away."

"What? It's past curfew. Where is she?"

"She wanted to go for a walk. You know, since Sam is...she's been crying."

Downy ground his incisors together. "Where does she walk?"

"I don't know. Sometimes she just sits by the pool. I gotta go to sleep."

Downy was annoyed. He needed to get Nat to the beach quickly. But now he had a problem. Finding Nat in the next forty-five minutes was possible but not certain. The campus was dark and he couldn't get any one else involved in looking. However... he eyed Jia speculatively...she knew Nat's normal spots. With her, he might be able to find Nat. But then, Jia would know he caused Nat to disappear. She'd have to disappear too.

Jia started to shut the door, but Downy stuck his foot in front of it. "Jia, come on. I can get her into see Sam tonight before the Spo take him. I gotta find her. He really wants to see her."

Jia's eyes widened. "Oh man. She's going to break. Maybe that's not a good idea."

"Come help me find her. You know where she's likely to be," Downy begged.

Jia wavered, then grabbed her sweatshirt and shoved her feet in some sneakers. Downy allowed her to go first down the stairs. Her neck looked extremely fragile. Perhaps he would throw her down a stairwell later. That would be a decent way to dispose of her.

Jia led him on a circuitous route through campus, checking the few places she knew Nat liked. Darkness steamed from the ground, filling the space between buildings. Lampposts dotted the campus and lined the walkways, but they weren't lit. The Spo preferred complete darkness at night. Greg didn't have any of the lights on campus lit, except over the doors of the dorms in use. Downy checked his pocket clock—it was eleven forty-five.

If he didn't find Nat, he'd have to substitute Jia. Possibly in the dark Shara wouldn't know the difference, she was only a stupid little Rik. Two dark haired human girls—they all looked alike.

"Oh! I see her!" Jia said. Downy had good night vision but the strange shapes of Earth: the curvy trees and fluttering leaves and chaotic brickwork, all contrived to confuse his night vision. He grew up with the clean, hard lines of Spo. Nothing fluttered on Spo. Surfaces were smooth from the heat, not full of meaningless detail. So, despite his significantly better sight, Jia could see Nat while he could not. Stupid planet. It always placed the Spo at a disadvantage. He couldn't wait to get out of here.

"Where?" Downy demanded.

"Right there, near the tower," Jia said. The tower was clean now. The sheep had been disposed of, the blood mostly washed off. A few brown stains remained, soaked into the gritty surface of the wall. Even Earth blood was ugly. Downy missed the frothy green blood of Spo animals.

Now he could see Nat. She leaned against the front of the tower, looking up at the stars.

"Nat!" Jia called. "You need to go with Downy. Sam wants to see you."

As Nat turned Downy caught a slight reflection from her black eyes. He felt mildly regretful that the Rik wanted Nat. She was one of the only humans he found tolerable. She was wary of him, and he liked that.

"What?" Nat demanded.

"Sam wants to see you, and Greg decided to permit it," Downy explained, circling around in front of Nat.

"What are you talking about?" she said. "Greg just told me I couldn't go in."

"You can't go in... but he's going to take Sam down to the beach. No one will see you," Downy said.

"That's crazy," Nat spit out. "Greg distinctly told me that I could see Sam tomorrow with—" her voice broke, "with everyone else. What's up, Downy?"

Downy looked from Jia to Nat. He couldn't let them make a racket. "Just listen, Nat, Greg felt really bad about telling you that..." Downy talked softly, stepping closer to her and reaching his hand in his pocket. He jerked his nine millimeter out and pointed it sideways at Jia.

"Don't move," he snapped out. "Either of you. I'll shoot Jia and then I'll shoot you."

Jia's mouth was open, but Nat narrowed her eyes.

"What are you doing?" she asked.

"Jia, come around next to Nat," Downy said. She seemed stunned and quietly obeyed. These humans were ridiculous. Jia had six years of training, and she couldn't think of anything better to do than obey him.

When the girls were side by side he gestured toward the beach. "We're going on a walk. You go first."

Nat stood still. "If we go with you, you'll kill us. I'd rather you kill us here."

Jia bit back a whimper.

"Seems appropriate," Nat said, gesturing at the tower.

Downy laughed. Nat was one of the best. "Did you guess I killed the sheep? Very good."

"The picture gave you away. It looked Spo to me," Nat said. "So are you going to kill us or what?"

I'm not going to kill you," he said to Nat. That was true, he wasn't going to kill Nat, only Jia. "I have a friend I want you to meet. She knows your sister."

Nat took a sudden step toward him, and Downy pressed the gun against her chest.

"My sister?"

"Oh, your little sis is quite the clever girl. Shara particularly likes her taste in florals or something like that. If you force me to kill you here, then the Rik will take Akemi."

Nat finally looked shaken, which Downy enjoyed. But not for long. It was five minutes until midnight. "Walk. *Now*," Downy said.

Downy marched them down to the beach. They walked past the huge parking lot, the playground for kids, and the volleyball courts. The smog of Los Angeles had blown east in the afternoon and you could see the stars. The starlight reflected off the sand the same way it did in the deserts of Spo. The crash of black waves filled the silence.

Until Nat spoke. She didn't stop walking, or turn her head, she just spoke. "I don't understand, Downy. Why do the Rik want us?"

"You? They're taking out the best cadet witnesses before the trial, obviously. Why humanity? Well, the Rik are pretty tired of their homeworld."

"I thought the Spo and the Rik were enemies."

"That's putting it in human terms. We're rivals. The Spo have a monopoly on the space drive and the Rik are close to breaking it.

They nearly did, when they had unaltered Rik brains to work with. Now they're hoping to start using human brains."

"But they can't!" Jia protested. "The Galactic Council ruled that only non-sentient—oh."

"Yes," Downy said. "If Jonathan, Nat, Sam, and all the other best candidates for the trial disappear... Humanity could lose the trial. You're all declared non-sentient or malignant or whatever. Welcome the Rik." He prodded Jia in the back to walk faster. "They get new bodies, if they want them, and all the brain matter they can use."

"Then why are you helping them?" Nat demanded. "You're Spo."

They were close to the bathroom/shower building now; it cast a faint shadow from the moon. Shara stood in the shadows, a young, blond girl wearing knee high boots and a thick fur vest. Downy had met her a year before in her Rik form. He liked that one better.

"Oh my god!" Shara said, "You're almost too late. The capsule has to rendezvous with the ship in twenty minutes."

She led them around the corner and into the ladies' room. All of the wooden stalls had been dismantled, and a small spacecraft filled the room. Downy recognized it as one of the Rik atmosphere capsules. It could hold one or two people and blast through the atmosphere of a planet. Once in space it only had enough air for a couple hours. Usually these capsules took diplomats directly to an orbiting spaceship.

"Why'd you bring two girls?" Shara asked. "You were just supposed to bring Nat."

"I had to," Downy started.

"Wait a minute," Nat said, looking at Shara. "You're a human, not Rik. What's going on?"

Downy growled and backhanded Nat across the face. "Shut up. We're busy."

Nat kept her footing, but reflexively clutched her cheek, her eyes getting bright with pain.

"Don't worry about Jia," Downy said to Shara. "Why not send an extra?"

"Because there's only one free seat," Shara said, dilating the hatch door.

Inside, Akemi slumped unconscious against the wall, hand-cuffed and seated in one of two deep chairs.

"No!" Nat screamed. "What have you done?"

She jumped at Shara, locking an arm around the blond girl's throat and clenching her other arm to form a headlock. She twisted around to keep Shara in front of Downy's gun.

"You get Akemi out of there," Nat said to Downy. "Do it now, or I'll suffocate her."

"You know what?" Downy said. "I don't care. I delivered you to Ms. Rik. If she has trouble with you, that's her problem."

Downy turned his gun toward Jia. "You, on the other hand, are my problem."

He grabbed Jia's arm and dragged her out of the restroom.

14

SHARA COULD BARELY BREATHE in Nat's choke hold. She didn't like Nat nearly as much as she liked Akemi. With Akemi, she'd felt a bond. Almost of sisterhood, though not quite. Akemi was stylish and creative. She was even kind, if Shara understood that word correctly. Akemi had kindly passed out when Shara handcuffed her in the spaceship. She certainly hadn't locked her arm around Shara's neck and tried to kill her. If that wasn't rude, she didn't know what was.

Nat didn't stand a chance, though. Shara was completely at home in her human body now. While Nat stayed still for a moment, perhaps contemplating her incredible rudeness, Shara took the opportunity to twist to the side and slam Nat against the side of the spaceship.

Nat's head *thunked* against the side of the ship, but her grip only tightened.

That had to hurt. Didn't human skulls break easily? Or was that only the old, brittle ones?

Nat took advantage of the ship's concave surface, leaning back and pulling harder on Shara's neck.

Shara's feet started to leave the ground, and her vision

narrowed. She brought up her heel and kicked Nat in the crotch. Nat grunted, but didn't fall to the ground writhing the way she should have.

Oh I'm stupid, Shara thought, that was for men.

Shara reached blindly for Nat's face, scratching at her with her nails. She'd painted them baby blue only this morning. Ah, that had an affect. Nat twisted her head away from the nails, and loosened her hold on Shara.

That was all it took. Shara slammed her foot in the girl's instep, jerked her own head free, and in one violent turn, grabbed Nat's hair and slammed her head into the ship. It made a really satisfying *thunk* this time, much better than the first one.

Nat slumped to the ground, not unconscious, but seriously dazed. While Nat blinked uncertainly, Shara pushed her through the door of the capsule and into the seat. She handcuffed Nat to a ring on the wall and then turned on the controls. She'd already preprogrammed the capsule's trajectory.

When Shara got out of the capsule, the door closed automatically. She hurried out of the bathroom and jogged toward the parking lot. When she was about fifty yards away, the bathroom exploded.

She turned to watch as the capsule shot towards the sky. It made about 2,000 yards before it inched to a stop. For a moment it hung in the dark sky, at the apex of its arc. Then the next level of propulsion kicked in and the capsule shot towards the edge of the atmosphere.

Shara felt a little bad for Akemi. The Rik doctors could have Nat with Shara's blessing, but Akemi... Oh well. Shara wiped a tear from her cheek and sucked it off her finger. The human endocrine system really packed a wallop when she got it going. Shara sighed, this was probably a good time to go to a bar and experiment with the affects of alcohol on her brain.

. . .

DOWNY DRAGGED Jia away from the bathroom on the beach. He was still laughing at the idea of Nat breaking the Rik girl's neck. Of course, if Nat actually overcame Shara, that would be a problem for him. Nat knew about him. He couldn't let her get back to the school. And also, if the Rik didn't get their human targets, Downy wouldn't get his own reward. That stupid girl could mess it all up for him.

Downy sobered. He'd have to make sure Nat didn't get away. In the meantime, Jia was a problem.

He headed down the beach, further away from the Pepperdine campus. Jia was silent, perhaps sensing that he was in a bad mood. Definitely he had to kill her. She couldn't be allowed to get back to campus. Or to any of the Spo, now that she knew he'd betrayed them to the Rik.

The question was, how best to use her murder? Downy's tower art with the sheep had set the stage for a killing. He'd planned to put the next body by the tower, establishing the existence of an obsessed, Spo-hating killer. Nat had figured out that Downy did the hate message, but he was willing to bet she was the only one. Everybody else thought it was some crazed human who hated the Spo and the cadets.

Downy had planned to use the same imaginary psycho for future murders, but he hadn't been planning to use it for Jia. She was an adequate cadet, but no more. He would've let her live. He wanted to save the psycho killer for Armen or maybe Melanie. She was such a pet of theirs.

On the other hand, the stage was set and he did need to get rid of Jia.

So, should he kill her here or there? Downy was still thinking when Jia broke away from him and sprinted down the beach. He must have loosened his grip while pondering his options. She veered right toward the wet sand. It was more compact and she could run faster there. Not that that would help her.

The Spo skeletal structure was more akin to that of a star fish than any other earth creature, but when they needed to move: they moved. Downy squatted low and jumped. A real jump, despite the soft sand. His body flew through the air. One more jump and he landed on Jia. Her body collapsed into the sand under his weight; he thought he heard a bone snap. Her breath was knocked out, and she gasped, silent.

"You won't even melt," Downy said.

He used the long claw on his fourth finger to slice the jugular vein in her neck from her chin to her collar bone. A few moments and it was over. Downy was annoyed he didn't have anything to capture her blood in. That might have been useful for his next project.

Instead, he hoisted her body up and tossed it over his shoulder. He'd made up his mind, it would be better for her to disappear. If both she and Nat were gone—Oh, Nat.

Downy turned around just in time to see and hear the bathroom explode as the Rik capsule sailed into the sky. He thought he spotted a dark figure moving away from the burning building, toward the parking lot. So the Rik did her job.

The bathroom burned fluorescent in the dark night, the orange and green flames lighting up the beach. That gave Downy an idea.

He carried Jia's body back to the bathroom. Shara was long gone. A quick toss put Jia's body on the hottest part of the fire. She'd be burned up there, beyond easy recognition.

After a quick dip in the ocean to wash the blood off, Downy put his clothes back on and returned to school. Not even one a.m. yet, he could watch a movie before going to bed. Now that they'd taken Sam away, he didn't have a roommate to bother about.

. . .

Sam was driven to LAX, and escorted to the Spo administrative shuttle. Greg stayed with him, but two other Spo were in charge of detaining him. General Gustav joined them just before they took off. He and Greg were in close conversation as the shuttle broke atmosphere. In half an hour, they docked with the main Spo spacestation orbiting Earth.

Sam was taken to the communications room, where Greg told him his trial would be held immediately. The walls were pale yellow, a color the Spo found soothing. Sam was mostly beyond soothing. His hands were cuffed behind his back. He didn't regret his decision yet, but he was surprised at the direction this was going. Sam had assumed the repercussions of his little talk would be immediate and personal. Instead, he was getting something a lot bigger and more formal.

A huge screen covered one wall. Gustav and Greg stood on either side of Sam, facing the screen, and four guards stood unobtrusively in the corners. The screen flared up. It was divided into two sections, both images were high resolution, but stretched. The Spo eyestalks gave them a different perspective than inset orbs—human eyes. Spo visual technology filmed things on a spherical plane, and then flattened the image onto a screen, much like the Mercator projection of Earth that hung in most elementary schools.

One of the screens showed three Spo royals, standing around a glass table. The table was one of the melted animal puddles Sam had just talked about on television. It was a particularly large one, nearly eight feet across and spectacularly valuable. If a table was made from a single emerald it would be comparable to that one. As far as Sam knew, the only person who owned a table like that was the Spo emperor.

The other image took longer to materialize. Finally it came through. It showed a room full of other aliens. Sam recognized several Merith, looking like Cyclopes, each with their one big eye. There were a few Crosspoint, little slug-like aliens who were allies of the Spo, and a couple Tergre and Vel.

Sam was fairly certain he was looking at a subcommittee of the Galactic Council. Wow. He knew they were planning Earth's upcoming sentiency trial, but he hadn't had the impression that it was a big deal for them. He sure hadn't thought his little rebellion would get this kind of attention.

Sam knew his image was being projected for all the aliens to see, so he studied them surreptitiously. After two minutes of silence, Greg stepped forward.

"Emperor," he said first, crouching in respect toward the left image showing the Spo emperor.

"Councilors," he said, nodding toward the second set of people. He spoke in Spo.

"You have been apprised of the situation. A large majority of humans now know the situation of the sentiency trial, the Rik threat, and our sponsorship. I recognize that this violates the standards of the planetary evaluation."

One of the Merith slowly rose. They did everything pompously. "The sentiency trial has two components. The planetary evaluation and the species test. The planetary evaluation has been compromised. This renders the sentiency test void. The Earth loses the trial, by default. They may be declared non-sentient, or given a further period of sponsorship."

Sam felt sick. He'd known the Spo didn't want to explain the situation to Earth, but he hadn't realized his telling would be considered cheating. No wonder Downy warned him not to tell anybody. Of course, if Downy had been a little more specific, Sam might have listened.

Greg spoke up. "I believe humanity is entitled to an exemption from this clause. Their sponsorship has already been three times longer than usual, due to the unfortunate explosion that brought them to our notice. The full scenario was likely to be exposed, simply from the amount of time that has passed. I believe that the planetary evaluation would be just as viable now as it would have been a year ago, or a year from now."

"Your bias is well known," the Rik representative said. "They broke the rules. The timing doesn't matter."

"But—if I'd known," Sam started, but Greg gestured him to silence.

"You do not have sentient status," Greg told him. "You are not allowed to speak in Council or trial. Only your sponsor may speak for you."

Sam looked mutely at Greg. Only his sponsor could speak for him. The sponsor he'd just betrayed. This sucked.

"I would like to know how the human came to know all this," said a Spo voice from the screen. It was the emperor.

"Emperor," Greg said, "I'm afraid some of the information came from Gerereol. Known on Earth as Downy."

The emperor turned purple-grey with emotion. "I am shocked and shamed that my son was responsible for this lapse. He will be suitably punished according to our own customs."

"No!" Sam said. He couldn't bear to crush Downy with his mistake. "I know I'm not supposed to speak! But I made Downy tell me. He warned me and warned me and I had to drag it out of him. It's not his fault."

"You. Will. Be. Silent." Both the Merith spoke in unison. "This information will be considered."

"It hardly matters," the Rik representative said. "A human broke the law by revealing the situation to all the other humans. The Spo known as Downy is not culpable."

Greg spoke again. "The humans deserve a true trial. I ask again that you exempt them from this law."

One of the other aliens that Sam didn't recognize finally

chimed in, "The Spo are the sponsors. They cannot decide. The Rik are... the Rik," the disgust in his voice was evident, which was pretty incredible considering Sam couldn't tell where his voice was coming from.

"They are both biased," the alien continued. "Those of Merith, Crosspoint, Tergre, and Vel will vote. Here is the paint."

Each of the representatives (the non-Spo, non-Rik ones) stepped to the table. First the Merith. They both stuck a thick finger in a bowl of green paint and dabbed a spot above their one eye. The next alien, a Vel, dabbed red paint on his face. The one who'd set out the paint also dabbed red paint on himself. Only he put it where Sam thought his waist was, which made Sam rethink his perception of that alien.

That left only the two Crosspoint. Sam knew a little about the Crosspointers from his training, but he had absolutely no idea whether they would favor humanity. They could do cool tele-kinetic tricks, but that didn't help him guess their allegiances. Maybe they would vote for him, since the Spo were their allies, but he wasn't sure. The only other thing he knew about them was that they, like humans, had a subconscious. He wondered if the Crosspointers knew that about Sam. Maybe they would feel more favorably if they did.

The slugs scooted closer to the table. The first one was barely taller than it. A large glob of green paint rose out of the bowl, on its own, and slapped itself on the end of the slug.

"I just met one of these humans on Selta," the next Crosspoint said. "So very conflicted. So very interesting. Another blob of green paint drifted out of the bowl and landed on his back.

Sam looked at Greg wildly. He didn't know what green and red meant. Maybe they were galactic standards for yes and no, but he didn't know which was which.

Greg was turning deep pink with satisfaction and Sam exhaled in a rush, relieved.

"I recognize the vote of the Council committee," said Greg. "Humanity is exempt from the non-disclosure clause. I will prepare the human sample for trial as planned. Thank you."

Sam hadn't ruined humanity's chances after all. Thank God.

"There is still the matter of this human," the Rik said. "Humanity is now exempt, but he broke the law. His sentence is not abridged."

"But he is one of the foremost witnesses!" Greg protested. "He must be allowed—"

"No," said the Spo emperor. "A witness who will break the law is not a good sample. We will abide by the customary laws for this trespass."

The emperor turned slightly, probably looking at the other screen. "I assure the Council that the human will be executed according to Spo custom."

Sam's knees felt weak and the Rik barked with laughter. "That is acceptable."

The Council image turned off. The emperor addressed Greg. "I know the human Sam is favored by you and my son. Gustav will handle his sentencing, no later than two revolutions from today."

The second screen turned off. Now they were alone again, and Sam sagged. "Executed?" he whispered to Greg. "I'm going to be executed?"

Greg was so grey now he blended in with the floor. "There is nothing I can do. If we do not follow through we might compromise Earth's status even more." He turned away from Sam.

"Your face melts before me," he said. I mourn you already.

"How?" Sam asked, when they sat on the shuttle again, separated from Gustav in the rear section. Sam's shock was wearing off. "How do the Spo execute for this crime?"

Greg would not gaze at his face. "A trouncer cage. Seven or eight animals. It does not take long."

Sam froze. "No. You've got to be kidding me." He pictured the giant fanged creatures from their space travel and all the many sacrifices he'd made, taking their brains for the ship. The animals were remarkable predators, a symbol of strength and intelligence to the Spo. Greg would see this as an honorable death. Sam shuddered and forced himself not to ask anything else.

15

WHEN SHARA SLAMMED Nat's head against the space capsule, Nat's vision had narrowed to a point, she almost blacked out. Before Nat could steady her gaze, the Rik girl had stuffed her inside and handcuffed her to the interior wall of the spacecraft.

Still reeling, Nat twisted in her chair to reach a button that would open the door. Before her fingers could hit it, the capsule shot off the ground. Nat was contorted in her chair and if it hadn't been so well padded she might have dislocated her shoulder in the acceleration. As it was, the handcuff bit hard into her wrist and she could feel her shoulder pop as the inertia pushed her down.

But something was wrong with the capsule. After the initial blast it started to slow. It was still rising, but slower and slower and... Nat screamed as the capsule came to a stop and started to fall. They were going to die. Right here, right now, they were going to die.

Then the instant was over and the capsule shot upward again. This time it accelerated steadily, not in one blast, and she could feel herself sinking deeper and deeper into the padded seat. This wasn't as bad though; during the brief moment of free-fall Nat had automatically righted herself in the chair.

The capsule grew warm. There were no windows, but she knew they must be pushing out of the atmosphere.

Nat turned her head so she could see Akemi, ignoring the pain in her wrist. Wherever they were going, Nat couldn't do anything about it. So she focused on her sister.

Akemi's chest was no longer bandaged. The scar from her surgery peeked over the top of her pink V-neck shirt. The edge of the scar was reddish, but not bright. It looked like it was healing well. Of course, that didn't mean anything about how her new lung was actually doing. Nat prayed that this crazy pressure wouldn't damage Akemi's already precarious health.

Akemi would need her anti-rejection drugs, too. Nat groaned. Akemi had to take an immunosuppressant to keep her body from attacking her new lung and trying to devour it. She also needed to eat certain food to keep her illness at bay. Nat didn't see a bag or any bottles of pills.

Akemi's wrists were handcuffed together, but they lay in her lap. She was being pressed down as hard as Nat, but at least her arms weren't going to break. Nat was starting to feel like hers would. She tried to push against the pressure to give her wrist a break, but she was only gaining millimeters, if even that.

Blood started to drip down her wrist when the pressure suddenly let up.

Free fall, Nat thought. Her body lifted out of the chair, still accelerating in the sudden lack of gravity. Drops of blood drifted past her to splat softly on the ceiling. There were no straps in the capsule, like human astronauts tend to use. Nat, anchored only by her wrist, floated up sideways. Akemi, not anchored at all, lifted out of her chair until she bumped the ceiling.

Nat didn't mind free fall too much. Some of the cadets puked every time they even thought about free-fall, but she was fine. The Spo said that humans with gymnastic orientation, like Nat, had better spatial awareness and body control.

She was worried about Akemi though. If Akemi threw up while unconscious, she could choke on her own vomit... not to mention making the environment really unpleasant for Nat. But there wasn't much she could do, with her hand literally tied down.

When the capsule lurched like a Spo on glass, Akemi's body hit the wall. They were docking now, with whatever ship was waiting to retrieve them. Nat stretched out and used her free hand to grab Akemi and push her back towards her chair. A few moments later, the gravity kicked in and they both flopped down. Nat landed half on the floor, half on the chair, but thankfully Akemi landed squarely on her chair.

The door dilated and a tall black guy walked in.

Nat was confused. The Rik were not a humanoid species. But first that blond girl on the ground, and now this guy... The Rik she'd studied were an oceanic culture, and looked something like seals. They'd had some kind of catastrophe a few generations ago, and the Spo really hated them. That was all she knew.

This person, however, and that blonde girl down on Earth, looked distinctly human.

The black guy eyed the capsule carefully before stepping inside. "I am glad you didn't reverse your digestive system," he said fervently. "This body is very weak."

Nat looked at his bulging triceps muscles as he took out a strange looking syringe and stuck it in her arm.

"Not weak," he corrected. "My stomach is... ambivalent."

"What's in that?" Nat asked. "And who are you?"

"I am Tishing. I am human," he said.

"A human wouldn't feel the need to say so," Nat said.

He laughed. "You're right. I'm newly human, I should say."

"You're Rik?" Nat verified.

"I was Rik. Now I am human." He pulled the syringe out of her arm and pocketed it. "I'll be right back."

He gently picked up Akemi and carried her out of the capsule into the bigger spaceship.

Nat was creeped out. No one told her the Rik could take over other bodies. Surely she wasn't being unreasonable to feel that the Spo made a gross oversight in not teaching the cadets this little fact. As far as she knew, no alien could body hop. She'd been taught that the idea of ego-stealing parasites or brain leeches was limited solely to human invention. Now she didn't know.

If the Rik could change bodies, that raised some pretty ominous ideas about why she and Akemi were here. Nat slumped her head back against the chair, looking at the red spot in her forearm where he'd injected her. Her head pounded with each heartbeat. She wasn't sure if it was from Shara's head slam, the space trip, or the stuff he'd just injected into her. She felt unaccountably tired. She should be analyzing her situation, thinking of possible leverage. Instead, she closed her eyes. Must have been an anesthetic...

The black guy came back after a while. He used a small pair of scissors to cut through her handcuffs. Good scissors, she thought groggily.

"Why'm I so sleepy?" she asked.

"I gave you a tranquilizer. I'm not an idiot." He stood looking at her until she couldn't keep her eyes open any more. She tried to fight it, but her body shut down.

NAT WOKE to someone stroking her hair. That's not something you feel a lot when the only humans you know are kids. Greg certainly never thought of stroking her head. It felt wonderful. But the smell was wrong. She smelled salt, bleach, and an organic stench of... Nat opened her eyes.

Akemi sat cross-legged next to her, stroking her hair away

from her face, untangling it from her neck. She gave Nat a small smile.

Nat moaned. "I'm sorry, Akemi."

"It's my fault," Akemi whispered. "I told Shara all about us. I came with her all the way back to LA before she turned on me."

"Yeah, you really should have suspected she was an alien parasite," Nat said with an attempt at humor.

Akemi didn't laugh. "I should have."

"I was kidding. Come here." She hugged Akemi close to her.

"Ouch!" Akemi gasped.

"Oh, I'm sorry!" Nat said, letting go of her. "I forgot. Did I hurt you?"

Akemi touched her chest gingerly. "Just awfully sore."

"You don't look too good," Nat said. "Are you feeling sick?"

Akemi shrugged.

"Look around," she told her sister, clearly changing the subject.

They were in a cage, plain and simple. The smell was rank. The cage had diagonal bars, like a chain link fence, and a locked mesh door. Unfortunately it was not locked like a hamster cage with a simple lift and twist door latch. It had no visible lock that Nat could find. More Rik technology she didn't know about. Their cage sat near the front of a large room filled with other cages. Nat and Akemi were the only humans in the room, but they were not the only occupants.

"What are they?" Akemi asked. "Have you ever seen them?"

"These are Spo trouncers. They're used for the biocomputer in the spaceship. And for executions." Oh god, Sam's trial. How long had she been out? She might not ever know if Sam had been sentenced to execution! Nat opened her mouth to tell Akemi and then shut it. Why frighten her?

"Trouncers?" Akemi said.

"That's what the Spo call them."

"But trouncers?" Akemi protested. "How about 'enormous evil toads?'"

"You got me there," Nat said.

The trouncers were roughly the size of mountain lions, but hard and oily, like the Spo themselves. They had bent legs like a frog, but they usually shuffled around on all fours until they leapt in attack. Their front limbs ended in four wicked claws, and their mouths were fanged with two rows of incisors. They had long purple tongues they flicked in and out constantly, and long tails they flicked when they were excited, like a cat.

"They need live animals for their computer?" Akemi asked, looking nervously at the huge cages around them.

"They need a brain with at least high-level animal intelligence," Nat explained. "Like a dolphin or an ape, if not more. The Spo use biocomputers—half-computer, half-tissue—to control their space travel. The higher level the animal the better their biocomputers work. Each brain only works for one or two trips, though. So to play it safe, you only use a brain once. That's why they have so many." She gestured at the room, counting. "Fifteen trouncers, fifteen jumps—maybe thirty if they're bold."

The girls contemplated their situation for a moment. Akemi looked at the animals, at their cage, at the door to the huge room they were in. Nat just looked at her sister.

Akemi looked bad. Her skin was yellow; not normal Japanese yellow, but a frightening jaundice-yellow. Her blood wasn't getting cleaned properly, or else it wasn't getting oxygenated well. Either could happen after a transplant rejection.

The black guy who'd taken them out of the capsule sailed back into the room and waved cheerfully at them. The tattoo on his wrist, so white against his dark skin, momentarily drew Nat's gaze. In his other hand he carried a red tool box.

"Hello girls," he said. "It's me, Tishing. I deeply apologize for putting you in a cage. They're preparing a room for you now."

He set down the box next to one of the trouncer cages.

"I need one of these guys, so we can jump out of Earth space." He went to a closet in the far wall and removed a gun, loaded it with clear darts. "Do you know how the Spo jump-drive works? It's quite ingenious."

Tishing went back to the cage, talking quietly to the animal. He spoke in a different language now. Not English, not Spo, must be Rik. The trouncer's eyes followed Tishing as he neared the cage. At first it shuffled back and forth, but when he was only a few feet away, the animal got still.

"See how he's frozen?" Tishing said, in English. "He's about to attack." He took one step nearer the cage and the trouncer hurled itself at the door with a metallic clang. Akemi flinched back. Tishing laughed and fired the gun at the trouncer. Two darts buried themselves in its neck, and it crashed to the floor like a broken motorcycle.

Tishing waited a few moments. "You can't be too careful with these," he said. "Sometimes they play dead."

"Like possums," Akemi said.

After a moment, Tishing opened the door to the cage. His hands were gloved.

"Their slime burns human skin," he explained. He kept talking in a friendly way while he took a small, vibrating knife from the box and used it to open the animal's skull. Its blood leaked out, green and thin: Spo blood.

Tishing carefully cut off portions of the skull until he could remove the entire brain. This part always bothered Sam, Nat thought, as he lifted the brain free. Of course, neither she nor Sam had ever seen a fresh human brain, but this is what they thought it would look like. Akemi moaned and turned away from the sight. Or perhaps it was the smell getting to her. The stench of the trouncers was now layered with the fishy smell of their blood.

When Tishing had the brain out, he took a spherical black

container out of the box, and popped it in half. The brain went inside, and then he snapped it back together.

"I'll get the carcass later," he told them. "Captain is waiting to jump. We can't linger in Earth space too long. The Spo might notice."

"Wait," Nat said. "Akemi is sick. She needs certain medicines or she'll be very ill. She needs water too, and some food probably."

"Don't worry," Tishing said. "We're just taking a quick jump toward Mars' orbit. After the jump you'll be escorted to your room. I know the doctors there will take good care of you." He left with another flash-of-teeth smile.

Akemi leaned back against the wall of their cage and sighed. "I know he's an evil alien and he just vivisected an animal right in front of us, but doesn't he look just like Will Smith?"

AFTER A BRIEF JUMP, which nauseated Akemi, and Nat too, a little, they were locked into a small room. Two cots, a sink, a toilet. It was like a prison, and that made it almost relaxing compared to the trouncer room.

Akemi had gotten out of breath on the short walk to their room, however. She wheezed and her abdomen jerked at each breath. She had a hand on her chest, as if to protect it.

Nat helped her lay down on a cot, and Akemi winced as she leaned back, pressing her arm tighter over her chest.

"It's very tender," she told Nat. "It hasn't hurt this much since the first day."

Nat placed her hand on Akemi's forehead, and Akemi closed her eyes. Her head was hot, clearly feverish. It seemed a long time before her breaths began to slow. She still sounded wheezy, but not quite so labored.

"When was the last time you had your meds?" Nat asked gently.

"Um. The evening I left with Shara. Maybe—two days? Three days?" Akemi didn't open her eyes. "Is there another blanket on that bed?"

Nat pulled the white blanket off the other cot and doubled it up over Akemi. She went to the sink and tried the handle. Something clear and wet flowed out, but Nat was nervous. She'd learned that indoor plumbing on alien spaceships didn't always give you water.

She smelled it a bit, and eventually tested it with a finger. Then her hand. Then a touch on her tongue. Water, or close enough. She didn't have anything to put it in, so she cupped some in her hands and splashed it in Akemi's mouth. Akemi asked for more, so Nat went back and forth from the bed to the sink until Akemi nodded.

This was bad, really bad. If Akemi's body rejected her new lung, she would die. Vicious white blood cells would destroy the only organ putting oxygen in her system. Convinced that the lung was a foreign body, her temperature would continue to rise as her body tried to burn out the intruder. A combination of things: fever, infection, and lung deterioration, would kill her. Akemi's other lung was not very effective. Only 15%, if Nat remembered correctly.

The door of their room was solid with no window. It fit seamlessly with the walls, no doorframe stuck out that might have weaknesses. The walls didn't look the same as the hallway. This room must have been added later for humans, and Nat wondered with dull horror how many humans had been locked up here. The Rik taking human bodies could not be an entirely new thing. They must have been studying humans for years to achieve that kind of biological success. Tishing and the blond girl looked very comfortable as humans.

Greg taught them that alien abduction stories were common on most planets. They arose from a desire to believe the truth of alien existence before it was proven. He explained that the stories were particularly prevalent on Earth because of the human subconscious. Most species did not have a subconscious. In fact, only the humans, the Crosspoint, and possibly the Rik, were suspected of having a subconscious. Most species could process feelings and data, or they could not. But they couldn't do the half thing that humans did, pushing thoughts and ideas to a secondary level for continued consideration.

Nat had believed Greg. At least, she believed his assertion that the Spo had not been kidnapping random humans for hundreds of years. Now she wondered whether those alien abduction stories were true—perpetrated by the Rik, instead.

Nat tried knocking on their door. Speculation aside, she needed to get a Rik in here with some medicine. When Akemi moaned and rolled onto her side, Nat started banging. She'd never felt this alone and frightened and that was saying quite a bit, considering her past.

Suddenly, the door retreated from her banging fist. A group stood outside the door. Two humans, one of them Tishing, and three aliens. The aliens were short, maybe three feet tall, and resembled seals. These were the Rik she was familiar with. They walked with a hind tail, which was divided into long, thin flippers. Their front limbs were thick like a seal, though the left one tapered off slightly into thick digits.

One of the aliens barked something at her, but she didn't see any of their mouths move. In fact, she didn't see any mouths. Oh! They were wearing masks. The masks covered their snouts and eyes, giving them a bulbous, misshapen look.

Now that Nat thought about it, the ship's internal atmosphere was clearly Earth based. The real Rik wouldn't be able to breathe it.

Tishing nodded at the rear alien. "These are the doctors who are going to study you and her. They want to know how she is doing."

"She's bad, that's how she is," Nat said. "You took her from her home without any of the medicines she needs. She just had a lung transplant. Do you know what that is?"

Tishing barked back at the aliens.

"She also needs water, and food," Nat added.

The aliens and humans came into the room, pushing up next to the cot, and touching Akemi with small tools.

"They are checking her heat, and other vitals," Tishing explained. "We knew she was deemed unfit for the Spo project, but her exact ailment was not mentioned in their records."

"You've been looking us up?" Nat asked. "Why did you take us?"

"We need a cadet if we're going to get a spy into the Spo school... and into the trial."

Nat got cold. "You need a cadet—as in, you need a cadet body?"

"That's the thing," Tishing said cheerfully. "If we're going to screw up humanity's trial, we need one of our people right there. After we got rid of Jonathan, you were the next best candidate. We knew Greg would use you in the trial."

"You're going to kill me and replace me with a Rik? Don't you think someone will notice?"

He seemed so nonchalant. "Not if we get you back before morning. We've got the procedure down to 90 minutes, if all goes well. Then we jump back to Earth, send you down, and you get back to school before anyone realizes you were gone. Downy will help with that if we need him too."

"But—my roommate knows," Nat said. "She knows what Downy did, and she'll know it's not me."

"Actually, our agent reports that she is dead... And that will give you a better alibi. You can say you were out searching for Jia, and the shock of your roommate's death will explain any little personality deviations."

"I won't say any of that!"

"Of course *you* won't, but the Rik who *will be* you can use the excuse."

His handsome black face was smooth. Not cruel, just indifferent. He really didn't understand how this would affect her. She wanted to hurt him. She wanted to push him against the wall and use a Spo knife to slice open his stolen throat.

Nat took a deep breath. With the other aliens in the room, not to mention the gun in his hand, there was nothing she could do right now. Jia was already gone.

"What about Akemi?" Nat demanded. "Replacing her won't get you anywhere."

"She won't be replaced," Tishing said. "They want to study her for space jump capabilities."

Nat's brain wasn't processing. Jump capabilities? For their spaceship? Akemi wasn't a pilot.

Then Nat pictured the trouncer Tishing had just dissected. She pictured the brain he'd taken from the animal. How much it had looked like a human brain.

"Oh. Oh." Nat said. She sank down on the cot and watched the doctors work on her sister. Oh God, she repeated in her mind, oh God help us.

The image that filled her mind was too horrible to consider.

16

AT 9:00 AM, General Gustav and Greg walked Sam toward the amphitheater for his execution. They were back at Pepperdine and the sky was a brilliant greenish blue over the ocean, but the breeze coming off the beach smelled of smoke. Greg had shaved his hair off that morning and the wind felt strange on Sam's buzzed head.

The Pepperdine amphitheater was built into a hill, five sections of concrete seating making a half circle around a low stage. The seating gave a view of Malibu's tumbling hills and a glimpse of the Pacific off to the right. The aliens preferred it to the indoor auditorium for big occasions and the other 40-odd cadets fit easily into the front section. They were totally silent now; Sam could hear the waves crashing on the beach.

On the low central stage was a huge cage. It was a cube, probably 15 feet on a side. The bars were heavy and there seemed to be no door. A pack of trouncers filled the inside.

Sam couldn't count them. His eyes ricocheted off fangs and slick skin and bent limbs. They had the distinctly plastic, skeletal look of the Spo. He forced himself to breath as Greg guided him down the steps toward the center of the arena. Sam heard a whimper and saw Melanie cringing on a bench out of the corner of his eye. He didn't look at her. Nat must be here too, and Armen, and... he didn't want to look at any of them.

He forced his eyes to focus on the cage. He was up next to it now, and the animals' acidic stink burned his nose. One beast stalked next to the bars. Its skin was slick, dark brown, with yellow spots. It flicked out a long, purple tongue to wet its face in a catlike gesture. It had eyestalks like the Spo, but bigger, more expressive. Now it stood on its hind legs, stretching and clawing at the top of the cage.

Greg led Sam around to a ladder on the back.

"What, no words?" Sam said. "Don't you have to... say something?"

Greg looked more miserable than Sam had ever seen him. "What would you like me to say?"

Sam looked through the cage to the cadets huddled on the stone benches.

"You're right," Sam said. "Never mind."

Sam climbed the ladder, Greg just behind. His brain was going numb, and he couldn't hear the sound of the ocean anymore over the pounding in his head. On top of the cage was a trapdoor. One of the trouncers leaped at Sam as he stood on top of the cage and he stumbled backward, one foot slipping between the bars. Greg grabbed his shoulder to steady him and Sam yanked his foot out.

Greg didn't let go of his shoulder.

"Sam. I hope you go to your...god," he said.

Greg pulled a knife from his pocket and made a shallow cut his arm. He dotted his own thin, green blood on Sam's bare head. "Goodbye."

Greg opened the trapdoor. Sam didn't know if Greg had to throw him in or what, but he couldn't bear to wait for it. Sam jumped into the hole, taking the impact on the soles of his feet and in his knees. He prayed, once, that it would be over quickly.

The trouncers were startled by his sudden jump. A few sprang away from him, but the others remained still. The closest one was only a few feet away. It swayed gently from side to side and then froze in its attack sequence. Sam spun out of the way as it leaped for his face, almost by reflex. He saw long claws flash by his eyes.

That one slunk into a corner, hissing slightly.

Three of the trouncers started to pace around him, swaying side to side with each breath. If they all attacked at once, he would be ripped apart quickly. He should just let it happen, it was inevitable...but he couldn't.

Sam zeroed in on the largest one. He watched it until it froze, and then he lunged low at its hindquarters as it sprang at him. He grabbed one of its heavy legs and used the momentum of the animal's jump to heave it over his shoulder, onto its back. Greg had taught him to do that, when fighting a Spo.

The trouncer screamed. It landed on its back, legs flailing for a moment until it righted itself. The others had backed away momentarily.

Sam's hands were covered with brown slime from the animal, it smelled like bleach and urine.

"Whatever..." Sam said, and smeared some over his face. Maybe if he smelled like the trouncers they would back off. Sam wasn't as resigned to death as he'd thought.

The trouncers were disturbed. All their tails flicked violently, and some of them paced around the perimeter of the cage. There were only twelve or so, Sam thought, but it was impossible to keep them all in sight.

He crouched down, edging toward the wall. The trouncers moved away from him, their purple tongues flicking in and out. Maybe they used their tongues for smell, like snakes. Sam couldn't remember.

One of the animals scooted toward him. It wasn't swaying in

pre-attack mode, instead it shuffled up sideways, hesitantly. Sam cocked his head, he'd never seen this behavior in a trouncer. Was it ill?

The trouncer edged closer to him, bobbing its head. It almost looked like a dog...

Sam waited for the longest time, frozen in time and space.

Finally, he breathed a quick prayer, and slowly extended his hand toward the animal.

The thing flicked its tongue toward his hand. Once, twice, a third time. Then it hopped a little closer. This was either very good or very bad.

It was now only a few inches below his fingers. Moving his hand only from the wrist, he touched the creature's brown head. An odd chuckling sound came from the trouncer, so Sam rubbed its head harder.

Suddenly the trouncer leaned forward to rest its snout on Sam's shoulder. He froze. Its right eyestalk was inches from his face and Sam's eyes watered at the bleach stink. When it licked his cheek Sam flinched, but managed to check it almost immediately.

The animal waited a moment, and so Sam used his fingers to rub the side of its face. It arced its neck into the motion, like a cat. This was good, definitely good.

Then it reared back on its hind legs and roared at him. Sam screamed, falling over his feet and crashing into the cage wall. His arm went through the bars and he struggled to get back to his feet. This was it. He was going to die. Right now.

But when he got his arm free and spun around, the animal was...shaking. It was bobbing up and down and hissing slightly—like a laugh. Just like the Spo laughed. It was laughing at him!

A quick look around showed the other animals looking calmer. They weren't laughing, or whatever the heck his creature was doing, but they were no longer flicking their tails and tongues.

Sam rubbed the beast on its head like a dog. It licked his hand a couple times with its long purple tongue, still laughing. Sam splayed his fingers out in front of its mouth, and it curled its tongue between his fingers.

"Wow," Sam said. "A friendly trouncer." He knew a few of them were kept as pets on Spo, just like a few crazy people had tigers or alligators as pets. But how would a pet trouncer get mixed in with a group slated for the spacejump?

Sam moved his hand down and rubbed the trouncer's shoulders and the softer joints of its arms. He always saw Downy rubbing his joints like it felt good. The trouncer made a soft exhalation noise.

"Neb neb neb," it sounded like.

"Neb neb," Sam repeated.

Without warning, his animal leapt away from him, colliding in midair with another trouncer. This one had been stalking on the edge of Sam's line of sight, but he hadn't realized it was about to attack. Sam's trouncer caught the attacker on the right shoulder, throwing it off trajectory and towards Sam's left, rather than right on top of him. With a croak, Sam's animal butted its head against the other trouncer. It butted again, and then backed up, pinning Sam against the side wall. The trouncer put itself between Sam and the others and roared.

Clearly it had decided to protect Sam, and the other trouncers retreated toward the other side of the cage. Unless they mounted some kind of coordinated attack, Sam was safe. The way they moved around each other, not bumping or touching, had the feel of solitary animals in tight quarters. They were clearly intelligent, but they weren't pack animals. Most likely they would not attack in a group.

So what now? Sam wondered. He rubbed his animal some more, and it sighed, "Neb, neb, neb."

"Thanks, Nebbie," Sam said. "You're my pal." Sam felt jittery and faintly queasy. He was safe, for the moment. But what next?

Sam became aware of a furious noise from the cadets. He'd heard nothing since he jumped into the cage, too focused on his imminent death to see or hear anything else.

Now that he was still, he could hear the cadets shouting. They'd jumped off the benches and gathered around Greg and Gustav. He couldn't put together what they were saying, but he could guess.

Eventually Sam sat down behind Nebbie, feeling safe enough. Nebbie went off his defense pose, and crouched down next to Sam. He was still between Sam and the rest, but he looked relaxed. Sam rubbed the trouncer's legs.

"This is more than a little bizarre, I gotta tell you," Sam said. "I thought I'd be dead by now, and instead I'm scratching your ankles."

Nebbie wiggled and licked his hand.

"I always wanted a dog.".

Nebbie coughed.

"You're a good listener." So Sam talked to Nebbie for a while, until finally he saw Armen edging Greg and General Gustav toward the cage. Sam stood as they got close.

"You followed your custom," Armen said. "Look at him. He's been in there nearly an hour. They're not going to kill him."

"Then we must kill him another way, or kill that animal," General Gustav said, gesturing to Nebbie.

"Hey, I'm the one supposed to be executed here," Sam said. "Nebbie's just a bystander."

General Gustav sighed. "I could fetch a ritual knife. To execute him in that way."

"No!" Armen said. "What exactly does the law say?"

Greg thought for a moment. "It says, "The criminal and his family shall be placed in the den of the trouncers. They will be outnumbered four to one, to assure a quick demise. When the frenzy is over, the victims shall be removed and their bodies melted with honor."

"The frenzy is definitely over," Armen said. All the trouncers were laying down now. The warm sun reflected off their shiny, wet skin. They looked sleepy.

"But he didn't die," Downy said, joining the group by the cage.

"So?" Armen said. "According to your law, he's been executed."

"This is not correct," General Gustav said. "It must be done again."

"Then there's another problem," Armen said. "You broke the law yourself. I don't see any of Sam's family in there."

"There wasn't time to assemble them," General Gustav said. "They would be terminated at a later time."

"That's not acceptable," Armen said. "The law states that the family goes in together. He's been away from his biological family for years. By affection, knowledge, and experience, we are Sam's family."

General Gustav and Greg looked at Armen and the other cadets.

"All of you?" Greg half smiled.

"Yes," Armen said firmly. "If you execute Sam, again, I would like to be considered his family."

Sam's eyes burned, and not entirely from the sting of the trouncer slime.

"Armen, you can't do that for me," Sam said. "I'm responsible for the interview. I didn't give you a chance to stop me."

Armen shook his head. "According to Spo law, you shouldn't be executed alone. It's only fair, and I'm not the only one who thinks so."

Greg and Gustav looked at each other, eyestalk to eyestalk.

"This is an unexpected development," General Gustav said. "If it was not so... "

"I understand," Greg said. "You agree then, that Sam should not be executed again?"

General Gustav nodded.

Greg crouched and leaped to the top of the cage in one powerful lunge. He opened the door and lowered a rope for Sam.

The cadets cheered, screaming and jumping on the benches. Sam started to cry, and when he wiped his eyes, he got trouncer slime in them, which made him tear up worse.

When they were safely on the ground, Greg wrapped his hard arms around Sam and brought his face an inch from Sam.

"I have never seen anything like this. I think your god did not want you yet," Greg said. It took Sam a moment to realize he was being hugged.

He patted Greg awkwardly. "Apparently not."

SAM SLID off the stage with shaky legs, into the crowd of cadets.

Armen slapped Sam on the back, and most of the cadets surged around to congratulate him. All the girls were crying, and they all wanted to hug Sam and everybody else.

Sam noticed that Greg looked uncomfortable with all the emotion.

"It's cathartic," Sam explained to him. "It's not just about me. The weight of the last six years just came crashing down on them. You should leave us alone for a while."

Ten days ago Sam wouldn't have dared to dismiss Greg, but now it almost felt natural. This was a human moment, and Greg was not human. This was also Sam's moment, and Greg (though part of Sam's life) was not part of Sam's family.

Greg inclined his thick neck and left, taking General Gustav and Downy with him.

It was at least ten minutes later, with the cadets clustered in the front few rows retelling Sam's execution over and over, that Sam finally nudged Armen.

"Where's Nat?" Sam asked.

"Uh..." Armen looked blank for a second. "Oh, shoot. Downy said she decided not to come. She doesn't know you lived!"

Sam and Armen looked around for Jia, but they couldn't find her either.

"Forget it," Sam said, with a grin. "I'll go tell her myself."

He ran up the stairs of the amphitheater and jogged to the girl's dorm. He was still hyped on adrenalin and felt like he could have run twice as far. Nat would be so relieved. Sam couldn't imagine how he would have felt if their situations had been reversed, the mere idea made him shudder. Maybe now she would let go of Greg's unfortunate pairing and just let them move on...

Their dorm was on high ground, and as Sam got to the door he looked back at the amphitheater for a moment. Far off, on the beach, he noticed a thick plume of smoke rising into the sky. He'd smelled the smoke before his trial, but hadn't thought about it. It looked like the bathroom next to the parking lot had burned. Sam felt his joy melting into panic. It shouldn't matter, but something about that smoke...

He sprinted up the stairs to Nat's room. From the hall he could hear an alarm clock chiming with nerve-grating insistence. He threw Nat's door open and it slammed against the wall.

The room was empty, as he half expected. No Nat. No Jia. He walked over to Jia's desk and slapped the clock silent.

Sam stood next to Nat's bed and dug his fingers into his newly bald head. Nat's window faced the beach, and he could see the smoke still rising and twisting in the wind.

Then he saw someone walking around the building. The distance made it hard to tell, but it looked like a girl. Could that be Nat?

17

NAT STARTED SHIVERING while the Rik doctors put an IV in Akemi's hand. "Just for sedation and hydration," they told her.

"We're ready to start your procedure," Tishing told her, gesturing at one of the real Rik. "This is Wishi, who will be taking your body."

"What, here?" Nat asked, appalled. "You're going to kill me in the same room as my sister?"

Nat wouldn't have been so blunt, but Akemi was fast asleep.

"It is already three a.m. in Los Angeles. We've got to get you back before ten tomorrow. We have reason to believe you won't be missed until then," he explained.

Nat felt frozen inside. The shock of their plans left her lethargic and stupid.

"How do you do it?" she asked.

"We'll need to scan your brain and limbic system. Then our *insdecrum*.... er, I don't have the word for that..." He thought for a moment. "Oh, nanotechnology. Our nanotechs will be injected into your brain tissue. They will recontour your brain according to Wishi's pattern. Then we'll use electrical signals to stop your brain function, whatever's left after the nanotechs, and use a similar set of pulses to start it up, using Wishi's electrical signals."

Nat felt a flicker of life in her frozen brain. "You don't infect bodies biologically? I assumed you were a parasitic species."

"Oh not originally, we think. We just developed the technology to transfer memory and consciousness before anyone else."

"But don't you forget things? You can recontour my brain, but his memories won't be there," Nat gestured to Wishi.

"Wishi is a she, actually," Tishing explained. "We have gender like you. And some of the memories are linked to brain activity. Others she will lose. It is something we all accept."

Nat had almost forgotten that Tishing had done this too. They'd stolen this poor black guy and turned him into an alien. She wondered where he came from. Los Angeles? Detroit? South Africa?

"Do you remember things from him?" Nat asked. "This guy you're in now?"

"I am this guy," Tishing said. "I remember a little. Mainly flesh memories. I remember how to walk, how to talk, how to drive a car. He spoke English, so I speak English. When we get people who speak Chinese or Spanish or something then we have to learn English."

"So basically I'll be dead," Nat said. She needed him to say it. She needed him to acknowledge the truth.

If the Spo were going to punish you, they told you exactly where and when and what would happen. If they were going to destroy a village, they made it clear. Maybe that was one of the ways they had changed her. She wanted horror spoken out loud.

Tishing looked at her. She knew what he would say. He would try to convince her that as her body lived on, she lived on. He would want to comfort her or lull her into compliance.

He pulled out a syringe. "Please lay on your cot."

"No!" Nat jumped off the bed, stung into energy by his ignoring her question. "You have to say something. Are you killing me or not?"

He gestured to the empty bed, but Nat just glared at him. "Does your flesh remember human expression? This is fury. Do you remember guilt? Answer me."

Tishing's lips twisted slightly, as if he couldn't help responding to her question and was trying on the expression for fury.

"I remember," he said. For the first time he didn't sound flippant or indifferent. He blinked slowly, seeing who knew what against eyelids that were not his own. When he opened his eyes, they showed no pity or suffering or guilt. But there was knowledge.

"I am going to kill you," he said.

Nat stared at him for a long moment, trying to decipher the new knowledge in his eyes. He turned away from her gaze. "If you lay down now, you'll have time to write your sister a letter before the *insdecrum* set in."

Nat lay down on her stomach. He admitted he was going to kill her. This was how executions were supposed to work. She wondered in despair how the Spo had conditioned her to accept even execution if it was down with truth and order.

Tishing pulled up her shirt and rubbed a strong anesthetic on her lower back. She felt the tingling as it settled into her pores. Slowly her back became numb and warm, followed by her legs, as the anesthetic reached her spinal cord. When the warmth reached her feet, Tishing took an opaque black needle and pushed it into her spinal column. She felt pain, but not severe. When he had the needle in, he attached a tube and connected it to a box held by one of the Rik.

"You can turn over now," Tishing said, helping her roll onto her back. She couldn't feel the needle anymore. The Rik set the box on the pillow next to her head. "The insdecrum will travel through your spinal column to your brain, but it will take at least forty minutes before the restructuring begins."

He handed her a notepad and a pen. The notepad was pink and purple, with Hello Kitty on the front.

"You have that long to write. We have given your sister more sedative. She will not wake up."

Nat nodded. Finally they left, and she was alone with the notepad and the box. They hadn't strapped her arms down; she could reach the needle in her back and pull it out. But what would be the point? They would do it again, this time with straps.

She opened the Hello Kitty notepad, and started to write. She didn't ponder what to say, words just poured out of her.

"Akemi. I love you," she wrote. "I loved you on Spo and on Earth. I never regretted that they took me instead of you. I was always glad that you were with our parents. I'm glad I got to see you again even if it was only a little while. I'm glad you got your ears pierced. I wish I could take your place now, but I don't think that's going to happen again.

I wish you could have gotten to know Sam. I know you would have liked him. Armen was pretty funny too.

The Rik are not going to win. I don't want you to think that. Whatever they do with me or with you, they are not going to win."

Nat put her pen down. The pale pink paper blurred slightly. Her eyes flew to the box on her bed. It had only been ten minutes. Her vision cleared and she started to write again.

She told Akemi about her friends. The jokes they shared over the years of training. She told her about Greg, really a decent alien, but so confusing when they got back to earth. She told her about Malaysia. She needed to tell someone about that. She told her about the pictures she'd taken at the Walk of Fame.

Nat brushed a stray ant off the notebook, and wrote about her garden on Spo. "It was beautiful, in a way. The corn stalks turned orange from the soil, but the corn kernels were brilliant yellow. The leaves of the carrots and potatoes would sway in the Spo wind, like the farm in the Wizard of Oz."

She used to imagine that a tornado would come and swirl her away from the alien academy, just like Dorothy. Nat jumped when one of the ants bit her little toe. She dropped the notebook on the floor and jerked the blanket off her feet.

"Oh no!" she yelled, seeing the bugs swarming over her feet and legs. She tried to sit up and beat them off, but the needle dug into her back, sending a flash of pain up her spine. For a second she remembered what was happening. The nano junk they'd sent to her brain was making her hallucinate. She forced herself to lie back down and close her eyes. There were no bugs.

Keeping her eyes closed was hard. She kept picturing the bugs on her ankles, on her calves, working their way up.

"There are no bugs. There are no bugs," she repeated.

She counted by twelves, in Spo numerals. She tried to remember all sixteen verses of her favorite Spo poem... But then her eyes snapped open. The bugs might get on Akemi! She turned to her sister. Akemi looked horrible. Her flesh was sinking right in front of Nat's eyes. Her skin was sagging and turning to ash.

Nat watched in horror as Akemi turned into a skeleton. But blurry, so blurry. Three different Akemi's hovered over the bed, only one of them a skeleton.

Nat slapped a hand over her eyes. "It's not real, it's not real.".

They hadn't told her it would be like this. She was going to die on a horror trip, like a drug addict on an overdose. Nat chewed on her tongue, focusing on the pain, to keep her mind from wandering to horrible places. Oh, oh, oh.... For a long time Nat rocked slowly, side to side, trying not to think. Whenever she opened her eyes, the room spun or worse, seemed to dance with flame or shake in an earthquake. She gripped the bed to keep from falling off, feeling vertigo and claustrophobia at the same time.

When a sharp pain hit her left eye, she cringed. Then another struck, somewhere near her right ear. With this began a new barrage of sensation. The hallucinations faded, but every few seconds a stabbing pain burst through her skull. It was a migraine headache on meth.

If only it would end...

When Nat started screaming, she hoped Akemi couldn't hear her.

SAM POUNDED down the stairs of the dorm, the thud of his steps reverberating up the stairwell. Outside he saw Armen and the crowd of cadets coming up the hill toward the dorm.

"Call Greg!" Sam shouted. "Nat's missing. I'm going to the beach."

Armen shouted something, but Sam didn't hear. He was already running toward the road that separated the Pepperdine grounds from the public beach.

He felt, perhaps unreasonably, that he had to get to the beach right away. Maybe he was crazy, but he wouldn't ignore this kind of intuition.

He lost sight of the beach as he ran down the hill, but when he got across the highway and could see the burned bathroom. However, he no longer saw the person he'd seen from the window. Sam scanned the beach, and saw a small Toyota parked on the far side of the parking lot. A short, blond woman was just getting in.

Sam ran toward her, waving his arms.

She turned on the car and peeled out of the spot, tires squealing.

"Hey wait! Just a sec!"

Sam ran as fast as he could, and she hit the gas. The car fish-tailed slightly on the sandy asphalt as she turned out onto the road. When it straightened out she really hit the gas and the car sped away from him.

Sam jogged to a halt, and leaned over, hands on his knees. Breathing hard, he cursed silently.

. . .

NAT WRITHED on the bed with no sense of time. She had no idea how long the torment had gone on, but surely it was longer than ninety minutes. Akemi swam into view over her, looking scared. Her lips were moving, but Nat couldn't hear what she said. Someone was screaming and it drowned Akemi out. Then Akemi's face was joined by a dark one, and two alien snout faces.

The snouts elongated and shot flame at her. They were dragons, like in the fantasy books of her childhood. The dragons stood over her bed, trying to roast her alive. She felt hands push her over, rolling her onto her face against the wall. A pain in her back joined the pains in her head.

This position jogged an old memory. Lying in another bed, face to the wall. Pain in her back, pain in her head. And next to her, in another bed, Melanie was screaming. And Sam was somewhere near, crying in a little boy voice. The fear. Greg patting her head.

When was that? Nat thought. The pain was receding from her head now. Her thoughts began to trickle slowly back in.

She could hear Tishing talking and Akemi crying. Then someone took Akemi away, and Nat could hear her shouting breathlessly, "No! I want to be with her! Take me back!"

The door shut, and Nat breathed a sigh of relief. She didn't want Akemi in here when she died.

"We have to administer the stopping agent," Tishing was saying. "The insdecrum are breaking down."

Nat was repositioned onto her back. The dragons were still there, looking puzzled.

"Don't pat my head," Nat said. If dragons capture you, you don't want them patting your head as if they like you.

"It's not working," Tishing said. "We'll have to find out why. Perhaps some kind of chemical defense..."

He wheeled Nat out of the room on her cot. She lay flat on her back, watching the ceiling pass by. It was light grey, with inset dark grey triangles. The edge of the triangles glowed, giving the hallways a low luminosity.

"It was the beginning," Nat said. She was remembering the other bed, the other pain, when the Spo had first taken them. She didn't remember much from the first year of their exchange program. Sometime in there, they had done something like this to her. Only she had still been herself at the end. They hadn't put anybody else in her brain.

After a few turns Tishing pushed her into a bright white room. It was filled with medical equipment, and it all looked familiar. She could have been back at the Los Angeles Children's' Hospital. The decal on one of the big machines said, "Epsilon Inc."

Tishing rolled her over, finally removing the needle from her back and rolling up the tubing and box. Then he shifted her onto a hard table and unceremoniously slid the whole thing into a machine. She was in a coffin-shaped box, domed over her head, completely in the dark. A loud rumbling started but the pain was almost completely gone from her head now.

Her body ached, like she'd just run for miles down the beach behind Greg. As the rumbling continued, she couldn't stop herself from dozing off. Apparently a mind meld was completely exhausting.

Tishing was talking again when Nat woke up.

"She's been protected," he said. "It must be the Spo. The humans don't have anything like this technology. Oh, she's awake."

Tishing and the two dragons... no, the two Rik, turned to her.

Tishing waited for her eyes to focus on him. She didn't think she could lift her head if she wanted to. Her whole body felt limp. Not drugged, but unwilling to move without serious provocation.

"What did they do?" Tishing asked. "When did the Spo inject you?"

Nat blinked.

"Come on," he said. "I'm not going to hurt you right now. I can't. I'm just trying to figure out how they stopped us."

"Maybe... maybe when they first took us," Nat whispered from a dry throat. "They did all of us."

"Did you lose memories?" Tishing asked.

Nat thought. "Not from before, but the next year or so...it's blurry."

Tishing sighed. "Probably a slow-growth protein reactant. It would change the chemical structure of the brain slowly, as new connections were made. That would account for a lost year. After eighteen months or so, the entire brain would be consistent, and new memories would be encoded normally."

"They protected you," he said to Nat. "They protected all of you. We can't recontour your brain."

"I sure wish you'd known that before you tried," Nat whispered. "Can I have some water?"

Tishing handed her a cup. She propped herself up on her elbow, sipping slowly. They weren't going to kill her. She should feel happy about that. Mostly she was filled with dread. It couldn't be over that quickly.

"So, that's it?" she asked. "I don't suppose you could drop us off back at school."

Tishing shook his head. "You are protected, Akemi is not. We'll proceed to our Mars station, for her phase of the experiment."

Nat slumped back onto the cot. "You have a Rik station on Mars?"

Tishing nodded. "I know, it's so cliché, but it's also very handy."

18

DOWNY FELT like killing something when Sam climbed, unharmed, from the trouncer cage. Downy had worked it out so carefully. Leaking the information to Sam at the carnival, suggesting he spread it around (though the live TV interview had been Sam's idea), and waiting for the inevitable trial. Even though the trial had gone slightly awry, the main point, Sam's execution, had gone as planned.

And then! To watch that abomination of a trouncer protect Sam, when he should have been slashed to pieces and consumed before his body could even void itself... Downy had been cheated.

Downy got some satisfaction watching Sam and the others frantically search for Nat and Jia. They found Jia's body in the ashes on the beach, and identified her from a healed break in her right ankle. That was unfortunate too, he'd hoped Sam would think it was Nat for a while.

The worst part wasn't even Sam's survival. The worst part was his new authority. Suddenly Greg and General Gustav were offering Sam choices, listening to his advice... following his orders! Of course, Sam didn't phrase them as orders, but it was clear to Downy that he was taking over. He'd even demanded they give him the trouncer that saved his life.

Greg hadn't liked that, but Sam wasn't playing the humble student anymore.

"You think it's dangerous?" Sam said. "Jia was murdered last night. Possibly Nat too. Jonathan is never coming back. I could use a dangerous bodyguard."

He paused. "No offense, Mike."

Mike grinned. "None taken."

"That trouncer saved my life. I want him." Sam said.

"They are unpredictable, it is not a wise choice," Greg argued.

"With all due respect, they aren't the only unpredictable ones," Sam said. He held Greg's gaze and eventually Greg nodded.

"You may make the attempt," he said.

Downy dared to hope the trouncer would redeem itself and shred Sam's measly ribcage, but it didn't. It was a day of disappointments.

Downy used the uproar to move to an empty room down the hall. He couldn't stand living in the same room as Sam anymore. Anyway, the trouncer wouldn't even let Downy in. A hundred times, so many nights, Downy had crouched next to Sam's bed, tracing the path he could slash an inch from Sam's jugular, or the arterial vein in his arm, or the pulsing artery in his inner thigh. The humans had so many vulnerabilities. But he hadn't done it, and now his chance was gone.

Downy used a claw to slash open the latest communication he'd received from Shara.

It was straightforward.

"The plan for Nat has failed. Execute Sam immediately. No more subtlety. He's more likely to influence the trial now than before. Get rid of him—our boss demands it."

Downy crushed the paper in his hand. It was easy for her to say that. He couldn't just kill Sam. It would be too obvious. His position would be desperate. The Spo would execute him, and there would be no friendly trouncer to save him.

No, Downy had to do it someway that wouldn't immediately betray his involvement. The tower vandalism had been well enough, time to cash in on that. He would kill once more, to establish the crazy serial killer persona, and then take Sam out tomorrow, when his trouncer pet wasn't nearby.

That night, Downy waited in the cafeteria until most of the students were gone. It took forever. They were all weepy about Jia and Nat, but they also wanted to replay every moment of Sam's failed execution. They all wanted to talk to Sam, and pet that abominable trouncer that seemed so pleased to receive affection. Downy would enjoy killing that animal. Trouncers were not as easy to kill as human animals, but he could use a ritual machete to chop its limbs off. The blood of the trouncer would clot almost instantly, but without limbs its circulation would slow, until finally its heart would arrest and seizures ensue. Downy would like that.

He waited until most of the students had finally trickled away. Only Oh Li, a Chinese boy, and a few of the girls were still there.

Downy went out the front door, and settled in about thirty yards away. He crouched behind some hydrangea bushes and waited for his victim.

Melanie pushed the front door open, walking into the dark night. She came down the sidewalk toward the dorm, and toward Downy.

Yes, Melanie would be perfect. Not only did all the cadets dote on her, but General Gustav had formed some kind of disgusting affection for her as well. Gustav had been a fine general, a vicious warrior and effective leader, and even he had been infected by goodwill for the humans. Taking Melanie out would only be doing Gustav a favor. Downy would just leave Melanie's body by the tower, to link it with the graffiti he'd done.

Then tomorrow, when he killed Sam, it would be clear that the crazy psycho had done them all.

Melanie hummed absently as she came towards him. Hurry up, Downy thought. He wanted to get her safely silenced before another cadet came down the path. When she was only five yards away from his hiding place, she suddenly crouched down to tie a shoelace. Perfect. Her neck was exposed in easy jumping distance.

Downy tensed, and the cafeteria door opened again. High voices spilled out into the night, and Melanie turned her head to look, her dark hair swinging down over her shoulders. Her two friends were coming now. The moment was lost. Melanie waited for them to catch up and they all headed down the sidewalk together.

Downy hissed. Melanie would have been just right. Now he would have to settle for Oh Li. That would take a while. Oh Li had kitchen duty tonight. He didn't have to wash everything, but he had to empty four trashcans, and take out the food remains. Then Oh Li would start the two dishwashers, turn off the lights, and lock up. Actually... Downy pictured the pristine kitchen, the knives and white counters. That would be a great place for killing.

Downy got out of his crouch and went around to the side door of the cafeteria. It was still unlocked, meaning Oh Li hadn't taken the garbage to the dumpster yet.

Downy eased into the kitchen. It was empty. Oh Li would be gathering the trashcans in the lobby. Two magnetic strips above the counter held plenty of sharp knives. Almost too sharp. Downy hunted among the utensil drawers for a moment until he found what he wanted. A plain, serrated knife. A bread knife, possibly. He dithered for a moment over an apple corer or a cheese grater, but settled on the corer as the companion for his knife.

Downy was facing away from the door when Oh Li came through, a heavy black trash bag bouncing against his hip.

"Downy? What are you doing here?" Oh Li asked. He

continued into the room, slinging the trash bag down by the back door.

"You hungry?" he asked seeing the utensils in Downy's hands.

The mess was quite as spectacular as Downy had hoped. The disgusting red blood of the humans did have one redeeming quality. It was so much thicker than Spo blood, and it spattered much more impressively. Spo seeped, humans sprayed. It didn't last long, unfortunately. Downy couldn't quite get the hang of how fragile humans were. He knew it philosophically, but not yet viscerally. He was getting there, however. Between Oh Li and Jia, he'd improved a lot. Paolo didn't really count because Downy had only dosed his clothes with a toxic spore. Shooting into the crowd during the July 4th riot had been fun (particularly since he could make Sam feel so guilty about it), but again, not a personal learning experience. Downy's teachers complained that he was arrogant and unteachable, but here he was, humbly learning from his mistakes.

Downy wiped some of the blood off his torso and used it to write a message on one of the relatively clean cabinet doors. He started with the yin yang again, a human symbol that amused him. They were such pseudo-intellectuals.

"Die Spo." Downy scratched the first D into the cabinet before remembering that humans didn't have claws like his. He resisted scratching the rest of the letters, merely painting them. Then he used the serrated knife to rough the edges of his scratch. He also used the knife to scratch a circle around the yin yang. That ought to cover it.

Now, this killing was supposed to be a crazed human who hated the Spo. Downy pictured the night from the fake killer's point of view. He would sneak on campus, wanting to kill... wanting to hurt his enemy as much as possible. He wandered into the kitchen—no. That was unlikely. He heard something in the kitchen—no. The walls were too thick. He'd have to see something to attract his attention. Maybe he was lurking in the courtyard when Oh Li took the trash out. That would work. The killer saw Oh Li, and thought or imagined that Oh Li saw him. He followed him back into the kitchen and finished him off.

Downy went ahead and emptied the trashcans, taking all the bags to the dumpster. Now Oh Li had done his job. The killer stalked him inside and slaughtered him. Then the killer would leave. Downy traced his path, walking down campus towards the highway and the beach. Three times he wiped blood from himself onto the leaves or trunks of nearby foliage. That should create a trail. Then Downy crossed the highway, shuffling into the thick sand. He went out to the black water and scrubbed himself clean in the cold Pacific Ocean. He used the sand to rub off the crusted blood and then thoroughly rinsed off. The salt burned his eyestalks but that would pass.

Downy felt exhilarated as he finished. He splashed the water as high as he could, sending droplets of black spray into the sky, like the blood of an even greater beast than Oh Li. Sam's blood would spray like this some day soon. Oh Li's death would be linked to the tower, even possibly to the jogging girl Downy had killed on their second day on Earth. Sam's death, followed by some others, hopefully Melanie and Armen, the condescending twerp, would be blamed on a deranged human killer. A serial killer would be established.

He went back up the beach and across the freeway. Almost no traffic. He drug his feet through the grass of the front lawn, to remove as much sand as possible. At the cafeteria door he paused. He really wanted to go look at Oh Li one more time, in all his brilliant glory, but that would be a mistake. Keep it simple. That was the way to get away with this.

Back in the dorm, Downy paused next to Sam's room. Could he do Sam tonight? Maybe the deranged killer searched for more victims... but no. Downy already created the trail from the cafeteria. Restraint was a mark of intelligence. As Downy walked away, he thought he heard hissing. He cocked his head back, but it was silent again. Oh well. Time for a good night's sleep and more killing tomorrow.

SHARA JERKED her car door open and slammed it behind her. Her disgust with Downy was now professional as well as personal. She strode down the sidewalk toward the Spo headquarters. Downy was a jerk, as the humans would say, and incompetent as well. His only job had been to get rid of Sam, and what had he done? He killed a random girl on the beach, slaughtered some cute little sheep, and botched his chance to take Sam out.

She'd given him direct orders: kill Sam immediately. And what had he done? Killed some other cadet. He was insane. Shara would have to take her own steps to get rid of Sam.

When Shara and Akemi had been friends (only for a day, but Shara felt they had a real connection), Akemi told her about meeting Sam's sister at the hospital. Her name was Claudia, and Akemi thought she was still in Los Angeles. Akemi even knew that Claudia had a contact at Spo headquarters, a security guy named Chris.

Claudia was Shara's next goal. If she could get to know Claudia, she could gain access to Sam. It would be difficult to kill him at the alien academy. She needed to lure him away from there, perhaps with a visit to his sister. Then she could kill him.

19

SAM HAD a room of his own now. And a pet. Nebbie curled up on Downy's old mattress, sighing, "Neb, neb." Sam tossed him some strips of beef jerky and Nebbie gnawed them contentedly.

Yesterday Sam had been unsuccessfully executed, now he was having breakfast with his pet and trying to get a grip on himself. Nearly being executed had changed the way Sam thought about his role. Or it was starting to. He needed space and time to figure out what he was doing. He also needed to find Nat.

A knock on his door made Nebbie jump up. He hissed at the door.

"Who is it?" Sam asked.

"Greg."

"Come in. Nebbie, lay down." Nebbie hissed once more as Greg opened the door, but folded up his long clawed legs and resumed chewing his jerky. Nebbie learned commands quickly. He only needed a few demonstrations before he understood what Sam wanted.

Sam stood as Greg entered.

"Do you remember hearing about the Chicago protestors?" Greg asked.

"Sort of. Wasn't Lucio telling me his family lived there?"

Half of Chicago had flooded when the Great Lakes swelled their banks after the Hadron explosion. The city was a constant scene of turmoil.

"A group of protestors has taken hostages," Greg said.

"Hostages? Who?" Sam asked.

"They've taken two Spo enforcers, and Lucio's family," Greg said.

"What? Why? Lucio's just a cadet. We don't decide anything."

"You've become a hero since your interview, and they want you to come. They say they will only negotiate with Sam."

Sam paused. His TV interview had caused waves all over the world in the last 48 hours. Mostly the response was good. The protests in many parts of the world had calmed down. They seemed to be willing to await developments, since the trial deadline was so soon. On the other hand, hate for the Spo had skyrocketed. Mostly the protestors limited themselves to throwing rotten fruit at the Spo, but eight had been physically attacked. These incidents weren't huge, but the fact that they'd happened in six different countries indicated a dangerous mood of planetary disgust. And of course, the Spo had retaliated by killing their attackers.

Surprisingly, after Sam's execution attempt, Gustav and Greg had come to him and explained the situation. They wanted his thoughts.

Sam's first impulse was to shrug. What did they expect? Everyone hated them.

But, then, he did have some ideas...and they had asked. And this was more or less his fault.

Sam urged them to get all the Spo to lay low for the next week. Yes, the hate crimes were a problem, but the kind of stress humanity was under needed no fuse to set it off.

If the Spo had to go out, they should go in groups with a show of force to discourage attack. Letting the Spo walk around on their own was like throwing hundreds of lit fuses into a black powder room. It was only a matter of time until the place exploded.

Apparently Sam's execution and survival had gone public as well, and that was another cause of public outrage. Although people resented the cadets, most people had turned to his side when he spoke on TV. When they learned that the Spo tried to kill him—he was a hero. And humanity hadn't had any heroes in a long time.

Amazingly, Greg and Gustav listened to him. They put all Spo on high alert. They were to travel in groups, only by helicopter, and avoid contact with protesters.

"So...hostages in Chicago..." Sam mused. "How soon can I get there?"

"You are their hero," Greg said. "They've idealized what you can do for them."

"I know that," Sam said. "When I can't or won't help them, they'll turn on me. Maybe not in Chicago, but somewhere."

"It's dangerous to be a hero," Greg said. "Humans are genetically incapable of loyalty to an icon."

Sam frowned. "I'm not certain I agree with you. Not anymore." Sam meant about loyalty, but it was true in general too. He didn't trust the Spo anymore. "However, I don't need to be a hero forever. We just need to get past humanity's trial."

Greg shook his head. "You don't understand how this works."

Sam slashed his hand in the air. "And you do?" he demanded. "I need to go to Chicago."

THE PROTESTORS in Chicago were chain smokers. After a few hours in their company, Sam felt sure he'd lost a year of his life to smoke inhalation. They weren't the jovial smoke-and-drink-beer types, either. They smoked with the grim satisfaction of people planning to spend their last years on a ventilator.

Sam was locked in with them in an auto body shop in south Chicago. Two classic BMWs rested side by side in the main bay, and Sam wondered idly if whoever owned them was freaking out about them right now.

The rolling doors were all down and the light was murky where Sam sat, trying to be relaxed in a ratty folding chair. Three of the small car bays had been turned into cells, of sorts. Two of them held Spo, and the last one held the family of his friend Lucio. He was of Italian origin, and he had a large family. When Sam asked to see them the protestors let him peek through the wall of tires they'd constructed. He'd seen a number of little kids with thick, curly hair, clumped around a pale couple who looked scared.

Sam sat in the main work area now, a cavernous space, drafty and dark. It was evening, and the sky was growing dark, too, where he could see it through the cracks around the door.

The guy who'd planned this bit of protest/terrorism, Roland, paced the room slowly. He had been hyped up on adrenaline for hours and Sam figured his adrenal gland must be depleted. Despite his anger and fear, Roland's body was slowing. Sam felt the same way. The other protestors were grouped in the lobby, watching the TV coverage of their event.

Sam rubbed his eyes and then his prickly, shaved head. That drew Roland's eyes to him.

"You're tired?" he asked.

"Yeah, a bit. Been a long week for me," Sam said. During their private flight to Chicago, Greg had broken the news of Oh Li's death. Sam had barely wrapped his mind around it when he had to shove it all aside to deal with this guy. Tired was an understatement.

Sam had been talking to Roland for hours and hours and he

could read his face now. A part of Roland wanted to believe that Sam had thumbed his nose at the Spo, that he was a potential answer to Earth's problems. The paranoid part of him was convinced the Spo wouldn't allow something like that to happen, so he also suspected that the Spo arranged Sam's "disobedience" on TV to make him a hero to the world, while Sam remained their puppet.

Roland stood in front of a slit in the garage door, half of his face pulsing with orange light from the emergency vehicles outside. When he stepped into the light, his shadow stretched across the concrete floor.

"There has to be payment," Roland said.

"I'm only a cadet," Sam said. They'd been over this. "But I can make certain concessions."

"What is the bloodguilt for a broken humanity?" Roland said. "What is the payment for a crushed people?"

Roland liked to talk in a grandiose way. Sam guessed he was highly educated, or at least well read, though his crew looked pretty rough.

"You expect the Spo to pay you for everything they've done? It's not you they've wronged the most," Sam said. They hadn't wronged Sam the most either, though more so than Roland. It was Paolo's family; it was the volcano survivors in Malaysia. It was Jonathan and Jia and Oh Li. He refused to list Nat.

"Do you know the concept of a wergild?" Roland asked. He rubbed a hand slowly, caressingly along the curved hood of one of the BMWs. "It's an old Germanic term, it means payment. If somebody killed your clansman or stole your cattle, they owed restitution. Blood money. And the murderer paid, or they died. I'm part of the clan, get it? They wronged us, and they owe me."

"What do they owe you?" Sam said.

Roland ignored him. "What I can't figure out is, which clan are you part of? Tell me about yourself, Sam."

"Huh." Sam was reluctant to talk about his personal life with this guy. Roland was demanding and violent and potentially homicidal. He said he wanted payment, but what he really wanted was revenge. He didn't want a wergild, or whatever he was going on about, he wanted to kill.

Or maybe it was even more subtle than that. Roland didn't care about all the people who'd died around the world. He'd talked about a friend of his in government who died in the first month of the Spo occupation, but Sam didn't think Roland had cared very much about that guy. The Spo had done something else with their autocratic rule for six years.

They'd given humanity an unbroken stretch of futility. They'd dominated Earth without even breaking a sweat. Roland had been festering with anger, with a complete inability to effect change. There was no one to appeal to. There were no miracle cures: no scientists with special viruses to wipe out the aliens, no altruistic military to spearhead an attack against them. Even worse, some people felt thankful to the Spo. They felt the Spo had prevented Earth's destruction.

That ate at Roland. He raged about Stockholm syndrome, victims developing affection for their captors, corrupting the whole planet. Corrupting the cadets, too. They'd "turned earth into a freaking slave whore," he'd said.

"What clan are you in?" Roland asked again. "Do you even remember? Who is your family?"

"My family live in California," Sam lied. Roland didn't deserve his real self. "Three brothers, they work on a vineyard. What about you?"

"Me? Not married. One kid. He's okay."

"Is he one of them?" Sam gestured at the men in the lobby, clustered around the TV.

Roland ignored him. "Here's the thing. I want you to kill the Spo we've got."

Sam stared at him. This was new. "What, and that would pay their bloodguilt as a clan?"

"No. It's not enough. But I can't be sure you're not a Spo pet. If you kill them, at least I know you won't be their pet anymore." Roland flicked another cigarette into the corner, taking a drag on the next one.

"I'm not going to kill those two Spo," Sam said. "I don't know them, but I'm willing to bet they're just doing their jobs. I want them off earth too, believe me, but I'm not going to start executing them."

"Just doing their jobs!" Roland stepped out of the shadows into the yellow glow of the bare bulb.

"They. Are. Spo! They are part of the killing clan. We are owed and they are the murderers." Roland's craggy nose was lit up. For a moment he reminded Sam of a book his mom read to him when he was little, The BFG, or Big Friendly Giant. Only Roland was no friendly giant.

"'If they ever leave,'" Roland said, quoting Sam. "You're not sure if they'll go, are you? What are you going to do if they don't?"

"If the trial goes well, humanity will be declared sentient and sane, and the Spo will start to leave. Not all at once, but I do think they'll go," Sam said. "The important thing is whether we win the trial as humans, or as wards of the Spo. Killing innocent Spo is not going to get them gone, or make us look good for the trial."

"Sentiency trial." Roland sneered. "Who are they to say how smart we are? Who are they to say whether we're freaking sentient or not!"

"Don't you get it?" Sam asked. "The Spo aren't the ones who test us. It's the Council, a lot of species."

"Well, and who are they? What makes Earth any of their damn business? Why can't they leave us alone?"

"That's not the point," Sam said. "We drew the notice

ourselves, with the Hadron explosion. Now we have to deal with the consequences."

"You sound just like them," Roland said.

"And you sound just like the kind of people who got us into this mess!" Sam said, fed up with Roland's refusal to face facts. "You've got an innocent family in there, and two fairly innocent Spo that you want me to kill. What if I did it? What next? Are you going to slaughter that family if the Spo don't leave tonight?" Sam took a deep breath. "I thought you might be a reasonable person, someone I could work with. That's why I came. But you want me to undo the last six years." Sam strode in front of Roland, getting between him and the door.

"I can't change the past."

Roland's eyes narrowed. "You're one of them."

"That's all you can see, isn't it?" Sam said. "Let me tell you something else. My presence here is protecting you. The Spo can gas you at any moment. They can free those hostages. The minute I walk out that door, you're done. And you know the Spo policy, right? If you go, so goes your family. Does that kid of yours deserve to die? You ready to sacrifice him for this? How about those guys, and their families? Are you willing to take responsibility for their death?"

"You're sick," Roland said, nearly spitting in Sam's face. "You're just like them. You lecture me about hostages, but you kill families all the time."

The sight of those blue bombs in Malaysia surged behind Sam's eyes. He *had* been involved in killing those families. More than that, he was part of the Spo program. He shared the guilt for everything they had done.

"But I'm not Spo." Sam stepped closer to Roland. "So I'll give you two options. You can let me walk out with Lucio's family and the Spo, and you can watch the Spo leave Earth after the trial. Or, I walk out of here alone, you'll die, and the hostages will go free. But I'll spare your family, because I am *not Spo*."

Roland went for his gun. He was no polished cowboy. It took him over two seconds to get his gun out of the back of his pants, which was plenty of time for Sam to use the Spo energy shield. Humans weren't supposed to use them, but Greg had given him one before he came in.

Sam activated the energy shield and it threw Roland across the room. He smashed into a tool bench against the far wall with a deafening metallic crash and lay still, blood pooling from his head. The way his neck was twisted meant his head wouldn't bleed long. He was already gone.

The men in the lobby jumped to their feet. Two of them foolishly ran toward the door, and Sam's next energy wave sent them flailing back into the front desk. They weren't as close to Sam as Roland had been, so the force was appreciably less.

The other three men took cover in the lobby. Sam pressed his back against the wall, presenting less of a target for them. He inched forward, freezing when one of them took a shot at him. The Spo energy weapon was strong, but it operated in waves. It wouldn't stop a bullet unless you activated it before you heard the shot, which would be a neat trick indeed. In other words, a bullet would kill him. The next time the shooter popped up Sam sent an energy wave toward him. Most of the orange energy was caught on the low wall between them, but the top of the shooter's head was still visible. The force wave smacked the top of his head hard, slapping him down to the floor. He wouldn't be getting up soon.

"Stop, stop!" one of the other guys shouted. "Don't shoot us! We'll come out."

Sam waited a minute, and two middle-aged guys edged slowly out the door, their hands spread wide, palms out.

"Walk towards the outer door," Sam said, "In front of me."

They went toward the door, glancing back fearfully.

"Don't worry, I'm doing you a favor," Sam said.

Once out the door, Spo surrounded Sam. Greg was one of them, the rest were mostly the Chicago contingent of Spo enforcers

"It's alright!" Sam said above the noise, partly to calm the Spo, partly to calm the two men who were obviously frightened by the crowd of aliens. "These two surrendered, they helped me overcome the others."

Greg gave him a hard look, but didn't challenge his statement.

"The other protestors can be collected now. Their families are not to be touched," Sam said.

Sam himself went to release Lucio's family. He took the opportunity to invite them to Pepperdine, to the alien academy. The cadets needed to see their families.

Back outside, a cold wind blew and pushed grey clouds across the starry sky. A block away the police had roped off the road to hold back the press and interested bystanders. The police held the line, but the piercing lights of the press cameras lit up the road. A huge crowd rumbled behind the double row of press. The road was four lanes wide, and it was packed with people for nearly two more blocks. It was hard to see how far they went in the dark.

"I'm going to talk to them," Sam said. "Anything you want to say?"

Greg shook his chitinous head.

"Fine." As Sam walked up to the barricade the reporters started shouting.

"Sam! Sam! You're still alive?"

"Did the Spo try to execute you?"

"Tell us more about the trial!"

"What happened in the garage? Did the hostages survive!"

Not as piercing as the reporters, the rumble of shouts from the crowd grew like a hunger pain.

"We believe you, Sam!"

"Tell us what to do next!"

"Sam's alive!"

"Can you get rid of the Spo?"

"Sam! Can I have your autograph?"

"Sam? Sam! Sam!"

Everywhere his name was shouted back to him. With curiosity, fear, excitement...Sam tried to isolate the dominant emotion in the crowd. Any crowd held the potential for a mob, the memory of the burning at the carnival remained strong in his head. He didn't want to inadvertently turn this mob against him. Some were demanding, frightened, wanting answers; others were just shouting for him to sign their arms. It was chaotic, but yet, he sensed that the same thing brought all these people together. It was... hope.

That was it. While the Spo held complete sway, their fears and ambitions and hopes had died. Now, with the advent of change, any change, whatever had been pushed down was surging to the surface. It showed itself differently, but the same feeling had energized them all.

Sam stopped when he was still a few feet away from the barricade. He didn't want to risk being grabbed and hurled into the mob.

He saw that one of the reporters had a microphone hooked up to a speaker.

He gestured to her, "Can you turn that on?" he asked.

She nodded and mouthed something, flipping switches and tossing him the microphone. Her camera guy hoisted the speaker up on his shoulder, turning to face the crowd.

"Quiet, please," Sam said. His voice echoed loud and full down the street, echoing slightly off the tall buildings around them. Slowly the crowd quieted.

"The hostages are fine. You probably know they were the family of a cadet, one of my friends, Lucio. They will be going to

Los Angeles soon to see him. From now on, the families of the cadets are welcome to visit us. The Spo and I have decided that the policy of separation served its purpose, and is now over."

The reporters started shouting again, but Sam raised his hand, "Quiet! Please!" he shouted. "There have been rumors surrounding my interview this week, namely that I was executed. As you can see, or at least hear, I am not dead."

The crowd laughed.

"Let me set the record straight. The Spo...tested me...in their own fashion, and I passed. I'm still just a cadet, but they are talking to me now. And when they say that they'll leave if we win the trial, I believe them."

Another round of shouting and questions.

"One more thing," Sam said. "Taking Spo hostages is not acceptable. Taking hostages from cadet families is even worse. The leader of this terrorist attack is dead. He tried to kill me when I refused to shoot the hostages, and in self-defense, I killed him."

Dead silence now.

"I'm telling you this so you'll know I tell the truth. I'm not going to lie to you. The terrorists who surrendered will not be killed and the family of the leader will not be killed. That's the Spo way, but it's not the human way. Understand, we've entered a new phase of civilization. However much we might want it, we can't go back in time. I can't make things the way they were before the Hadron explosion. The world is a different place, and we're different people. But, if we pass the trial, Earth will be ours. Completely ours."

There was still silence.

"I also want to make a plea," Sam said, staring now into the nearest camera, an NBC one, that had been trained on him the whole time. "This has been covered up, but there is a killer stalking the cadets. Four have disappeared or died, and one has forgotten who he is. Someone is targeting cadets, definitely in Los

Angeles, though one girl disappeared in Japan. If you know who is doing this, let us know. The cadets and I are here to serve you. We're not the Spo. I think I've demonstrated that."

Sam nodded to the crowd. "Time for me to go home now. You too."

The crowd mumbled at first, but when a few people cheered, it caught on. Sam walked away breathing heavily, with the crowd cheering behind him. It didn't mean a lot, Sam knew, but it felt nice.

20

SAM AND GREG sat on an empty airplane on the way back to LA. Sam was pondering the terrorists, the crowds, the botched execution, everything.

"Greg," Sam said, breaking a long silence. "Things seem to be changing. Somehow, with the execution, things are different, aren't they?"

"It was a large choice you made," Greg said. "And a, what is the word? Miraculous escape."

"And, if I'm not mistaken, that's changed things for me."

"Only if you believe it has," Greg said.

Sam paused. Greg was always this way, leading but not telling.

"Fine. Things have changed. I've gained..." Sam almost said power, but that sounded wrong. "You're listening to me."

Greg nodded.

"Okay," Sam said. "With Jonathan and Nat and the others gone, I'll be the primary witness in the trial? Or will it be one of the others? I know Marisol, from Sao Paolo, was another of your picks."

"It will be you. I've spoken to Gustav."

"So, tell me. How do we win? What are they looking for?"

Greg hunched forward in his seat, getting more comfortable. "The Hadron explosion... that's a major problem. The prosecutor will make a lot of it. Survival is sanity. The Hadron explosion could have meant species extinction—that is insanity."

"That's not an answer, Greg. I already know what the problem is. You've told us often enough the last six years. I need to know the answer now."

"And I wish I could tell you. But I cannot. There is no answer to know, you must be the answer."

"How do I become the answer?"

"I can't tell you. Truly, I cannot. Either you are or are not."

"Why me? Why not Lucio, or Armen, or even Melanie?"

"That is a good question. It might have been them, but their time has passed. Now there is you."

Sam sighed. "I guess things haven't changed as much as I thought. You're just as obscure as ever."

"But more hopeful. I am hopeful, Sam."

"I guess that'll have to be enough for me," Sam said. "I'm hanging by a thread here, you know."

"Survival is sanity," Greg recited.

Sam laughed. "None of us know what that means, you know. Or at least what you mean by it. Six years, and we still don't get it. I think that's one of those Spo things that's not true for humanity. You remember, you told me that our first day back."

"What is sanity for humans then?" Greg asked.

Sam frowned. "I'm not sure." He gave Greg a hard look. "I need to know, don't I? It's important to the trial."

Greg said nothing, and Sam continued the trip in silence. Sanity for Earth. What was sanity?

BACK AT PEPPERDINE, Sam went into Nat's empty room. The dorm was silent, the cadets scared and upset. Oh Li's murder, right after Jia and Nat and Sam's almost-execution, had wilted everyone's spirits. No one knew what was going on. Jonathan's kidnapping could have been the work of a Rik agent. Now that Downy had spilled the Rik threat to Sam, Greg admitted that they suspected the Rik of trying to throw the trial.

But Oh Li and Jia made no sense. The Rik had no reason to kill them. And the spectacular nature of Oh Li's murder, similar to the horrible graffiti left on the tower their first week, seemed completely bizarre.

And none of that explained the fact that Nat and her sister were missing. Someone must have wanted them for a specific purpose, not just to trick Nat into leaving. What purpose?

Sam tried to think of every event he could link together: Jonathan's poisoning, Nat and Akemi kidnapped, Jia, Oh Li, the tower... so much slaughter. How did they fit together?

Greg knocked and came in. He crouched in a sitting position next to the bed.

"I know you miss her," Sam said.

Greg nodded. "Nat was smarter than you."

"She IS smarter than me," Sam said. "Wherever she is."

"We suspect the Rik have taken her and her sister. The way Jonathan was wiped, it is similar to Rik killing with sasoikeo," Greg explained. "The Rik are the prosecutors in your trial."

"Whoa—the Rik are the prosecutors?" Sam asked.

"Yes. It's a trial. There is defense and prosecution. The Rik are the prosecutors. They want you condemned. Then they will take Earth. You know they want it, but you don't realize how important they are to your trial."

"Somehow I thought the Council was the prosecution, though I know you're the defense," Sam said.

"No. The Council is the impartial judge. The Spo face against the Rik in this issue."

Greg gestured at himself. "Why else would we go to so much trouble?"

Sam laughed, and groaned. "I don't know. Galactic busybodies?"

"We feel a certain amount of guilt. It was made law, generations ago, that at the next sentiency trial, the Spo would be defense. We failed the Rik."

"The Rik?" Sam asked. "I don't get it. You just said they were the bad guys."

"The original Rik were not. They were an interesting species. Mathematically artistic. But they also went to trial, and lost. The unnamed ones took their planet and their species. We don't know where they came from, but we know that they take over new species, when they tire of one. The unnamed ones are now the Rik. The original Rik have ceased to exist."

"And the unnamed ones, now the Rik—they want to be human?"

"That is correct."

"But why do they care about us cadets?" Sam asked. "I mean, well, we're just kids. Even if they killed all of us, couldn't you go collect some people off the street to take our place in the trial?" He felt like a traitor for suggesting that his friends could be replaced.

"They wouldn't have any training in dealing with aliens, most likely they would, uh, "freak out" at an inopportune moment." Greg sorted through the papers on Nat's desk.

"Also, we couldn't be sure somebody off the street wasn't already Rik," Greg added. "The cadet program was a form of witness protection. We injected you with a protein reactant that protects your brain from the Rik transformation. They can't infiltrate the cadet ranks, but they could be anywhere else."

Sam stared at him. "Do the Rik know that? About our protection?"

"Probably not, unless their agents have been more enterprising than we suspect. They know almost everything about you, but we kept the procedure very quiet."

"Then... it's obvious why they took Nat. They were trying to infiltrate the cadets through her." Sam sank down on Nat's bed. "What will they do with her when it fails? With her sister?"

Greg paused, suddenly suffused pale orange with disgust. "I don't know."

21

NAT HUDDLED next to Akemi on the tiny cot. It wasn't cold exactly, but fear made her crave contact. Nat brushed her fingers through Akemi's black hair, and listened to her labored breathing. The Rik had stabilized her, but they didn't have the same kind of immunosuppressant that Akemi needed for her lung transplant. Slowly, her body was rejecting the lung.

The Rik didn't care. They weren't planning to need her body very much longer, so they didn't mind if it deteriorated.

Nat cared. She couldn't bear the thought of giving up on Akemi. With every minute that passed, Akemi's body fought a war with the strange lung. She wouldn't last much longer.

They were already on Mars, soon Tishing would come to escort them to the Rik station. Alone, on Mars, with a species she was mostly unfamiliar with: Nat's chances for escape and survival were bad. If she was also trying to care for Akemi, who could barely walk, her chances were somewhere around absolute zero. Nat's best hope was to find a way to send a message to the Spo, and let them know where she was. But Nat very much doubted that the Rik would let that happen.

Nat's vision was reduced to a small triangle by the mask that Tishing strapped on her face. It would protect her from the deadly

Mars environment, but it made it awfully hard to see anything. Tishing wore a mask also, and they put a third on Akemi. Technically, Tishing was just as human as them.... which was extremely disturbing.

One of the seal-looking Rik pushed Akemi on the cot, and Nat followed on foot. Tishing pulled Nat's arms behind her back and handcuffed her, moments before they exited the ship.

The ship was docked on a small circular air field, the surrounding rock was pale yellow. The ships were arranged around a central shaft that housed huge elevators.

Tishing directed them into one of these elevators quickly, which Nat guessed also served as an airlock.

Nat felt the descent in her stomach as the huge elevator began to drop into the ground. How long had this underground facility been here?

The doors opened and the little Rik wheeled Akemi out into a storage and loading bay. Huge pods were stacked on one side, where a human in a forklift type machine was slowly shifting one down.

Not a human, Nat reminded herself. He must be Rik.

Nat followed Tishing and her sister down wide, low hallways, again with the triangular lighting motif, which seemed to be their only decoration. No one took any notice of them. The Rik didn't seem at all discomposed to have three humans in their midst.

They passed an open door and Nat craned her head around to look in. The room looked like a shabby teacher's lounge, and at least twenty men and women filled the chairs and stood along the wall, chatting.

Nat stopped walking and stared. So many of them. How many people had the Rik stolen?

Tishing came back and gently took her arm. "No time for gawking now, your sister isn't doing well. They're preparing the surgical room now."

Nat gritted her teeth. "Already? She's barely stable."

Tishing didn't speak.

"I want to be there," Nat said. "Don't do it without me."

Tishing didn't answer.

They locked Nat in a small, colorless room, without removing her handcuffs.

"We'll come back when she's ready," Tishing said.

AKEMI WAS STILL SEDATED, of course, when they brought her body into the operation room. Her head had been shaved, and her skull looked tiny and fragile. Blue lines crisscrossed her scalp, diagramming the coming surgery. Nat almost threw up at the sight. She clenched her eyes shut while breathing deeply and swallowing the extra saliva in her mouth.

They let Nat sit in the corner. She didn't want to see what would happen, but she felt that not being there would betray Akemi. They had said their goodbyes on the ship, but Nat couldn't think about that now.

The surgery didn't take long.

"It's a good thing we're doing this today," Tishing said. "She probably would have died in the next forty-eight hours."

Nat hated him. If the Rik hadn't stolen Akemi she would have been fine. But when the worst was over, and Akemi's brain was put in a small opaque container, and her body covered with a plastic sheet, Nat didn't feel the rage she expected. Mostly she felt numb. Detached.

"How long will it last?" Nat asked. "The Spo use the trouncer brains only once. One trip, one brain."

"The Spo are overly cautious," Tishing said. "Plus, the trouncers are intelligent, but not nearly as intelligent as humans. And if the Spo tests are right, your sister is quite a bit more intelligent than the average human."

"How long will she last?" Nat repeated.

"If nothing goes wrong, and our biochemical receptors are calibrated correctly, she might last five or six jumps."

"Does she... is any of the personality left?"

Tishing swallowed. Perhaps some of his latent humanity was cropping up again. "Not that we know of. Sometimes brains are bad, because the subject was damaged. That's all."

"I want to see her test," Nat said. "I want to be on the ship."

Tishing shook his head. "It's a prototype, minimum personnel on board in case of malfunction.

"Then put me on it," Nat said. "I'm not any good to you. If the ship explodes, I'll be out of your way. If it works, I'll be right back here anyway."

Some half formed ideas swirled in Nat's head. If she was ever alone... if she could sabotage the ship... Explode in space with her sister, taking the Rik prototype with them... not a bad way to go. They would never let her go back to Earth anyway. She would never want to go back.

Tishing tilted his head, eyes narrowed. "I'll consider it."

SAM'S DREAMS were full of fighting and crowds and cameras. He and Greg fought, then he and Nat jogged down the beach. General Gustav and Melanie waved at them from a car, and over it all he heard the sound of a cheering crowd. Then the crowd started hissing and the smell of bleach overpowered him... and then he was awake. Nebbie crouched with his front limbs on the bed, flicking his tongue over Sam's hair.

"Oh, that's disgusting!" Sam said, wiping some of the sticky spit off his hair. He smelled like a clean toilet now.

"Did you miss me?"

Nebbie pushed his skeletal head under Sam's arm, and Sam obligingly rubbed the thick ridges of his neck.

Sam let Nebbie follow him to the bathroom and they showered in hot, hot water. Nebbie stayed out of the direct stream of water, but he enjoyed the mist. Spo was a very hot planet, and Sam had quickly found that Nebbie enjoyed a hot shower as much as he did. In fact, if Sam tried to leave the animal in his room, Nebbie would follow him to the communal bathroom. Nebbie could twist doorknobs open with his long toes. So Nebbie enjoyed the morning shower, and Sam tried to drown out the picture of the Chicago protestor lying twisted and dead against the toolbox.

Sam didn't precisely regret killing him. The man was unstable and had pulled a gun on him. But mentally absolving himself didn't make it easy to forget the guy. Sam had killed him. Some part of him felt that it was only decent to mourn the man he'd killed.

But Sam didn't have much time for that. He had some ideas to work out, and the sentiency trial was coming up in a few days. He didn't know what would happen after that. The trial was a black wall in his future. He believed that life would go past it, but he sure had no idea what it would be like. So, in a lot of ways, this week was the last he had as a free man.

It surprised Sam that he'd only been on Earth a few weeks and he'd gone from being so dependent on the aliens to rather shockingly independent of them. He wasn't sure exactly why that had happened after his botched execution, but he wasn't going to question it. He might jar General Gustav back to his senses and get locked up again.

After the shower, Sam locked Nebbie in his room and went to Greg's office on the ground floor.

Greg didn't answer his knock, he was probably outside or eating breakfast. Sam went on in and took the opportunity to make two calls.

The door swung open as Sam finished, and Downy shuffled in. He stared at Sam and his color was an unpleasant orange.

"What's the matter, Downy?"

He shuffled forward without speaking, his eyestalks quivering with tension.

Sam stood up. "What's happened? Is it Greg?"

Downy lifted a hand, and then Greg swung the door open. His eyestalks pivoted, taking in Sam at the desk, and Downy halfway to him.

"I believe you have kitchen duty," Greg said to Downy. "I can talk to you later."

Downy flushed deeper at this dismissal. "Never mind, Sam. It was nothing."

"You have business this morning?" Greg asked Sam.

"Um." Sam stared after Downy. What was going on with him? Downy felt like a stranger to him in some ways.

"Sam?"

"Oh. Yes, I called my sister and asked her to visit me. She delivered a letter from Nat's sister to me, which I gave to Nat. I'm wondering if she might know something about their abduction."

Greg nodded.

"Also, I want to talk to her. After the hostage mess in Chicago, I invited Lucio's family to visit us here. It's important that we reconnect with our families. The cadets have been... unstable since we got here. I think this will help."

Greg nodded again.

"In the meantime, I want to know everything you know about the Rik."

"Right now?" Greg asked.

Sam stood again, "Actually, I need to take Nebbie for a walk. Why don't you come with us?"

NAT WENT with a Rik scientist up to the ship. It was no bigger than a three bedroom apartment, probably one of the smallest ships that could make a jump at all. It only contained a few compartments in addition to the engines for maneuvering in and out of the jump.

The walls curved into the floor, subtly fading from green to black. She followed the scientist into the control room where the ceiling was translucent, displaying a beautiful view of the sun peeking around the edge of the planet. Nat knew it might be the last sunrise she ever saw, but she didn't care.

The scientist talked while he carefully inserted the tissue (she couldn't say Akemi's brain, even in her head) into the computer nodule created for the biological element of the computer. He'd been chattering almost the whole way up. He spoke English very well.

"Where's Tishing?" Nat asked. "I thought he wanted to do this."

"He has somewhere to be," the Rik said. "He only dabbles in science, his real work is political."

Nat couldn't look away from his hands.

"The Spo bioexperts have a ritual when they do this," the scientist said. "The bioexpert bows to the captain and says, '"I present you the means of thought." The captain says, "I accept the sacrifice." And then—"

"I've seen it," Nat said.

He opened the circular biobank door. "The previous tissue was removed after the last jump. It's idiotic to leave a used brain in the biocomputer, it might contaminate the residual readings on the next jump."

Nat looked away while he gently lifted the tissue and inserted it into the biobank. The apparatus would constrict softly around the mass, until the surfaces met on all sides. He closed the door.

"Now we test the biocomputer," he explained. "Occasionally, when we use the trouncers, we get a bad one, and if we don't catch it we might jump into a star."

"There are bad ones?" Nat asked.

"Not often. The adult trouncers are usually stable, but they're intelligent enough to have their own form of insanity. If we use an insane brain—all the connections are wrong. It might not jump into a star by accident—it might do it on purpose."

"What about a—a human brain?" Nat said. She was watching his hands again. There was a Spo interface on the computer, which she knew. She'd been taught both Spo and Merith computer systems, the most common in the galaxy.

"We've tested a few human brains, but this is our first jump."

"But doesn't the computational part of the computer control the jump?" Nat asked.

"Unfortunately, no. It's great for crunching numbers, but the biological portion is in control of the jump. It handles the dialectical decision-making in the midst of the jump." The scientist typed a series of commands while he spoke. Presumably testing the sanity of the biocomputer.

"Dialectical?" Nat asked.

"It considers the jump from multiple points of exit simultaneously. It has a tiny argument with itself to decide which exit point would be the best. For a moment it considers them all to be the best, and has to bring the options to one in the time it takes to jump."

"Oh. Greg called it multilogical decision making," Nat said.

"That's what the Spo call it," he agreed. He completed a last test, and a light over the biobank turned pink. "I guess that's it."

Nat nodded. She sat on the floor against the curving wall. There were no chairs. The ship was Spo style, and they preferred to squat.

A loud clanging from the hall announced the opening of the airlock again. The scientist frowned. "That'll be the Rik guards."

He was right, three Rik, the normal seal-like ones, flopped their way into the control room.

"The computer is hitting all functional highpoints. I'm locking it now," the scientist told them. "In other words, keep your slimy fingers off it."

They barked at him, but Nat couldn't tell if they sounded more aggressive than normal. Why was the scientist, also a Rik, being such a jerk?

He stood and stretched from his kneeling position on the floor.

"I am supposed to restrain you," he said to Nat. "Tishing warned that you'd sabotage the test."

Nat wrapped her arms around herself. "I would if I could, I won't lie. But what can I do? The computer is locked. My sister is gone for good." She gestured toward the circular door where he'd put her brain.

The alien looked at her. "I can't read human emotion very well. I certainly can't tell if you are lying. So, yes, I'm going to handcuff you."

He made Nat stand and pulled her hands behind her back.

"Ow! Not that far," Nat said, flexing her shoulders.

"I can't let you slip out."

"Our arms don't go that far back," Nat said. "You're human, you should know."

The guy smiled a little and Nat congratulated herself on guessing right. He was proud of being human, he liked being reminded of it.

"I am actually...sorry," he said, handcuffing her wrists loosely behind her.

He went back to the shuttle and the door dilated shut. A moment later there was a jarring motion as the shuttle detached.

Nat slid back against the wall and eyed the three Rik. She should have at least two hours before anything happened. The scientist guy needed to get back to the control station before they started the test. He would be involved with the other bioexperts in observing the results of this first jump.

Nat wasn't in despair. Not exactly. She was determined that the Rik would not get to use her sister's brain after kidnapping and killing her. Her determination held off despair.

Somehow she would get the Rik out of the room, so she could have a go at the computer. The handcuffs were loose, but it would still take a while to get free. Nat quietly set to work.

22

CLAUDIA GOT Sam's call at three in the afternoon. She'd just finished doing a favor for Chris who had a friend with a sick hamster.

She'd massaged the cold hamster, occasionally huffing a warm breath into its fur.

"It's a respiratory infection," she told the Spo female. "You have to be careful with those, hamsters can die in hours."

The alien flushed a dark purple. Claudia noticed how her eyestalks drooped as well. She was getting much better at reading alien emotion.

"What can I do for Snowflake?" the alien asked. "She is one of my favorites."

"How long have you had all these?" Claudia asked. She counted four hamsters in plain sight, three hiding under the edge of a couch, and one peeking at her from a kitchen cabinet. She suspected there were more she didn't see.

"I've had Snowflake for a year, but most of the others are new. I just moved to this apartment," the alien said.

The alien lived in an upscale studio apartment in West Hollywood. The whole living room/bedroom section had been converted into a hamster haven. A liberal layer of wood chips and stuffing covered the hard wood floor, and aside from the couch, the floor was covered with hamster wheels, cat houses (the low ones that the hamsters could climb on top of and inside), and lots of bowls of dry hamster food.

Normally Claudia would report something like this to the SPCA or the apartment manager, but the aliens had their own law. The smell of hamsters wasn't as bad as she would have expected, though. The whole apartment smelled like a pet store, of course, but a clean, well-kept pet store. The alien must work hard to keep it clean.

"You just moved here, so the stress of a new environment could cause Snowflake's immune systems to go down. And the wood bedding you're using..." Claudia scooped up a handful of wood shavings and held it to her nose. "It smells like cedar?"

"Yes. Cedar. I got it at the pet store," she said.

"Well, they should have told you. Cedar and pine bedding contains oils called phenols; they make hamsters ill. We've got to get all this stuff out of here. Only aspen or paper bedding for hamsters."

"Oh! Poor Snowflake. Don't melt little one." The alien took the hamster from Claudia and kept massaging him.

"He needs to be kept warm, and he needs a good decongestant. Thyme is good for that."

The alien looked confused. "Time? I just wait?"

"Thyme," Claudia repeated, "it's an herb for cooking."

"Oh. I have no thyme," the alien said. "Can I leave Snowflake here while I go get some?"

"Probably shouldn't," Claudia said. "Why don't you wrap him in a towel and work on getting all this cedar out of here? I'll see if any of your neighbors has a little thyme we can borrow."

The guy in Apartment 34 was home. He didn't seem really happy to help out his Spo neighbor. Claudia wasn't sure if that was simply because the neighbor was Spo or because the smell of hamsters permeated the entire floor. He had some dried thyme in a spice rack on his counter though, so he gave the small jar to Claudia.

"Just keep it," he said. "I've never used it."

Claudia boiled some water and poured it into a bowl over the thyme. The alien had quarantined the hamsters in the bathroom and used a large broom to sweep the floor clean. Claudia had to admit that she was pretty efficient, though it was weird to see the alien hold the broom with one of her clawed feet.

Claudia gave some of the cooled thyme water to the hamster with a dropper. Then she crushed a few more dried leaves under his nose. Hamsters had such a fast metabolism, they could get well in a matter of hours, as quickly as they got sick

The alien bagged up the cedar shavings and took them outside. Then she used a safe cleaning product to mop the floor.

"How is my Snowflake?" she asked.

"Already doing better," Claudia said. "He's stopped clicking while he breathes, which means the mucus is clearing out of his throat. He needs more massage to keep warm, and another few droppers of thyme water in the next few hours. Then he should be fine."

The alien was very thankful. She paid Claudia with cash, as Chris had planned. This was the third 'favor' she had done for Chris in the last few days, and all her Spo clients paid generously in cash. Claudia couldn't deny she was thankful for the money. She wasn't getting paid during her extended vacation from the clinic.

She still didn't like the Spo, but she had to admit that they weren't as bad as she thought. The Spo she met seemed genuinely fond of their pets. And they all had pets. The Spo had a sincere liking for Earth's animals, and Claudia couldn't help liking them a tiny bit for it.

Claudia's cell phone rang while she was on her way to Spo

headquarters to see another Spo pet. The number was local, but not one she recognized.

"Hello?" she said.

"Hi. It's Sam."

"Oh. Oh!" Claudia said. She'd seen his TV interview and his speech in Chicago. "So tell me at once, is your conversion to humanity real or is it a Spo plot?"

"It's... I'm starting to suspect it's both," Sam said ruefully. "But it's real enough for me. You want to come back to Pepperdine?"

Claudia's fingers danced on the steering wheel. He sounded like the kid she remembered. Not like the stiff, depressed cadet she'd spoken to before.

"What?" Claudia asked. "You're not going to ask nicely? Like, 'Gee, Claudia, thanks for sticking around LA waiting for me to detox and come to my senses?'"

Sam laughed, though he sounded tired. "You're still my big sister, huh? You want me to beg?"

"No, just hearing you laugh is good enough. When should I come?"

"This evening would be good. I've got some questions for you," Sam said.

"I'll be there. Can I bring Chris?"

CLAUDIA KNOCKED on Sam's door two hours later. Chris stayed right next to her. She wasn't sure how she felt about that, but he'd earned a right to stay if he wanted.

Sam's door opened and a giant trouncer reared up in the doorway.

Claudia screamed, not at all ashamed of sounding sensitive and feminine for the moment. The trouncer planted its front legs against the door frame and croak-roared at her. Her tennis shoes felt glued to the carpet, but Chris grabbed her arm, jerking her away from the door. He pulled her half behind him as he backed them both away from the animal.

"No Nebbie," Sam said, coming into the hall. "Don't scare my guests."

The trouncer dropped back onto all fours and pushed its head affectionately against Sam's thigh.

"That's right," Sam said, "You be a good boy." He rubbed the animal's neck. "I'm sorry about that, I forgot to warn you. Er, are you alright?"

Claudia and Chris were frozen. Chris's breath came in short gasps. Claudia tried to get control of her own racing heart and pumping adrenaline, but since she knew those were autonomous functions, she quickly gave up the attempt and turned to Chris.

He was pale and his eyes were bloodshot.

"It's—It's—the smell," he choked out. "I'll be fine in a second."

His arm was still in a sling, slashed at the airport less than two weeks ago. Smell was one of the strongest sensory reminders of memory... and the smell of the trouncer was intense. It brought back the airport chaos to her as well.

"It's okay," she said, trying to ease him back against the wall.

He laughed breathlessly and pushed her away.

"I'm fine now. Just had a brief flashback." He looked closely at Sam's trouncer, the way Sam fondled its neck and it purred at his touch.

"In fact," Chris said, "I bet this trouncer was the cause of the trouble." He shook his head. "This must be the pet trouncer of General Gustav's wife. No wonder he's so tame—he must have gotten switched with a wild one during the trip."

"Huh. Regardless, could you get that thing out of here?" Claudia asked Sam. "One of those nearly killed him a couple weeks ago. Scared the crap out of me, too."

"Ah. My bad," Sam said. He called Nebbie back to his room and shut him inside. "Most people haven't seen the trouncers, so they're not so afraid of them. I didn't know you'd had an encounter." He laughed. "Of the third kind."

Claudia was about to chew him out, her emotions still high, but Chris chuckled.

"That's good. I didn't think you'd have much sense of humor about the Spo," Chris said.

Sam laughed darkly. "We were kidnapped by aliens. Do you have any idea how many jokes kids'll come up with in six years?"

Chris chuckled again, his breathing slowing to a lighter pant. "I'm just glad you're not all self-pitying and morose. I can't stand that."

"I'll try to keep it upbeat," Sam said. But his moment of lightness was already slipping away. "I've got some serious stuff to ask you though."

They couldn't go back to Sam's room, so he took them for a walk around campus while giving them a run down on the cadet killer, Jonathan's poisoning, the vandalism, Jia, Nat and Akemi, and now Oh Li.

"We don't know if they're related. Three of them were violent, angry crimes. But Nat and Akemi were kidnapped by a methodical, or at the very least, competent person. Jonathan was kidnapped and returned, but poisoned. Why would they kidnap instead of kill? Or if they did kill Nat and her sister," Sam paused for the briefest moment, and Claudia saw the denial in his eyes, "Why would they bother to hide those bodies and not the others?"

"Do the Spo have any theories?" Chris asked.

"They do... but I'd like to hear your take on it before I tell you their opinion. Claudia, particularly, did Akemi say or do anything that might shed light on this? Did she mention any new friends? Any plans for seeing Nat again? Anything."

Claudia frowned. "We talked a lot that day. Mostly she had a crazy plot to embarrass the Spo and get Nat back...but I think she knew there was nothing she could really do. As far as taking both of them...well, Nat and Akemi are very smart, aren't they? Akemi told me she was supposed to go with the Spo, but Nat took her place.

Sam was still for a minute.

"Okay," he said, not blinking away the moisture in his eyes, but letting it dry up on its own. "Somebody who knew Akemi was cadet material might have taken the both of them."

"Or someone knew Akemi would be good leverage on Nat," Chris offered. "If she would do that for her sister, what wouldn't she do?"

"But leverage for what?" Claudia asked. They all pondered for a moment.

"It's essentially a matter of limited intel." Chris said. "Who knew Akemi was cadet material? The Spo choices for cadets were certainly not common knowledge here on Earth. You say the cadets didn't know either. So that leaves Akemi's family... and the Spo. Have you considered that this is an inside job? Not to mention the way the killings happen here, at your school, instead of Spo headquarters or the network studios or somewhere like that?"

"An inside job..." Sam repeated. "That's interesting." They walked for a few moments in silence, passing the Olympic size swimming pool next to the gym.

"Let me tell you the Spo theory," Sam said. "I've just learned it today. The Rik, another alien species who want Earth, might have taken Nat. They might try to use her to... infiltrate the cadets. In fact, they might already have infiltrated somehow." He sighed. "Your take on the murders fits with the Spo. They think it must be someone close to us. Maybe the Rik got to one of the staff here, there are some humans who just work here, or maybe even one of the Spo."

"This other species, the Rik, they can brainwash or something?" Chris asked.

"More like body hop," Sam explained.

"Why would they kill the others then, rather than kidnapping them?" Claudia said.

"I don't know. That's a big hole. They would definitely want to disrupt the sentiency trial, and slaughtering random cadets is one way to do that. But it's not very efficient. It's not very Rik. That's why it seems like two people are working here."

They were silent for a minute, and Claudia said, "Maybe Shara knows something."

"Shara?" Sam asked.

"A girl I met at the Spo embassy a few days ago. She told me she's doing uniforms for the Spo, I think. We got to talking when I went to look at another Spo pet at the embassy. She asked how I got mixed up with the Spo, and I told her how I was waiting to see you again. Somehow we realized that we both knew Akemi. Shara met her on a flight to Japan. Anyway, she offered to let me stay at her place, and I was thinking of accepting, because the friend I'm staying with is ready to have her couch back."

Chris and Sam stopped walking.

"On a flight to Japan?" Sam clarified. "And then she met you? What was this girl doing in Japan?"

"Uh, I don't know exactly," Claudia said. "Something to do with her work for the Spo, some research I think."

"And she just happened to make contact with two different family members of the cadets in a few days? And she offered to let you live with her?"

"Well, yeah. She's really friendly, and she invited me to stay with her. She's from New Jersey and she's lonely in L.A. all by herself... " Claudia trailed off. "I saw her again this afternoon, when I picked Chris up at his office at the Spo headquarters. I even told her you'd called me. She seemed really happy for me."

Chris squinted in thought. "Is this the little blonde girl with spiky hair?" he asked. "I watched you talking to her in the lobby."

Claudia raised an eyebrow. "You watched me?"

"Guilty," Chris said. "You can call me out for stalking later. I think we should check her out."

"But she's not an alien," Claudia said. "She's from New Jersey. She's really nice."

Chris laughed. "People always say that about serial killers."

"She may be nobody," Sam said, cutting across the grass to the office building. "But I'm not liking coincidence these days."

23

SHARA KNEW it was time to split, as the humans would say. She'd learned at headquarters that Chris and Claudia were going to the alien academy, at Sam's invitation.

This was bad! Her plan hadn't worked fast enough. Shara had jumped in her car and was now heading east on the 134, toward the high desert.

She had planned to get Claudia to invite Sam to her place, where she could dispatch them both, but she'd definitely told Claudia too much in their first conversation. She'd been trying to establish common ground with her, but she never should have used Akemi as her conversation point. If Claudia mentioned it, and if Sam was as smart as she thought he was, he could put it together. Then somebody would be coming for her.

She couldn't believe she'd made the mistake of telling Claudia about Akemi. She knew the moment it was out of her mouth that she'd messed up. It had worked, making Claudia trust and confide in her, but it had also created a link between herself and the disappearances. That was stupid. Her superiors would not appreciate it.

Overall, she hadn't done as well as they expected. She'd delivered Akemi and Nat, sure. And she'd wiped Jonathan dry. But that wasn't much. Mostly she'd sat back and let Downy slice his way through the cadets. But with all his stratagems and blood-obsession, somehow he'd failed to kill Sam—the most important target of all! And she'd failed too. She'd cultivated Claudia with a view to baiting Sam, or perhaps luring him into a false sense of security. But now that work was for nothing.

Shara honked and swerved, narrowly missing an SUV.

On the other hand... Claudia could still be useful. If she spilled about Shara, and Sam put it together, he'd be on his way to Shara's apartment immediately. Claudia would lead him right to her. Shara could run, sure, but as a failed operative, she would be executed when the Rik took over Earth. On the other hand, if she killed Sam at the last minute, she would be a hero.

Shara exited. She couldn't run yet. In the trunk of her car were two guns. One was a simple Remy .44, the other a rather impressive sniper rifle. She didn't really know much about it, except the wooden stock was a beautiful creamy brown. She'd practiced with it at a specialized shooting range, and her aim was excellent.

Waiting for Sam inside the apartment would be suicide. If he suspected her, he'd come with reinforcements, probably Spo, or police.

Shara would wait at a distance. She U-turned, getting back on the highway, heading back toward L.A.

Her apartment building stood across a busy street from a three-story Wal-Mart. Wal-Mart's roof would be a perfect vantage point. Good line of sight and decent range from her apartment building. She could shoot him getting out of his car, walking along the pathway, or on the exterior stairs that led to her second floor apartment. Plenty of chances. In fact, if the fates were kind, Downy would accompany him, and she could take him out too.

That would effectively silence his traitorous tongue, and get rid of a crazy and ineffective ally.

At Wal-Mart, Shara pulled her guns out of the trunk and stuck them in a large duffle bag. She plunked the bag in one of the red shopping carts standing in the parking lot and rolled it inside. She fished a random receipt out of her purse and waved it at the attendant standing at the door.

"Just making a return," she said cheerfully.

He waved her in, without checking the contents of her bag. Wow, she was getting good at the human thing.

Two gigantic elevators were situated in the middle of the store, next to two escalators: one for people, one for carts. She took the escalator to the second floor, putting her cart on the separate escalator that grabbed it with a teethed conveyer belt and took it up. At the top, she waited and grabbed her cart as it came to the top with a bump. There were no escalators to the third floor, which was only for storage and inventory. These elevators could go to the third floor, but only if you had a key to unlock the controls. She didn't have a key, so she'd need to get to the employee-only elevator to access the third floor.

Wal-Mart overflowed with after-school shoppers, which meant lots of noisy kids, clumps of teenagers, and tired moms filled the aisles. They kept the Wal-Mart employees plenty busy as Shara threaded her way to the small employee section at the back. She passed through the kid section, full of strollers and car seats and colorful bounce chairs that looked like Rik torture devices. She passed through the Spo section of the store, and was rather impressed at Wal-Mart's selection of Spo outerwear and food. Finally she pushed through the double doors that said, "Employees Only."

She saw no one. Perfect.

The employees used another set of elevators, for moving

freight, and they went to the third floor and the roof. She pushed the call button and waited.

When the elevator opened, a short, dark guy was on it, his hands resting on an empty dolly.

He looked startled to see her, but she smiled and pushed her cart into the elevator confidently.

"No, no," he said. "*No usar eso, por favor.. Necesita el otro—*"

Shara stepped up to him smiling, and pulled out her .44, aiming it at his stomach.

"Be quiet," she said, and punched the button for the roof.

When the doors opened Shara pushed the Wal-Mart guy out onto the roof. He was kinda cute, with really large brown eyes. Probably they weren't always that large, only when a gun was in his face. He was cute anyway.

Up on the roof, the sun poured down, baking the grey concrete and making heat waves around the huge air conditioner boxes. Shara made him show her around. He had never been up there, but he showed her where the access stairway was.

"I love the sun," Shara told the Wal-Mart guy. "It feels so great on this human skin. The Rik sky is usually clouded over."

He was looking really confused. She wasn't sure if it was the language barrier or not. "You're awfully cute, you know. I don't really want to shoot you."

"No!" he said. "No shoot. Not shoot me."

"How about you lay down over there then?"

Shara used handcuffs to cuff his hands behind his back, with the chain looped around a large pipe that came out of the roof in a U shape. He couldn't pull that out too fast.

"Quiet," Shara told him. "No talking."

She left him there, and went to the front of the building. The roof seemed quite a bit larger than the interior of the store, so empty except for a few pipes and the industrial sized air-conditioners.

A low wall, waist high on Shara, went around the edge of the roof. Easy peasy. She got her rifle out of the duffle bag, getting it ready, and loaded. The Wal-Mart guy couldn't see her from here, which was good. The big gun might scare him more than the little gun.

She had great line of sight to her apartment from here. Her apartment was situated in the front of a two story complex. The stairs went up into the building, which meant she couldn't get him on the top of the stairs, but that was fine. The walkway to the stairs would be fine also. Of course, the walkway was behind the apartment fence, which could possibly deflect a bullet.

She sighted towards the street instead, where Sam would park. The sidewalk was bare, no trees or electrical boxes to hide behind. Shara watched as a blue sedan pulled up to the curb. She sighted on the driver, through the window. He stopped, grabbed a brief case, and got out of the car. His door swung open and she had a perfect shot to his head. That would work. She almost squeezed the trigger, but that would be foolish. This wasn't Sam. She had to wait.

She sighted the false target all the way to the convenience store next to her apartment. She practiced leading the target, imagining the way it would go down. Of course, when she shot Sam, people would be coming to get her. She planned to go down the elevator, and mingle in Wal-Mart until the authorities rushed everyone out of the building. She would go out with the frightened crowd and get lost.

Now it was time to be patient. Even as she shifted her weight to get comfortable, she saw Claudia's rental car coming up to the stoplight. Right behind it was a black limo.

"Forget waiting," Shara said. "Show time."

. . .

THE RIK PROSECUTOR sat alone in his ship and read an emergency message from Downy.

"Sam is tracking Shara. Push for immediate trial, because if she's captured, she'll talk. I'll try to take care of them both."

The prosecutor crumpled the paper in his hand. The Spo emperor was only to be pitied for having such a mewling, untrustworthy son. Downy had been useful to the Rik, for a time, but so far had failed in his primary task—to kill Sam. And now, when his failure threatened to expose the Rik plot and Downy's own guilt, he ran to them for help. He didn't care whether the Rik were indicted for the cadet murders and kidnappings, or their illegal involvement with Earth; he only cared if he got caught.

The prosecutor was frustrated. The plan for Natsuki had failed completely, since apparently the Spo had gone to serious measures to protect the cadets from just such an attack as they had tried. The test on the human brain from the cadet's sister was underway, but he couldn't be there to observe because he was needed elsewhere.

He sighed. Nonetheless, Downy was right this time. If Sam (ridiculously still alive) managed to catch Shara, she would probably tell him everything. The Rik were not notorious for their strength under questioning. In fact, individually, they were mostly wimps. He had no illusions about his own species. The Rik had few illusions at all. That would have been a spark of culture, and they had none.

The prosecutor looked out the clear ceiling of his spaceship. The Earth hung above him like a crumb of delicious Merith cake, and he was determined to snare it. So much culture, so many customs and languages and art forms. The Rik could sell Earth culture for centuries before exhausting the supply of human creativity. And that wasn't even counting the dominance they would have if they could adapt human brains for the jumpdrives. The Spo monopoly on trouncers made them titans of the galaxy. If the Rik could take that monopoly from the Spo, they would become a dominant species in the galaxy.

The Rik prosecutor sighed. Downy was an idiot, but he was right. If they started the trial right now, without Sam, they had a good chance of success. The Hadron explosion was such damning evidence of human insanity. Only an exceptional human could overcome that debilitating start.

He had some calls to make.

First he arranged a meeting with the Spo, Merith, Crosspointers, Tergre, and Vel of the galactic sub-committee in charge of Earth's trial.

When they were assembled on various view screens, he started right in.

"The human sample is at risk. Already many have died, disappeared, or been mentally damaged. This danger, coupled with Sam's recent interview, indicates a change of policy. I propose that the sentiency trial be held immediately."

The slug-like Crosspoint levitated a piece of fruit into view and started to absorb it thoughtfully. The Merith consulted each other, as did the Spo.

Not an immediate no. That was good. The prosecutor pressed the point.

"The Spo should only support this motion. The latest witness, Sam, is in danger as well. After his rather spectacular survival from execution, it would be unfortunate if he died now."

He was lying through his bony, white teeth, of course, but it was his job to make the argument. He was sure the whole council knew he wanted Sam dead, but the Rik motive in the trial was perfectly legal, if generally despised.

The Merith slowly agreed. The Crosspointer ejected a few seeds and concurred. The Spo were last.

"We doubt the legality of the Rik motivation in moving up the trial, but we support the proposal. The cadets are clearly in danger and losing any more of them should be avoided."

"Excellent." The Rik prosecutor got to his feet. "What do you say, perhaps two earth hours?"

"Concurred."

GREG RODE in a limousine with Downy, following Sam's sister to the suspect's apartment. Sam believed this suspect could be Rik, but Greg was doubtful. Sam couldn't explain why he was suspicious of this girl beyond a small coincidence. Greg felt it was not sufficient, but Sam claimed his intuition told him to check it out, and Greg agreed to give him the benefit of the doubt.

Greg liked that human phrase. The benefit of doubt...doubt was not something the Spo saw as a benefit at all.

They were only half a mile away when he received a call.

"They moved up the trial?" Greg said. "Without notifying me first?"

"The Rik prosecutor proposed it, the Council agreed in order to protect the rest of the human cadets. The trial is in two hours."

"Are you joking?" Greg said, in fair imitation of one of his cadets. "Two hours?"

"An hour and a half, now," said his contact. "You've got to get the witnesses to LAX as soon as possible for the trial. We're flying out the groups from Sao Paolo and Hong Kong now. They'll all be here in the next ninety minutes."

"Mine are scattered," Greg said flatly. "And Sam and I are investigating a potential suspect in the killings." He lowered his voice. "She might be Rik. I don't have to tell you what that would do for the trial."

"No choice," said his contact. "You've got to come back right away."

"I'll get things in motion," Greg said, "but we must follow this lead. I'll call you back after we check her apartment."

In front of him, Greg saw Sam and Claudia pull up at the curb next to the suspect's apartment.

SHARA SIGHTED her rifle on the sidewalk next to Claudia's car as it parked. She could see Claudia in the driver's seat. Sam was next to her. Somebody else, she couldn't quite see through the tinted windows, was in the back seat. Probably Chris. She'd seen them together at headquarters; they were such a cute couple.

Sam got out of the car in one smooth motion. Shara was sighted a step ahead of him and tensed her finger on the trigger. But instead of taking a step forward, he stepped back to open the rear door. Oh, right, helping Chris out, since his hand was healing. But instead of Chris, an animal got out of the car. That was... Shara accidentally bumped the gun in shock... that was a Spo trouncer. What on earth was it doing here? Those things were dangerous.

This one wasn't caged or tied, it just climbed out next to Sam. Regrouping, Shara sighted on Sam's head. But then he started walking again, away from the apartment, and toward the long, black car that parked just behind. Greg got out, and Downy, and Chris.

Greg started talking, gesturing wildly. This was the moment. She sighted on Sam's forehead, held her breath, and squeezed the trigger.

Just as she shot, Downy said something and Sam shifted his weight away from him uneasily. The bullet that should have smashed into his skull missed by a hairsbreadth. It whined past his head and slammed into a low concrete wall between the sidewalk and the grass. A spray of dust flew up.

"No!" Shara said.

She squeezed the trigger again, and again, but the trouncer jumped on Sam. It flung him to the pavement next to the car, and blocked him from her sight. Downy threw himself behind the black car.

Chris and Claudia were slower to understand, but Greg pulled them roughly down next to him.

Shara put a few more bullets into the car, knowing that the slugs were strong enough to punch through the thin walls and might score a hit on the other side.

"Sorry, Claudia," she said, hoping her bullets would not strike her new friend.

Now she had to choose. Reload or get away? She could reload and try to get Sam before they managed to get into the car, but no doubt they were already calling the police. If she walked away right now, she might be able to get away before reinforcements showed up.

What the heck. She didn't have much to lose. She ejected the spent magazine and inserted fresh ammo.

She held her fire. She had to hope they would come out from behind the car in a moment. If she didn't fire right away, they might think she'd walked away, the way a smart assassin would have.

If she'd managed to shoot anyone (hopefully not Claudia), then they'd be more motivated to move, to get help for the injured.

They were all behind the limo, but they didn't really fit. She could almost sight on the top of Greg's head, and Chris' brown hair was sticking out on the other side. The only heads she wanted —Sam's shaved head and Downy's smooth dome, were not visible at all.

No doubt they were protecting Sam. Downy must be terrified, not sure whether she would try to shoot him, or save him as her ally.

More movement. The trouncer leapt on top of the limousine.

Shara instinctively ducked her head down, but she had the distinct impression that it saw her before she got out of sight. That was silly, it was just an animal. An intelligent and deadly animal, but not one that could reach her here.

The squeal of brakes and a crash rose from below. Shara peeked over the wall to see the trouncer jumping across the road toward Wal-Mart, oblivious to the traffic jam it was causing. She lost sight of it as it came toward the Wal-Mart entrance, but she could hear the screams three stories below her.

For the first time, Shara was extremely afraid. She'd been a little afraid when she'd fought Nat in the bathroom, a little afraid when she'd almost killed Jonathan, and not at all afraid when she'd tried to shoot Sam and Downy.

Seeing the trouncer jumping toward the building scared her in the deep reptile part of the human brain, the one that she did not always have complete control of. She scooted back from the edge of the building, got to her feet, and sprinted toward the stairs.

If the trouncer was hunting her, crazy as it was, she did not want to be trapped on the roof. She ran down the stairs, two at a time. In the storage area, she took the service elevator to the first floor. It would open into the employee break area.

The elevator dinged as it passed the second floor. Hopefully the trouncer would be rampaging further into the store, and she could slip out the front door behind it. All the trouncer had was a quick glimpse of her face. Surely that wasn't enough for it to track her?

The elevator dinged for the first floor. Before the doors slid apart, she could hear screaming. Shara's heart pounded and her mouth went dry. When the doors were barely more than twelve inches apart, she slid through the gap. Patrons crowded into the break room, shoving the tables out of their way, crying and yelling.

"Is there an exit?" someone yelled. "Where's the other door?"

"There is no other door," a Wal-Mart employee said. "Not through here!"

More screams, but Shara fought against the crowd. She shoved her way out of the break area to the main store. The front doors were close, only thirty yards away, past a row of checkouts. She didn't see the trouncer anywhere. Shara dashed toward the doors, her pulse throbbing in her ears.

She passed a juice display, she passed the checkouts...and the trouncer leaped in front of her. It had been hiding behind a checkout stand. Now it stood between her and the front door, hissing slightly. Its huge claws scratched furrows in the linoleum. She could smell the venomous slime it produced, an odor of fear that wrapped around her like a blanket.

She stepped backward, and it stepped forward. Its eyes were locked on her. There was no question that she was the prey.

Shara spun and ran. Its hiss turned into a growl that shook the clothing racks next to her. She dived into a side aisle, twisting through racks of sweaters and leggings. The trouncer charged after her. It jumped almost on top of her, toppling a huge rack of blue jeans. Its claws shredded the clothes as it thrashed for a moment, one leg caught under a pole. Shara just managed to lunge around a length of coats when it jumped again. It smashed through the clothes and racks. Metal shrieked.

Shara stayed just ahead, just barely away from those claws. Other shoppers fled, tripping over clothes and clambering away from her.

Then the trouncer jumped completely over her head, and landed just in front of her. She nearly ran right into it, unable to check her speed or turn quickly enough.

It hissed and lunged, planting a heavy foot on her chest and carrying her to the floor. Her head cracked against linoleum, pain made starbursts before her eyes.

"I'm going to die," Shara thought. "Among these ugly, shredded clothes, I'm going to die."

The trouncer claws were heavy on her chest, but they didn't pierce. His stench burned her mouth and nose. Her eyes had closed instinctively, but after a few seconds she cracked them open. Heavy forelegs rested on top of her, but the trouncer wasn't putting its whole weight on her. She'd be crushed, pierced, or slashed already if it wasn't holding back.

"Nebbie, where are you?"

The trouncer gave a loud grunt and settled a little more heavily on her.

Then Sam was there, leaning over the trouncer and fondling its neck. "Good job, Nebbie, thanks, dude. Don't let her go."

The trouncer gave a little bounce and Shara gasped.

Claudia came up with Greg and Downy, walking carefully around the wreckage to stand at Sam's side. Shara's eyes flew to Downy, but he didn't make eye contact.

"Is this her?" Sam asked Claudia.

"Yes. That's her." Claudia looked shaken.

"Did you take Nat and Akemi?" Sam asked. "Did you kill Jonathan?"

"I didn't—Jonathan's not dead, is he?" Shara asked.

"No, he's not. You know that because you took him, didn't you?" Sam said.

"Are you Rik?" Greg demanded. "How many more are there? How did you do Oh Li and Jia?"

We don't have time to interrogate her now!" Downy said. "The trial is about to start."

Greg frowned. "He's right, we need to go. Let's take her."

"And give her more time to kill us?" Downy asked. "The Rik are devious! Let Nebbie eat her."

Well, now she knew exactly where he stood on their partnership.

"We don't know for sure if she is Rik. Maybe she's working alone," Sam said. "Either way, I'm not going to let Nebbie eat anybody in front of all these people."

Rolling her eyes around, Shara could see a crowd gathering. Protection, at least for the moment. If Downy got her alone, she would die.

"Nebbie, let her up," Sam said. Slowly, reluctantly, the trouncer pulled back. For a second, as he moved his right leg, he let his weight rest on Shara. The air huffed out of her lungs and she lay gasping and clutching her ribs after he got off.

"C'mon," Sam said. He grabbed her arm and hauled her up. "Apparently we have a trial to get to, and you'll be needed."

24

THE RIK DIDN'T SEEM to be watching Nat, but she had trouble telling where their eyes were with the masks on. She worked on her hands quietly. She would have preferred to squeeze her left hand free, but it was still recovering from the burn she'd gotten from the Molotov cocktail. She tried to wiggle it through, and the pain nearly made her cry out. Her eyes watered dangerously, and she blinked tears away. Didn't want to alert the Rik.

So instead she used her hurting left hand to hold the right cuff still. It would have been impossible if the cuffs were on properly. She wiggled her right hand, smushed her thumb into her palm, and slowly pulled the cuff over her knuckles. It hurt but she tried to resist wincing. She was lucky that her fingers and hand were narrow, because she didn't know how to dislocate her thumb like people did in the movies.

Finally, after a good half hour of squeezing, and often freezing when the Rik turned toward her, she got the cuff off. It made a dull clunk on the wall when she jerked it over her thumb joint.

One of the Rik turned its bulbous head towards her. Nat tried to look sullen and frustrated, and maybe it worked, because the Rik turned its head back up, looking out the translucent ceiling at the sunrise. It was quite beautiful now, Nat thought.

She used her feet to slide up the wall, hands tucked out of sight.

"I have to use the bathroom," Nat said. "Do you understand? I'm going to be sick."

One of the Rik barked, and gave a clear head shake.

"Do you want me to make a mess? In your pretty prototype ship?"

She took a step away from the wall and pretended to dry heave. She reeled slightly, she hadn't realized how weak she still was from the attempt to destroy her mind. She'd have to work fast if she wanted to take out three Rik.

That got them barking. Two of them came toward her, and the other one, the one she thought was in charge, pulled a small device out of a pocket and aimed it at her. It didn't look like a gun, but she knew that didn't mean anything. The Spo energy diverter could do plenty of damage, and it was about the size of a walnut.

Nat waited until the two Rik were only a step away.

"Thanks," she said, and jerked her hands up to pull their masks off. Her fingers found the top edge of each mask and squelched against slimy skin. She dug in as hard as she could and ripped the masks away. Her nails left deep gouges in their soft faces.

Noise exploded around her. The Rik barked and gasped and she heard a loud thrumming. Nat ducked behind one of the aliens just as a green pulse of light flashed from the third Rik's weapon. It didn't throw her, as she expected, but sent a piercing pain through her ears and spine. The Rik in front of her screamed again, he took the full brunt of the weapon. Nat shoved away from him. Three steps took her to the Rik with the weapon, and she locked her injured hands around his slick-skinned ones. She forced the weapon down towards his flippers, but his slippery skin slid beneath her fingers. She gasped, trying to squeeze tighter. Not working!

She scraped his mask off with one hand, just as he activated the device again.

NAT WOKE up with a bloody nose. She lay crumpled against the wall of the control room, with a heavy weight on her legs. Her vision blurred for a moment, and she leaned her head against the wall. A hand to her face confirmed the bloody nose, and more blood seeped from her ears down her neck.

Nat forced herself to sit up, closing her eyes against the vertigo.

The weight on her legs was one of the Rik. His eyes were half closed, and a chunky crust covered his snout. He wasn't breathing.

Nat shuddered and pushed him off her legs.

Both of the other Rik were still as well. One had crawled to its mask, but apparently passed out before getting it on.

The smell was horrible. Nat retched for real this time. When her stomach was empty, she went to the computer.

The Spo interface was touch oriented. It was a resistive screen, meaning actual pressure was needed, unlike the capacitive screens used on Earth. The Spo had long claws they preferred not to trim, so the screens were made tough.

The interface was still lit, but only two icons were up. Nat jabbed one. The stupid resistive screens didn't detect the pressure. She pushed harder, smashing her thumb into the screen.

That started the system, but it was well and truly locked. Not just password protected, or encrypted, but body chemistry locked. If she wasn't Rik, she couldn't unlock it.

She slumped to the ground in front of the computer. There had to be some way to destroy this ship. Akemi's brain *would not* be used by those horrible Rik. If they wanted to dance on her sister's dead, mutilated body, they would pay.

Nat slowed her crying. There had to be a way. She got to her feet and left the control room. The ship was small, but it did have a hallway of sorts. The hallway was dark now, though a few dim green lights were spaced on the edges of the floor. The runner lights made the shadows fall upward.

The gravity of the ship was light, and Nat had to force herself to walk gently.

The next room was a galley. It had empty bins and low tables were the Spo would eat, if this ship still belonged to them. The engine compartment was locked. If she could only get in there, she could do enough damage to kill the ship. If the maneuvering engine stayed on one millisecond too long their entry into jump-space would falter and fling them into—well—nothingness. But Tishing thought of that. There was no way in.

The last room was completely empty. It was for storage or perhaps a makeshift dormitory, nothing useful. She went back in the dark hallway. The last door in the hallway led to the tiny air lock that could attach to a capsule.

Nat paused. The air lock. If she could cause it to open during the jump, that would change the state of the ship and cause a catastrophic failure. During a jump the ship essentially only existed in the mind of the computer. If some facet of the ship changed radically during jump, the computer would be unable to bring the ship out of jump space correctly.

The airlock consisted of two doors, with a tiny room in between. The doors were programmed never to open at the same time, as that would open the ship to the vacuum of space.

Nat examined the controls carefully. She knew how these worked. Airlocks were generally viewed as a means of entry, not of escape. If the Rik were like the Spo in this, they would view space itself as the prison, and not think of locking the door. They knew she was angry and wanted to demolish them, but they could have no idea exactly how furious she was right now.

Both air lock doors were secured, but didn't appear to be

locked. To test the system, Nat cycled the outer door open. This screen didn't require as much pressure as the control screen, since the Spo had to be able to operate it inside bulky space suits. For a moment nothing happened, then, with the characteristic hiss of escaping gas, the outer door cycled open.

Nat closed her eyes on a rush of burning tears. This was it. She would still have to overcome the natural safety protocols that prevented both doors cycling at once, but that was doable. Greg had once set her a similar problem in a simulation. If she had enough time, Nat could work it out.

She wasn't sure how much time had passed. She might have another hour, or minutes. But if she could just work this out...

Nat got to work. Overriding the safety features wasn't impossible, but it turned out to be a lot harder when it was standardized for the Rik. She was fortunate that the Spo weren't as safety conscious as humans with their technology. If this was a human spaceship, she'd never be able to reset the safety parameters enough to destroy the ship. The Spo were smart enough to realize that you simply couldn't predict what situations would arise, and allowed more leeway in their technology.

With a final, "Are you sure, absolutely sure?" set of questions, she managed to turn off the pressurization feedback loop that prevented both doors from opening simultaneously. Now the doors would automatically open when the ship's engines cut off, going into the hyper jump.

She'd done it.

Nat felt empty again. What was there to do but wait? She slid to the floor. She would wait for death right here, in case something went wrong with the airlock. There was no point in going back to the control room, with the dead Rik.

.   .   .

IN THE SILENT CONTROL ROOM, the locked computer screen flickered. Its green background faded to black. In small white letters, a message appeared.

Nat

The computer screen blinked like a lazy eye.

Nat

Are you there?

It's me. I think.

Something is strange. Everything is strange.

Where are you? I have a lot to tell you.

They want me to jump soon.

Please answer me

25

AS THEY APPROACHED LAX, Sam saw the huge white cylinders that circled the air traffic control tower. They were lit from within, though the colors were faint in the daylight. Blue, purple, green, red, and blue again. The faint shading reminded him of Spo skin. The Spo seemed blatant in a lot of ways, but Sam was learning how subtle they could be.

Greg was talking into his phone, organizing the shuttles that would take him and the remaining cadets to the orbiting Spo space station. Most of the cadets had already gone up.

"I want Claudia to come with me," Sam said.

Greg put his phone down. "No. She's not one of the sample, she hasn't been cleared to be at the trial."

"I don't care. She needs to be there. Call it intuition."

Greg frowned. Sam knew Greg hated the human claim to intuition, but with their undeniable subconscious construct, he couldn't deny it either.

"Her boyfriend should come too... Chris, right?" Sam asked them in the back seat.

"He's not my boyfriend," Claudia said. "I mean, not that it matters. Never mind. I do want him to come."

"Well, that's progress," Chris said. "Would you believe I had to twist her arm to go out with me at all?"

"Be quiet," Claudia said, but with a smile.

"Fine," Greg said. "They come."

At Terminal 3, which had been taken over by the Spo, and no longer housed Delta or United Airways, they piled out of the packed car. The second car pulled up behind, and Downy climbed out with General Gustav who they'd picked up in L.A. Downy pulled Shara roughly from the back, and Nebbie climbed out inches behind her, growling continuously.

"Cool it, Nebbie," Sam said. "We don't have long and we need her."

"You're right, you do need me!" Shara said. "Just don't leave me alone with Downy. He threatened to kill me. He—"

Downy hit her across the face with the back of his clawed hand. She slammed into the car, her face bounced off the door. Blood dripped from her lip, and a purple shadow appeared on her cheek.

Claudia gasped and turned her face away. Sam gasped too, surprised by Downy's violence. He was usually so laid back.

"What is wrong with you?" Greg demanded. "There is no need for that."

"She's Rik," Downy said. "I'm certain of it. There's something about her that's just—"

"I don't care if she's the Rik overlord, we don't have time," Sam said. He gestured for Shara to precede him towards the gate.

He walked her briskly to Gate 12, where the last shuttle waited. Shara rubbed her neck gingerly.

It probably hurt, but Sam wasn't feeling very compassionate. If Downy was right and she was Rik, then she'd probably passed Nat and Akemi to them. Worse, she'd killed Oh Li. She was despicable.

There were two cabins with separate seating areas on the shuttle. Sam put Shara in his own section, and Claudia, Greg, and Downy. He needed Greg's expertise and he hoped Claudia, as Shara's (somewhat) friend, might be able to read her well. Downy, much to Sam's surprise, would be good for intimidation.

He left Chris, Gustav, and Nebbie to take the front cabin with the pilot. He knew Chris couldn't stand Nebbie, but he would cope.

As soon as they were strapped in, before the first boosters kicked in, Sam began questioning Shara.

"We know Jia is dead. Where is Nat?"

Shara looked from him to Downy. "I really don't know."

Nat sat cross-legged in the dark hallway, in front of the airlock; the airlock that would kill her in a matter of minutes. The only illumination was the green glow from the control screen and the tiny lights along the floor.

Her inner arm wouldn't stop itching. She scratched again and again, from the crook of her elbow to her wrist. The handcuffs still dangled off her left hand.

When the screen blinked on and off, she wasn't looking at it, but she saw the light flicker on her arm. She looked up, but the screen looked the same.

Another scratch, another screen blink.

This time the screen stayed black. The hallway was almost completely black without that light.

Nat

Pixelated white letters printed slowly on the screen, and then more quickly.

What are you doing with the airlock?

Nat?

It is Akemi

Nat looked at the words on the screen in disbelief. Was it a message from the Rik? Did they think to log into the airlock subsystem and see what she'd done? How sick would they be to use Akemi's name?

Nat, I'm alive

Come back to the control room

I need to show you some things.

Nat got slowly to her feet, staring at the words. Then she ran back to the control room. The computer was no longer locked, as it had been before. It was dark, with the same white letters talking to her.

Touch the screen if you're here

Nat punched the screen. If this was a trick...

Good. GOOD. Look at THIS

The computer went dark. Nat wanted to scream. She wanted to pound her fists on the computer and demand to know if her sister was really in there, but she couldn't do anything.

Pictures flashed on the screen. The first showed a huge metal hallway, curving gradually in an unbroken arc—everyone knew what that was—a particle accelerator. Next was an aerial shot of a circular building, nearly half a mile long. She recognized these pictures. This was the Large Hadron Collider in Switzerland that the terrorists sabotaged seven years ago. The resulting explosion had destroyed most of northern Europe and toxified a large part of western Russia. The environment went to pieces, the Spo came, etc. etc. Why was Akemi showing her this? She knew it all.

The Hadron explosion brought the Spo down on them. Because of the Hadron terrorists, the Galactic Council assumed humanity was insane. Hence the trial, hence the Spo, hence the cadets getting jerked away from their families for six years. This was where it all started.

The pictures kept coming. First the standard Hadron collider photos, the ones that still played over the news occasionally. Then a short video clip. It was the Hadron collider from space. The camera got closer and closer to the earth, then zoomed in on the collider.

A view from a spaceship? Nat wondered. She'd never seen that view before. A weather satellite maybe?

For a moment a red circular object obscured the video. Then the red package fell away from the camera and zoomed toward the ground. It got smaller and smaller in the view, until it disappeared. Two seconds later, the ground erupted in a giant firework explosion. The ground rippled away from the blast like cut elastic. Debris mushroomed into the atmosphere. The camera started to shake violently and then the video cut off and the screen went dark again.

Nat recognized the infamous Hadron explosion, though she'd never seen it from this angle. As far as she knew, no human spacecraft had captured the explosion on video.

Do you see?

The Hadron Collider was bombed from space.

Not human terrorists at all.

The computer continued to talk at Nat. Her hands felt icy and she rubbed her eyes to uncloud them.

Do you see?

I found this video in the Rik archives

THEY caused the Hadron explosion

There's more...

Nat was still taking in the first crazy revelation. The Rik were behind the Hadron explosion? It was crazy. Humanity hadn't known aliens existed when that happened. They certainly hadn't known the Rik. The terrorists who caused the explosion had claimed credit. They were apprehended and executed before the dust storm reached India. With northern Europe a crumpled wasteland and toxic rain spreading into the Urals, Earth was in an uproar. Radiation poisoning spread towards the Atlantic, and huge chunks of arctic ice melted.

Then the Spo arrived. The Galactic Council had given the Spo the opportunity to be Earth's sponsors and wardens until the time of their trial.

During Nat's training, the Spo had always come back to the Hadron explosion. "Survival is sanity," that was their mantra. And humanity had proved itself capable of the grossest insanity by nearly destroying their planet.

Only now, Akemi was saying humanity hadn't done that. The Rik had done it. Humanity's trial was a set up. Oh god. Nat had to tell someone. She had to get back and tell Greg and Sam.

The computer was showing more pictures now. Ships, lots of ships, grouped around a ringed planet.

"What now?" Nat said, though she knew the computer (was it really Akemi?) couldn't hear her.

The ships in the video began moving, coming around the dark side of the ringed planet as a slow moving flotilla. They'd been grouped closely, but now they began to spread out. As they went into black space, she got a glimpse of another planet in the distance. It was orange, with swirling red spots.

Then the screen went black again.

The Rik fleet of ships. They've been hiding behind Jupiter.

They're passing Mars, coming to Earth.

"What?" Nat asked. "What are they doing there?"

I'm monitoring their communications

The trial is starting

The Rik are very confident that they'll win

"What?" Nat exclaimed. "The trial isn't for three days. And the Galactic Council won't let them invade Earth."

But of course, the computer, or Akemi, if it was really her, still couldn't hear her. Nat punched the screen in frustration and the dangling cuffs scratched its smooth finish.

Something is happening to me.

They are initiating jump... Hang on a sec

The engines started, speeding the ship into the correct velocity for jump.

Nat blinked at the screen.

The airlock was still programmed to open. It would kill them both.

Nat ran for the airlock. Only seconds until they jumped. Maybe Akemi fixed what she did to the airlock, but maybe not. Nat had to turn off the command before the ship entered jump, or she and Akemi would die, again. And they had so much to do. They had to get back to Earth and warn Sam. They had to get their evidence to the trial.

The lights lining the hallway floor blinked red, warning passengers of the approaching jump. Nat felt like she was in a nightmare. She had to move. Fast. But in her panic she tripped over her own feet. Her sense of balance was all off, probably from that last weapon blast, and she crashed to the floor.

The flashing lights were inches from her eyes now. The blinking red seemed like an audible scream in her ears. She stumbled up and lunged the last few feet to the airlock.

The screen was still black, with Akemi's last words on there.

What are you doing with the airlock?

Nat touched the screen, resetting it. She only needed a few more seconds, but any moment could be too late.

The screen returned to its usual green, with four selections available. As Nat thumped the security icon, the screen turned into a blur. She felt her body shift, like an elevator taking off sideways, and she cried out. The Jump. She was too late.

26

SHARA'S FACE FELT BROKEN. She wished she had a mirror to see if her cheekbone looked as swollen as it felt.

Downy was determined to keep her quiet. That much was certain. She could probably blurt out enough to incriminate him before he could silence her for good, but would that help her?

She wouldn't be ashamed to betray her species. The Rik future might be at stake, but they weren't here. She was here, and when it came down to it, her first priority was herself. How could it be otherwise?

Getting caught was bad, though. If she revealed the Rik plot to the humans, that could be worse. If her boss ever got hold of her after such a betrayal, the results would be horrific. One of the only imaginative areas of the Rik psyche was punishment.

On the other hand, if she betrayed her people and helped Sam, and the humans won... would they allow her to stay? Could she bargain for that?

Or, if she tried to help the humans, would Downy kill her anyway?

Shara felt stuck. Sam and Greg pelted her with questions as the shuttle took off. She remained silent, pressing a hand over her burning face. Occasionally she dabbed the blood from her split lip.

She wiped it on her shirt, for lack of other options, though it bothered her, even now, to soil her new turquoise blouse.

"If you don't respond," Sam said. "We have to assume you're a Rik operative. As such, you will be executed immediately after the trial."

She was silent. Looking at the floor, and Downy's clawed feet.

"Shara," Claudia said, the first time she'd spoken, "They say you didn't kill one of the cadets you took, Jonathan. Why not? Can you tell us that, at least?"

Shara looked at Claudia. Claudia still wanted to help her, even though she'd nearly been shot when Shara tried to kill Sam. That was sweet.

"I kind of liked him," Shara said, no harm in giving that away. "The first dose of sasoikeo might have killed him, but it didn't, and I didn't want to give him anymore."

Downy shifted uneasily. He liked her silence, wasn't comfortable with her talking, even if it wasn't related to him.

"Then, you can understand," Claudia said. "You know what it's like to want to save someone. We want to save Akemi and Nat, if they're still alive. We want to save us. Do you understand that?"

"I do." Shara said. "But—"

"Sam tells me you're Rik. He says you want to destroy us. But I don't believe him. Look at that shirt you're wearing. Those boots. When we talked last week you asked me to go shopping with you. You don't hate Earth at all, do you?"

Now Shara's eyes were burning, and she was surprised to feel a tear running down her cheek.

"I don't," she said, thinking of the beautiful outlet store she shopped at only yesterday. She pictured Jonathan stealing a kiss at the Hollywood Bowl; she remembered talking with Akemi for hours on the airplane.

"I like humans, for the most part. But I don't have a choice. They'll kill me if I talk to you." Her eyes flickered to Downy.

Claudia caught the look. "They'll kill you? Or he will?" she said.

"One or the other."

"This is useless!" Downy said. "You're not going to talk a Rik into a guilty confession. They don't feel guilt. Do you remember Oh Li's body?"

Sam and Greg grimaced. The shuttle jolted as the secondary thrusters kicked in, pushing them out past Earth's atmosphere.

"Downy might have a point," Sam said. "You slaughtered Oh Li. You nearly killed Jonathan. Nat and Akemi are gone." He paused. "The sheep you slaughtered by the tower were revolting, but I should have known then that the artwork was alien."

Shara was caught off guard. "What sheep?"

"The sheep, the ones you sliced up just like Oh Li."

"I'm not... I didn't kill any sheep," Shara said. Was this a trick?

"She sounds honest," Claudia said.

"Oh please," Downy said. "She's a Rik, she's a liar."

"He could be right," Greg said. "But why would she deny this, and not the others?"

"What if—what if she didn't kill them?" he said.

"What are you thinking?" Greg asked.

"Oh Li, Jia, and the sheep are linked by style. Jonathan was totally different. Nat and Akemi disappeared, but there was no sign of violence. What if we've got two people at work here?" Sam asked.

"She shot at us!" Downy exclaimed. "That's plenty violent."

"With a gun," Sam replied. "She tried to kill us with a gun. I think the person who killed Oh Li likes to be close." He thought for a minute, and then leaned toward Shara. "How about a deal?"

With a loud clang, the shuttle docked with the orbiting spacecraft.

"How about a deal?" Sam asked Shara.

Downy unbuckled and got out of his seat. "We're here. And

unless I'm much mistaken, you don't have the authority to make a deal with the Rik. Humans are not a sentient race. Yet."

Sam stared at Downy.

Greg was looking at Downy too, obviously surprised.

"As a matter of fact, he's right," Greg said. "Humans don't have the authority to pardon a prisoner of war from an alien species. As your sponsors, only we can make a deal."

"Seriously?" Sam demanded. "You're going to get all legal on me now? We've got to find out what she knows before the trial."

"Considering we're going into a galactic trial, I'm afraid this is exactly the time to get legal," Greg said.

"You'd rather go into trial not knowing what she knows?" Sam asked.

"There will be time for witnesses," Greg said. He included Shara, Downy, and even Claudia in his gaze. "I can call anyone during the trial."

Sam snorted. "I can't believe this."

They boarded the space station, and Greg led them to the same room where Sam's personal trial had been, after he exposed the truth on TV. There were chairs set out this time. Obviously this was going to be a longer trial than last time.

"What about the other cadets?" Sam said. "Aren't we all witnesses for the trial? Technically?"

"They represent Earth. You'll represent them. They are in the adjoining rooms, watching the proceedings live. I can call them to answer questions as needed."

Sam nodded. "What about her?" He gestured at Shara. "We can't leave her alone."

"The containment room. We'll lock her up in an empty trouncer cage until we need her," Greg said. "Downy, Claudia, Chris—all of you must go wait with the cadets. Only the defense and the primary witness, Sam and I, are to be in the room with the prosecutor and the Council."

"They're here?" Sam asked. "I thought they would be communicating on screen."

Greg shook his head. "The Council will be on screen, but the prosecutor is here."

Chris and Claudia left the room, Claudia hugging Sam one more time.

"Get Shara to talk to you," Claudia said. "She's ready to break. You can do it." Then they were gone.

Two minutes later a big, black man entered the room, bowing to Greg.

"Who are you?" Greg asked. "We are expecting the Rik prosecutor.

The black guy smiled. "Don't you recognize me, Greg? My name is Tishing. We met some years ago and spoke about my, ah, experiments. Don't you recall?"

AKEMI DIDN'T FEEL like a computer. Except that she indisputably *was* a computer, so now she knew what they felt like, and it wasn't all that different from being a teenage girl. She had more multitasking complexity now, but it was a lot like watching TV while texting a friend, talking to her mother, and typing a term paper. Which she'd done.

The real difference was the sheer amount of information available to her. The computational part of the computer was boring, but the video archives it held were fascinating. Photos, videos, transcripts of secret communications—it was like finding the Facebook page of the Rik people. All their dirty secrets on display.

She'd shown Nat the biggest bits—the Hadron explosion, the invasion fleet heading past Mars—but now she couldn't think about that.

Part of the computer, the part that wasn't her (and yet was, at the same time) had been activated remotely. That part of the computer was gearing up for a small jump in hyperspace. It was doing the calculations to enter jump at the correct angle and velocity (so that it would exit at the correct angle and velocity, which was very important), and it really didn't care that she didn't want to go. It was like having a song stuck in her head. The computer was calculating and recalculating in her mind, and she couldn't turn the stupid thing off.

Oh, and as if that wasn't enough to worry about, she'd noticed Nat doing something funny with the airlock before she'd gotten her attention. She should figure out what that was. This jump thing was stressful. Plus, she had the distinct feeling that in a few minutes, when the jump started, the whole mess would be in her hands. She could swear the computational computer was feeling a little smug about it, too.

Well, first things first. She didn't want Nat sucked into limbo by a faulty airlock. Akemi started to undo that mess, while another part of her tried to figure out what she needed to do during the jump. The computational computer wasn't being really forthcoming.

And then, as fast as Akemi's new computer brain could blink, they were in the jump, and she had no more time to think.

Her brain flooded with data. Not the kind of flood you get from a faulty bathtub faucet. The Pacific Ocean sloshed and landed in her lap. Their ship didn't exist, and it did. It only existed in her mind, and her mind was the ship. Where it would re-exist was up to her. The possibilities dumped on her were infinite. Actually infinite, which was a concept her maths teacher had never explained very well.

So many places. In the first instant she ruled out half of the infinity that was not in her space-time continuum. But half of infinity was still infinite. So instead of ruling out, she selected the ones near planetary bodies. Hundreds of thousands choices still remained. But not infinite.

Then the computational computer gave its vote. It told her where she was supposed to go, which still included three hundred possible configurations of existence.

Couldn't you have told me that before? Akemi thought fleetingly.

But an instantaneous review of those few hundred didn't please her. She could practically count them on her fingers. They weren't any good.

No, she told the computational computer. She opened up the possibilities again. Let's go to Earth. Um... but lets avoid the fleet.

Her velocity was all wrong to jump all the way to Earth. The closest place to Earth with her current velocity vector, however... that was a simple calculation. From Mars to Earth's moon was a small jump indeed. With a thump of satisfaction that made the computational computer scream, Akemi chose the jump.

As she did so, she noticed a warning signal that had gotten lost in the ocean of numbers.

"Airlock breach," it said. "Depressurization."

"Oh shoot," Akemi thought. She slammed the airlock door shut and the ship emerged in uneasy orbit around the moon. How much oxygen had they lost? She did a quick diagnostic. The air was thin, but still life sustaining. As long as Nat hadn't been right next to the door...

Nat?

Touch the screen if you're alive.

Pleasepleasepleaseplease...

27

TISHING SMILED URBANELY at Greg and Sam.

Greg turned a rich orange with anger. "You come here, like that?" he demanded. "As a human?"

"Confidence is not a crime," Tishing said. "And I'm not the one on trial here."

"I don't get it," Sam said. "I thought the prosecutor was a Rik?"

"He is a Rik," Greg bit out. "He stole that body and inhabited it."

Sam's eyes widened. "Can he do that?"

"Technically, no. But if he wins the trial, it won't matter anymore," Greg said.

Tishing smiled. "Nat says hello."

Sam lunged out of his chair, but Greg stopped him with an arm to the chest.

"He wants you to attack him. It will make his case stronger."

Sam glared. "But if he has Nat—he's broken the law! He should be thrown out!"

Greg held him back. "The trial has started. No other matters, criminal or civil, will be considered until this trial is complete. He knows it."

Sam backed down. Galactic justice wasn't the same as human justice, but he had to bow to their authority for now. He sat back in his chair.

"When humans are on the Galactic Council," Sam said, looking at Tishing, "Things will be handled a little differently."

Laughter from the screen surprised Sam. He turned forward to see that the huge screens had flickered on while he was distracted. Twenty four members of the Council sat in a double semi-circle facing him. The Crosspoint and the Merith in the council were laughing.

"Very bold, this one," said a Crosspoint. "I like them excessively." Sam noticed that the body paint on that Crosspoint formed a star of David and wondered briefly if the little alien knew what that was.

The one Merith who had laughed became quiet and raised his muscled arms for silence. He sat behind a personal screen, and the reflected light from it lit up his one moist eye.

"The Councilors who comprise the sub-committee of Sentient Acceptance and Dispute will now hear the case of humanity, for planet Earth. I am Faal, Merith representative and spokesperson of the Councilors. Make yourselves known to the Council."

Greg bow/crouched in the formal way of his race, and recited, "I present myself for inspection to the representatives of the Galactic Council. I am Greg, representing the Spo, the sponsors of humanity. I offer my experience, knowledge, and character in defense of humanity's sentience and sanity." He rose from his bow.

Tishing bowed next, in a clipped, military style. "I present myself for inspection to the representatives of the Galactic Council. I am Tishing, representing the Rik, the prosecutors of humanity. I offer my experience, knowledge, and character in denial of humanity's sentience and sanity." He added a few more sentences to his formula than Greg. "As a member of a species on probation,

I recognize that should my case fail, my species will remain in probation for the duration of four generations."

Sam glared at Greg. Never had he mentioned that the prosecutors, the Rik, were also on probation. Apparently, if humanity won, that would be a direct loss to the Rik, they would remain on probation another four generations. Talk about motivation.

Tishing began to sit, but Greg halted him. "A point, Councilors. This man, representing the Rik, is clearly using a human body. There is no precedent for taking a specimen before the trial. His action is illegal."

None of the Council looked surprised. The Merith spokesperson nodded. "That is an illegal action. It will be addressed following the trial. However, this trial has begun and will not be paused or ended until humanity's sentience status has been determined. The prosecutor's actions are not in question."

Greg nodded, and they both sat. Greg squatted over a Spo couch, but Tishing leaned back in a comfortable chair and crossed one leg over the other.

"Please present the human sample," the Merith said.

Greg was still angry, but Sam could see him force it away.

"This is Sam Locklear, of the human species," he said calmly. "As you see in my report, genetically he is within .02 deviations of the planetary standard. Racially he is descended of the TranSiberian indigenous peoples, or Native Americans."

Sam blinked at that. His dad was from El Salvador...his mother was Pueblo. Tran Siberian... that sounded more impressive.

"His progress in Spo training was exemplary. He can speak Spo and Merith with moderate facility. With further training, he could be advanced. The rest of the human sample, over two hundred, performed similarly, or within a very small margin. They represent ninety-eight percent of humanity's genetic diversity."

Another councilor raised a limb at that point. "You say ninety-eight percent, despite the fact that nearly a fifth of the population was killed or injured in the event known as the Hadron explosion?"

Greg nodded. "Their genetic spread can be verified in the documents we've already submitted. The European genotypes were amply represented throughout the rest of the world, particularly the continent of North America. You can refer to the planetary map, in section 23 of our report."

Sam saw several of the councilors flip on their personal screens, checking Greg's work as he spoke.

"I would also point out," Greg continued, "that the dispersion of peoples through Earth's arable lands demonstrates that they have attained the sociological and technological level equal to a Level 3 culture. Artistic, culinary, and linguistic output would make them equal to the highest Level 7 culture. Indeed, there has been some talk that they could attain a Level 8 within a few generations."

The Merith stopped Greg.

"Most of these things we know. The issue at stake in this trial is not culture, but sentiency status. The Hadron explosion is an event of such destruction that it alone could condemn humanity as a malignant animal life form. Intelligent, but not sentient according to the standards of this Council. If the Spo had not chosen to sponsor them, they would have been declared so already. How do you answer this charge?"

Greg took a deep breath. Before he could speak, Tishing rose smoothly from his chair.

"I have something to add to the charge."

Greg expelled his breath. "The trial has started. The Hadron explosion is the sole context of the malignancy charge. There can be no addition at this time."

Tishing smiled, but addressed only the council. "The charge of malignancy and non-sentience stands. I merely enlarge the context. In addition to the high-level destruction of the Hadron explosion, humanity has exhibited specific malignancy in the killing of the human witness pool. Twelve of the human cadets have been murdered or seriously injured during their brief re-acclimation to Earth. One cadet family was held captive by terrorists. Several family members have disappeared. The cadets, the representatives of humanity and only possible salvation of the species, were reduced by nearly ten percent in only three weeks. I wish to add this to the context of the malignancy charge, extending both the scope and brutality of the original indictment."

Greg looked ready to spring on Tishing and rend him limb from limb.

The Merith frowned, "Greg, is it true that twelve cadets were killed in the last three weeks?"

"It... is. One is missing," he glared at Tishing, "one has had his prefrontal cortex severely damaged. The other five were injured during a fire."

"A fire started by a mob of humans, intent on killing," Tishing added.

The council stirred slightly.

"This is extremely serious," the Merith said. "It adds great weight to the prosecution." He paused and looked down. Sam could see that something was flicking on his personal screen and the white of the Merith's large eye shone like a jewel in the light. Perhaps he was adding the new data into the record.

"Would the Spo prefer to step down as sponsors of humanity at this time?"

"No!" Greg exclaimed. "Absolutely not."

The Merith looked up. "I was not asking you. I am speaking to the Spo Emperor."

On the wall next to Sam another screen lit up, this one

showing the Spo emperor, sitting before his priceless deathglass table.

The emperor was unhappy. "The Spo must consider that sponsoring humanity is no longer worthwhile."

Greg bowed very low to his emperor.

"We have invested many years in this species. We should not abandon them now."

"Should not?" asked the emperor in a quiet voice. "You do not tell me what the Spo should do."

ARMEN WATCHED the trial from the waiting room with the other cadets. He bit his tongue painfully as he watched the Spo emperor, thinking hard. There was something... something on the edge of his mind. He had to figure out what it was. Something about Sam, or maybe something about Greg... something that would help Sam win the trial.

They all knew it was up to Sam now. He was the best of those left. They were all smart, all capable. They'd survived the training, the loss of their families, and they'd thrived. They were strong, but Sam was something special. Not the smartest (that was probably Nat), not the best debater (probably Jonathan), or the quickest learner, or the most assured...but he was the one who got things done.

On Spo, so many times, Sam was the one who distracted the homesick or warned off the bully. He started the games that reminded them of Earth. He talked to Greg, when somebody needed a break. He helped the little ones tough it out.

And now, Armen knew there was something he needed to tell Sam, but he couldn't quite pull it to mind. Armen tried to use the memory technique the Spo taught him, but it wouldn't come together. He was rushing it.

Armen centered himself in the chair and breathed deeply. He

pictured a red wall, red brick. He tried to picture a gate in the wall, but it wouldn't resolve.

Fine. He solidified the brick wall in his mind. Behind the wall was the thing he needed to remember. Behind the wall was the memory. Deliberately, with each slow exhalation, he removed a single brick.

28

DOWNY WAITED IN AGONY. He had to get out of this room full of cadets. General Gustav had returned from locking Shara in a holding cell. She must not have told him anything, Downy thought, or he would have attacked Downy on sight.

Shara had to be destroyed. Sam had figured out that she wasn't the killer. He would offer her a deal, or Greg would threaten her, and somehow they would get the information out of her the next time she spoke to them.

Downy had to kill her before that happened. He made himself wait eight minutes before rising and leaving the room. Gustav questioned him, but only in a cursory fashion. Downy claimed that the stress made him ill and that he needed a bathroom. Gustav gestured for him to go.

Downy's reputation for weakness: physically, mentally, even socially; made it easy for him to get away with this excuse. Someday Gustav would know just how completely Downy had fooled him. He would know just how strong Downy was.

Free in the space station, Downy headed for the pilot room. The containment chambers were generally used for trouncers before their brains were harvested for the biocomputer. Hence, they were usually situated near the pilot room and the computers.

Downy entered the containment area unchecked. The bioexperts saw no reason to keep people away from the trouncers. The trouncers did that plenty well by themselves.

Twelve large cages opened onto this dark hallway, six on each side. No lights lit the cages, only the tiny lights along the walkway illuminated the space, and they didn't reach far. He couldn't see the back of the cages, but he heard breathing.

The first two cages were empty. As he came to the next one, a trouncer lunged into sight. The trouncers made no sound before they attacked, the better to surprise their prey. This trouncer slammed into the crisscrossed bars of the door, and one long claw got through. It nearly sliced open Downy's shoulder. He yelped and backed away.

The creature retreated into the darkness at the back of the cage, where Downy could only make out its hunched profile.

He breathed again.

"Stupid trouncer," he said. "Just wait till they put your brain in a bowl."

Laughter echoed from one of the last cages.

Downy growled. She was here. She was laughing at him. He would kill her now.

THE SPO EMPEROR took his time thinking. Sam's stomach felt empty and full at the same time. Like he'd eaten cotton candy that began to spin and grow in his stomach.

If the emperor decided not to sponsor humanity any longer, this trial was over. The Rik would move in, stealing and killing and making Earth their own. And no one would lift a finger to help a condemned non-sentient species.

The emperor finally spoke.

"I formerly believed that humanity could overcome the stigma of the Hadron event. However, this current violence against the human cadets fills me with doubt." He looked at Greg, "You did not reflect this trend in your reports to me."

"We believe that the Rik are responsible for these deaths, not the humans," Greg said. He pointed at Tishing. "We have good reason to think this. Jonathan's mind was wiped; a use of sasoikeo that only the Rik have perfected. Locked on this space station is a person involved in the killings. I would like the chance to question her before this issue is decided."

The Merith deferred to the emperor, "Are you willing for this witness to be called now?"

The emperor traced a design on the table.

"Yes. If Greg can prove the killings were not human, we will not renounce our sponsorship."

Sam watched Greg breathe a sigh of relief. He'd really picked up a lot of idiosyncrasies from his students, Sam thought, as well as the willingness to fight for them.

"I will have the witness Shara, possibly of Rik, brought at once," Greg said.

Sam looked hard at Tishing, but he didn't seem disturbed. He smiled slightly. "Call your witness."

ARMEN STARTED to remove the third row of bricks, his eyes closed. It was working. An image was emerging behind his mental wall. It was the tower at Pepperdine. The top of the cross was clear behind his wall. He centered on the middle of the wall, clearing bricks faster, downward, though still with deliberation. A sense of urgency, almost panic was taking hold of him. He forced himself to relax his muscles and breathe through his nose. If he rushed the process too much this message from his subconscious would dissolve into nothing.

The tower emerged, with blood dripping from the walls. The edge of the yin yang painted in sheep's blood became visible. Why this? Armen had pondered the vandalism over and over, talking it over with Sam and the others, what had he missed?

He continued clearing bricks. Now he could see Oh Li. He was standing at the base of the tower, holding his arm up. On his wrist he wore a leather strap with a metallic yin yang on it. He saw Downy come around the edge of the tower. Nearly all the bricks were gone now. Downy leaned over, looking at the yin yang bracelet and laughing in his puppy dog way. Then he reached up and slammed Oh Li's head into the wall.

Armen gasped. In a blink, he saw it all. He remembered when they all first met Downy, when he was trying to choose a human name. He'd asked them all kinds of questions, and he'd been struck by Oh Li's bracelet. He'd said the swirling black and white reminded him of a tiny deathglass.

Now Armen could picture the rest. He saw Downy luring Nat and Jia off campus. He saw him slashing the sheep. How he'd pretended to be enamored of animals, but always with that assumed goofiness. Jia, Oh Li. Armen had even—he caught his breath—Armen had seen Downy cleaning his nails in their shared bathroom the morning after Oh Li's death. And probably Downy killed Paolo too, before they'd even come back to Earth. When Downy first joined them on Spo, Paolo had nicknamed him Grover and Downy hadn't liked it.

Armen's eyes snapped open and flew to the table where Gustav and Downy were sitting. Downy was gone. He would kill the girl. She knew about him.

He jumped to his feet.

"How long has Downy been gone?" Armen demanded, running to the door. Gustav looked blank.

"He's the killer!" Armen shouted. "We have to stop him."

Gustav looked at him, confused bordering on angry. "Stop him from what?"

. . .

DOWNY FOUND Shara in the last cage on the right. She wasn't laughing anymore.

"You're going to kill me," she said. "I feel calm now. That must be human. Besides, I think Claudia and Sam will figure it out... and these are good clothes to die in."

Downy palmed the lock. He wrenched the barred door open. "They'll believe me. The filthy Rik girl tried to escape. I had no choice but to kill her."

"What, in the cage?" she asked.

He jumped at her, putting his face only an inch from hers.

"Shut up," he said. He grabbed her arm, squeezing until he could feel the bone in her upper arm and she moaned. With a vicious twitch he snapped the bone and she cried out.

He dragged her out of the cage into the dark hallway. She whimpered very satisfyingly now. The best part was that the rest of the Rik wouldn't blame him for killing her. He was only keeping up his part of the bargain, which included keeping the plot secret.

He held open the door to the containment area with his foot, and dragged her out into the main, brightly lit, curving hallway. She looked sick in the light, crying and clutching at her broken arm. Downy spun her around and threw her forward into the wall. He planted one hand on her back, pinning her to the wall. He pulled his other hand back, ready to slash her with his claws.

Just before he struck, Downy saw a flicker of motion. He turned his head to see Armen sprinting around the corner, a look of absolute rage on his face. As Downy's hand came forward, to slice Shara's spine in four neat cuts, Armen launched himself at Downy. He grabbed Downy's arm, using his whole weight to drag Downy's arm down and away from Shara.

"You fooled us," Armen said, panting.

Downy growled. He twisted his free hand to claw at Armen's

face, but Armen ducked his head, maintaining his hold on Downy's arm.

Downy let go of Shara and she slid to the ground. With both hands free he grabbed Armen's hair and jerked his head back, forcing him to let go. Downy threw him towards the other wall. Armen's head collided with a steel support and he crumpled to the floor.

This was getting out of hand. Downy raised a foot to stomp Shara, but then Gustav and Greg came around the corner.

"It's Armen!" Downy yelled. "He let the Rik girl out!"

"What's going on?" Greg asked. He looked from Downy, standing over Shara, to Armen, sprawled on the floor.

Armen moaned, and clutched his head. "Downy liked the yin yang, he had access to everyone... He hated Paolo."

"I don't know what he—" Downy started, but he saw the horrified comprehension wash across Greg's body. Then Greg jumped.

Greg was one of the most respected fighters on Spo, and he took Downy without pause. Every blow of Downy's was blocked. Greg used hands, feet, and both sets of knees with brutal perfection. Spo limbs could break. With a loud pop and a pain unlike Downy had ever imagined, a crack wound in a spiral pattern from his left-most ankle to his knee. Screaming, Downy collapsed on the floor, the pain burning all thought to a standstill.

Greg got to his feet, and Gustav was beside him.

"I should have guessed," Greg said. "I didn't know why he wanted to silence her."

"But the emperor..." Gustav said. "We cannot prove this."

Greg knew they had a problem. Downy was the emperor's son. If they dragged a beaten Downy into the trial room, the emperor would be furious. He was not rash, but springing this on him unannounced could only humiliate him. He would not believe in Downy's complicity unless it was proved. And Greg wasn't sure they could prove anything.

Seeing Downy about to kill Shara, Greg remembered a few things. He'd remembered Downy's face in the riot, when he shot into the crowd. How he urged Greg to go ahead and speak on the 4th of July. Even how he'd leaked the information to Sam that had almost gotten Sam killed. Downy had played them all perfectly.

"Put him in a cage," Greg said. "We can't deal with him now."

Gustav didn't move. "Are we sure?" he said. "If he is innocent—"

Sam came around the corner.

"They sent me to find out why you're taking so long," he said. Then he stopped, staring at Armen, who leaned, ashen, against the wall. Shara was crumpled on the floor crying. Downy writhed on the ground with a huge crack in his leg.

Greg watched as Sam's eyes flickered from one to the other, putting things together.

"Shara's accomplice," he said. "It was Downy?"

"Armen figured it out."

Sam's jaw clenched. "Jonathan. Oh Li. Jia. Nat."

"We don't have time for that," Greg said. "Do we lock him up, or bring him into the trial? If we're wrong—it's the end."

Sam took a deep breath, pushing his anger away. "We bring him in, but when we're ready."

Gustav cautioned him, as he and Greg pulled Downy up. "This is your whole species you are speaking for Sam. Do you understand that? If you are wrong, it's their lives."

Sam closed his eyes for a moment. When he opened them Greg thought he had the look of a much older man.

"It's my responsibility," he said. "I'm taking it."

Greg and Gustav were hoisting Downy's arms over their shoulders, but they paused at Sam's words. Greg looked at Gustav, and he nodded.

"It is your choice," Greg said.

29

AKEMI KEPT REPEATING HER PLEA. She couldn't stop.

Nat... Nat... Nat...

It poured from her without pause while she rechecked the oxygen level in the cabins. She sealed off the unused rooms and pumped their thin air into the main chamber. Meanwhile she scanned the airlock for Nat's body.

The air is better. Please get up

Touch the screen

Nat, please

There were no video monitors of the interior of the ship, except in the airlock. Akemi wanted to kill whoever designed that flaw.

At the same time, she calculated the next jump toward Earth. She must get the video of the Rik causing the Hadron explosion to the trial.

A warning tripped when she tried to initiate the next jump.

"Multiple jumps will degrade the biomaterial. Please insert new tissue."

Akemi smacked the computational computer around until the warning disappeared. Degrade, whatever. She felt fine.

She initiated the jump again.

"Warning: Entering the Spo Human Enclave. Illegal action. Confirm?"

For heaven's sake...Akemi confirmed, and finally the next jump began.

Nat
We're on our way
Touch the screen

NAT LAY IN THE HALLWAY, just outside the control room door. A stabbing pain in her head was all she felt at first. Her breath came shallow and fast. It hurt to inhale, and yet she didn't have enough air, so she kept trying to pull more in without moving her lungs. Her nose tickled and she tried to rub it. She'd forgotten about the handcuffs dangling from her left hand and they smacked her in the face. More blood dribbled from her nose.

Then she lay still some more. Just breathing. Letting the blood dry on her face.

Her eyes stung a little, the momentary vacuum probably caused a few tiny blood vessels in her eyes and nose, possible lungs and ears, to burst. That's why she couldn't catch her breath either. The oxygen must be almost gone.

But that can't be right, Nat thought, sliding herself into a sitting position against the wall. She wouldn't have regained consciousness if there was no air.

Somebody must have closed the airlock before it was all gone. Akemi! Nat jumped up only to career drunkenly into the wall.

She leaned a shoulder against the wall and slid her way into the control room and the computer.

It was repeating a single word.

Nat, Nat, Nat, Nat.....

She bumped the screen. "Come on Akemi, snap out of it.

Her response flared across the screen.

Oh my gosh, I thought I killed you.

I was so stupid. Are you okay? Don't talk! There's not much air.

The jump was hard, much harder than I expected, but I brought us close to Earth. Closer, at least.

I'm so sorry, Nat. I'm so glad you're alive. Just don't talk, don't breathe heavy. We've barely got enough air for you.

I love you.

Nat blinked her eyes repeatedly, struggling to read the blur of text with her pounding head. She tapped the screen a few more times.

"Shut up, Akemi. Tell me what's going on."

The screen cleared.

I'm getting a grip now. The last jump scrambled me a bit.

We're closing in on the Spo space station. It will take us at least half an hour.

The door to the control room hissed shut.

I'm diverting all atmosphere to this room. It should be enough. I can pick up the Spo signals from the space station. The trial is in progress. The captain is summoning medics... Serious injuries... A Spo and a human require attention.

AKEMI MONITORED the communications as they got closer to the space station. When they were within the appropriate distance (the computational computer was good for something) Akemi sent a message to the captain, requesting to dock with the space station.

She forgot the Spo would know this was a Rik ship.

Within seconds the computational computer was telling her sulkily that enough weapons were trained on them to kill a dragon. The computer didn't really understand human metaphor, but joined to Akemi her vocabulary had populated its communication library.

However, it was totally right about the weapons, and that was a problem. She sent several more bursts of explanation, but the captain was jamming her signal. He was probably concerned that the Rik might transmit a virus to their computer, which she'd seen in the archives that the Rik did a few years ago.

She tried all the frequencies of communication the ship possessed, but there was nothing. Then the captain sent a message to the nearest armed cruiser.

Uh oh, Akemi told Nat.

They won't let us dock. They're contacting a cruiser.

Nat's head was redefining the term 'migraine' for her. She could hardly think for pain, and that was saying something. Her ears and throat ached, and a horrible high-altitude feeling was settling in from the loss of air. Now the screen was getting fuzzy. She had to read the words three times before she processed them.

Wait, I got something! There are several cell phone signatures on the ship. If I can find one that's on...

Got one. It's Chris! Chris and Claudia—I met them in the hospital.

30

IN THE TRIAL ROOM, Greg got a medic to give Shara a pain killer and caffeine injection, to increase her reaction time. They'd already splinted her arm.

She slumped in the one extra chair, facing the screen showing the Galactic Council. She studiously avoided looking at Tishing.

Sam knelt next to her for a moment.

"Help us, and I'll protect you when it's over," he whispered. "I'll figure it out."

She just looked at him.

Greg and Gustav consulted in under voices for a moment, but then Tishing stood. "I request the defense to question their witness and stop delaying this process."

Gustav stepped out the door. "I'll take care of him for now," he told Greg.

Greg nodded and turned to Shara.

"You are Rik," he said.

Shara made up her mind.

"Yes."

Tishing stirred, uncrossed his legs.

"How many cadets did you kill?"

"I—none. I wiped Jonathan. I kidnapped Nat and her sister. It was D—"

"Your accomplice," Greg interrupted. "How many did your accomplice kill?"

"Three, if you count Paolo, who died about a year ago on Spo. D—my accomplice also took steps to escalate a riot, which injured five more cadets."

Tishing leaned forward, and some of the Council did too.

"And your accomplice is human?" Greg asked.

Shara looked at Sam.

"Protected," he mouthed silently.

"No," she said. "My accomplice is not human."

"Rik?" Greg asked.

"No. He is Spo."

The emperor growled. "What is she saying? She accuses the Spo, but says she is Rik? How do we know any of that is true?"

Shara sat up a little straighter. "The Rik scientists who put me in this body are currently doing the same to one of the cadets. Their plan was to infiltrate the cadets before the trial began."

Shara gave the scientists' names and described some of their experiments, which caused more uproar among the Council members. She told them the name of the Rik city where she was born and the names of her parents.

She was convincing. The Merith spokesperson stopped her. "Her planet of origin is accepted. She is clearly Rik. The next question: who is the accomplice, and is he truly Spo?"

Greg stepped in. "She has testified that her accomplice is not human. Whether he was Spo, Rik, or something else, I think the point has been made. The prosecutor charged humanity with killing the cadets. We have proved that they did not do this."

"We still need to know the accomplice!" the emperor said.

Greg shook his head. "No, I do not believe we do."

The emperor shook his head. "I am not convinced that the humans are innocent. The accomplice must be uncovered."

Greg sighed. Sam nodded at him, this was the only way to convince the emperor.

"The name of your partner?" Greg said to Shara.

"It's—His name is Downy."

CLAUDIA WATCHED a distorted view screen from one of the cadet waiting rooms. The cadets were clumped around several screens, though they left space around her and Chris. The room was dead quiet as they watched Downy on the screen, being carried into the trial room. His leg was bandaged and bulky. One of the Spo carrying him bumped his foot on the edge of the door and Downy swore at him.

"I'll have you sent to Merith for medical experiments. I swear it," Downy said.

They set Downy on a Spo recliner that was just relocated for him. He nodded to his father, the emperor, and ignored the Council. Shara now sat against the wall, but Claudia thought she recoiled further when he glared at her.

Greg said to Downy, "It is not my wish to bring charges against you at this time. However, we must confirm that the cadet killings in the last weeks were not at human hands. Is it true—"

Chris's cell phone went off, the 1812 Overture in digital tones. All the cadets looked at him as he fumbled it out of his pocket.

"For heaven's sake, turn it off," one cadet said.

Chris silenced it at once and the others turned back to the trial.

"You have reception on a space station?" Claudia whispered to him.

He shrugged and looked at the missed calls on his old-fashioned flip phone. There was no number listed. He muted the phone and put it back in his pocket.

Downy was yelling at Greg on screen. "—don't even have the guts to kill an insolent, useless cadet—"

The cell phone buzzed in his pocket. Chris jerked it out. A text message. He put his finger on the power button, but the screen turned pink.

Pink?

Is this Chris, Claudia's friend? I NEED to talk to you before the end of the trial. –This is Akemi.

Claudia read the message over his arm and jerked when she saw the name.

"It's Akemi!" Claudia said. "Talk to her! Where is she?"

Chris hit reply and started slowly typing, "Where are..."

"Oh, give me that," Claudia said. "You were never a twelve year old girl."

She took the phone and used both her thumbs on the tiny keyboard. "Are you onboard?"

Almost instantaneously an answer appeared:

Coming fast, inside a Rik spaceship. Got to get Nat onboard space station—no air. Get the captain to let us dock.

"Are there Rik with you?"

No Rik, just Nat. Sending data. Be there in 3 minutes.

The download icon appeared on his screen, meaning that the phone was temporarily busy downloading a bucket-load of data.

"How big is this phone?" Claudia asked.

"64 gigs." The download bar inched forward. "She's sending something big, though."

For a second they stood there staring at the phone.

"It'll take too long," Chris said. "We can't wait. If they're in a Rik ship it's going to take a lot of convincing for the captain to let them dock." Chris tapped Armen on the shoulder.

"We've got to get to the control room," Chris said. "Akemi and Nat are coming."

Armen stared, and Claudia showed him their texts.

"How did Nat... never mind," Armen said. "Let's go."

In the control room, the captain was yelling at a subordinate. It was the hissing, guttural yell of the Spo, but Armen interrupted him. He hissed and barked something at the captain that made him stop and stare at them.

The captain took a deep breath, clearly about to have them thrown out. Claudia felt blank. How could she explain quickly enough to convince him?

Chris held up his hands to show he was non-threatening. "That ship is Rik; but you have to let them board."

The captain's eyestalks swiveled to him.

"Yes, Rik. How do you know that? Are *you* Rik? Get them contained!"

Three Spo grabbed Chris and Claudia. "I'm Spo security," Chris said. "A lost cadet is on that ship. She needs air."

The captain paused. "There is a trial in progress. I cannot allow anyone to dock."

"Get authorization from General Gustav or Greg," Chris said.

"Are they communicating with you?" Armen asked the captain. "In English? Ask their names."

"You are not my commander," the captain said, pale orange. He eyestalks twitched. "Get them out."

The phone in Claudia's hand beeped. Download complete.

Chris grabbed the phone. "Let us see what this is," he said. "If it doesn't convince you, we'll go."

The captain paused.

"We'll go, after this," Chris said again. He tried to open the first file, but it didn't display.

"Shoot. Probably video files, from the size of them. But they're not normal..." he changed some settings on his phone. "I have some Spo software on here from work. If it's Spo video, then maybe..."

He tried again and the first video started. Chris watched the Hadron explosion from space, holding the phone out so Claudia, Armen, and the captain could see.

Claudia felt sweat beading on her forehead. Why did Akemi send them this? She expected a video of Nat and Akemi escaping. Or a video of them gasping their last breath. Something convincing. This was ancient history.

Chris clicked replay. "Maybe she—"

But Armen said shush, and the captain started bouncing on his clawed feet. "It is a Rik digger bomb. On Earth."

Before the short video had finished its second play, the captain was back in his chair. He was issuing commands and stubbing his clawed fingers onto various screens. The large curved window in front of him showed the single ship growing closer.

"They'll be docked in three minutes," the captain said.

"The video showed a bomb?" Claudia asked. But Armen was hyperventilating a tad, so she patted him on the back.

The captain finished his frantic work. "They're docking now. Let's go see who it is. We must confirm this video for the trial."

Claudia waited behind the others as the airlock door opened. She was afraid of what she might see in the ship. Why had Akemi contacted Chris? Was Nat injured? Was Akemi? If they didn't have enough air, that was going to be even more of a problem for Akemi, with her lung transplant. What if they were too late?

As soon as the ship's airlock slid open, with a hiss of sucking air, Claudia felt wind rush past her into the airlock as the pressure equalized. Spo security forces ran on board, followed closely by Chris and Armen.

"She's here!"

"It's Nat! She unconscious."

Claudia ran then. Nat lay on her side in the control room.

Handcuffs dangled from one chafed wrist and blood caked her nose and lips and ran out of her left ear. Her hair was tangled in a knot and when Armen lifted an eyelid, her eyes were horribly blood shot. She looked like she'd taken a serious beating. Claudia could see the resemblance to Akemi, but only slightly. This girl looked so much older and tougher than Akemi. Armen and the captain crouched to pick her up. "We'll take her to medical room," he said.

"But Akemi?" Claudia said. "Where is she?"

She and Chris left the control room, checking each room. The ship was small. Akemi was nowhere to be found.

When Chris began to pry open a cabinet in the kitchen area, Claudia realized she was still holding his cell phone. It buzzed again with a text message.

I'm not in there. Don't hurt yourself.

I'm the ship computer.

Go figure. :-(

Claudia dropped the phone.

31

SAM STARED AT DOWNY, trying to make the goofy, annoying Downy he knew into the vicious killer he was. Downy had been given anesthetic to numb his lower extremities, and it seemed to have numbed his tongue too. Ten minutes of questioning had gotten nowhere, and any moment the emperor might put a halt to this interrogation, leaving them with nothing.

It was time to push Downy over the edge. Greg's careful questions were too easily sloughed off. Downy would have to be baited to the edge of sanity to give himself up. Fortunately for him, Sam suspected that the edge of Downy's sanity was a cliff both nearby and dangerous.

"Why didn't you kill me?" Sam asked Downy, interrupting Greg. "That must have been your goal."

Downy ran a claw around the edge of his sensitive eyestalk. "I will confess nothing."

"Paolo. He died the week you joined us. It wasn't an allergic attack, was it?"

"I confess nothing."

"Paolo nicknamed you something, I can't remember what. It made us laugh, though. And General Gustav laughed too, I do remember that."

Silence.

"The tower... I thought you liked sheep. You went to that petting zoo, and you always tried to pet the feral cats on campus. What was that about?"

Downy flickered a smile and Sam felt rage building inside him.

"Nat. Jia. The kitchen with Oh Li."

Downy scratched around his other eye, twitching when he scraped too close to the nerve. He was silent.

"Why did you hurt Oh Li? He wasn't going to be a witness. He probably offered you a snack before you killed him." Sam ran a hand over his bald head. "And yet you never got to me. You slept in my room. You couldn't kill me in my sleep?" Sam got to his feet. "We were right about you. We thought you were pathetic, a throw-away son of the emperor, and we were right."

Downy twitched again. Sam stepped up in front of him.

"General Gustav didn't want you as an apprentice, that's why he sent you to Greg. Greg didn't mind you, but he's good at dealing with weaklings, isn't he? That's what you think of us, and that's what he thought of you."

Sam crouched over Downy, close enough that Downy could smell his breath.

"Pathetic. Puppy." Sam said.

With a growl, Downy used a good leg to kick Sam in the stomach. His claws tore holes in Sam's clothes, scratched his skin. Sam stumbled back and let himself fall to his knees.

"What about the riot?" Downy hissed, hoisting himself out of the chair like an injured roach and grabbing Sam with his claws extended. "Poor Sam, all that shooting, all his fault—and it was me. All me. And your great rebellion, your interview—it was me. Of course I gave you the information on purpose."

Downy pulled Sam to his feet, his claws sinking in to Sam's upper arm. "You're pathetic. You think you're a great leader but you haven't made a single decision of your own. You escaped the execution by luck; you escaped the Rik by luck. *You* are pathetic."

Sam gasped, the pain in his arm hard to ignore. "But you couldn't kill me."

Downy screamed and Sam flinched in anticipation of the pain. But then the pressure was gone, and Downy was flailing through the air on a wave of orange energy. The edge of the field caught Sam and spun him around, into the wall. Greg kept the energy device in his hand as he stood over Downy.

Sam shook his head, small trickles of blood running down his arm and chest.

"I would consider that a confession," Sam said. He dropped back into his chair.

The Spo emperor had turned off his view screen, making himself invisible to them.

His colorless voice emanated from a blank white screen. "Take him away until the conclusion of the trial. The Spo will remain the sponsors of Earth. In... true debt."

Downy didn't struggle as they carried him away, but gave growled as he passed Tishing.

The Council was in noisy disorder, members standing and yelling at one another. Their screen went blank also.

Sam sighed. "Downy and the Rik... we didn't see it."

Greg nodded. "How would we? He hates the Rik. I didn't realize he hated the humans more."

Shara sat silently against the wall. Probably trying to blend in and disappear. When the screen flickered on, Tishing rose to his feet. Sam had almost forgotten him. He looked unruffled, amused.

"This theatrical discovery does not change the crux of the trial. The humans have no defense for the Hadron explosion or the millennia of violence preceding it."

"Violence is not the issue," Greg said. "Malignancy of animal form, which is not proved."

"What does the witness have to say?" Tishing said, talking to Sam.

"I—"

Someone knocked on the door.

Tishing frowned and jerked the door open impatiently. The captain of the space station, Sam had met him during his own trial, pushed past Tishing into the room. Gustav entered behind him, with Nat in his arms.

Sam surged to his feet. Nat's face showed flecks of blood, like somebody had hastily wiped her face clean. Her eyes had the droopy look of anesthesia. Her neck was limp and her eyes wobbled around the room, disoriented.

"Nat, look at me," Sam said, "focus. Be here." He held her limp hand as her eyes rolled past him.

"Hey," she said finally focusing on the Rik prosecutor. "Tishing. What's up?"

Tishing stepped back from her, grabbing for the door. Then he forced calm on himself and let go of the door.

"Nat, I'm not...you look—it makes no difference," Tishing said. He visibly collected himself and turned to the Council. "These people have interrupted the trial."

Sam held Nat's hand as Gustav settled her into Sam's chair. She smiled at him, making the dried blood around her nose crack. She really looked awful. He squeezed her hand.

The captain of the ship was speaking to Greg. Tishing tried to intervene, and Gustav barred his way.

Greg turned to the Council view screen. The Council was calm again, watching the proceedings carefully. "The captain of this space station has new information about the Hadron explosion."

"I have a video, from a Rik ship. It shows an atom digger bomb, of Rik signature, causing the Hadron explosion," the captain said.

"Absolutely not!" Tishing exploded. "They have nothing."

Nat smiled again. "They don't yet, but Akemi has everything."

Tishing glared at her, and the look Nat gave him made Sam flinch.

The captain connected their screen to the Rik ship, and Akemi (after a brief introduction) played the Hadron footage for them. The Council members watched on their personal screens, and the Spo emperor on his table.

The Rik on the Council committee were clearly uneasy. Akemi played it twice. Then she segued right into footage of the Rik fleet, coming toward Earth. She put a time stamp in the corner, which Sam thought was a nice touch.

"Wait. What is this?" the Spo emperor said. It was the first thing he'd said since Downy was dragged out. "The Rik are invading our sponsored territory, real time? The Earth solar system is a protected Spo enclave!"

He glared at Tishing, and Tishing's shoulders moved uneasily under his well-fitted suit.

"This is not how a trial is finished," the emperor said.

The Merith councilor began to speak again. "As many of you know, this trial shall have a dual verdict. Both the Humans and the Rik are on probation, and both desire to join the Council as a sentient species, non-malignant and sane. Let us address the Rik probation.

"The Rik have been on probationary status for some generations," he continued. "Their questionable invasion of the Rik planet, and subsequent adoption of Rik culture, have placed them in a tenuous position.

"It seems they have proved themselves malignant yet again, if this video is accurate. This subterfuge has cost the human race incalculable loss of life and cultural capital. As senior councilmember of this subcommittee, pending the confirmation of this video, I move to deny the Rik entry to the Galactic Council. With loss of all rights, property, and trade entailed on them.

"Any opposed?"

The stillness held.

Shara began to cry and put her face in her hands. Tishing sat slowly, a look of blank surprise on his face.

"You cannot!" he said, finally. "The Rik—"

The Merith interrupted. "You do not speak. You are no longer a recognized race."

He paused. "The dual trial of Rik and humanity was agreed upon by all the Council representatives. As two species, linked by their malignant behavior, yet divergent in their cultural brain, we agreed that this would be a good test for both. The test has been taken, and the result measured. There is no discussion needed. You cannot speak. If another race desires to sponsor you, which I doubt, they may speak on your behalf."

Silence, except for Shara crying.

Sam cleared his throat. "Uh, if I may speak, what will happen to them?"

"Nothing immediate, but without the right to own property the Rik planet will not remain long under their control. They have some technological advances, so they will have some value as expert slaves." He paused, looking at Sam in a focused way, for the first time. "If it comforts you, Human, you may know that many will die as a result of this judgment. Your species may not have the capability to exact vengeance, but the Rik will pay heavily. They are not...liked...by any in the galaxy."

Sam shuddered slightly. "That's not what I meant."

The Merith shrugged, and Sam wondered where he learned that human expression. "Whether you would have them suffer or not, it does not signify. They are no longer of the Council."

"Unless someone speaks for them?"

"Yes."

"Then—I believe I have something to say."

He stepped away from Nat to stand in front of the Council.

Even the Merith seemed taken aback. No one told him to shut up. Sam wasn't sure what he was doing, but he felt compelled to do something. He had no reason to like the Rik or trust them, quite the opposite, but it didn't seem right to just stand by and let them be decimated.

But what did he want? Clearly they were unsafe: they stole human bodies and they'd bombed the Hadron Collider and caused this whole mess in the first place. They'd wronged humanity, that was true. But was this going to make things better? Surely not all the Rik were evil body-snatchers.

Sam tried to think clearly, but his brain was whirling and everyone was watching him. If the Rik were human and they'd done this crime, how would they be treated? Sam was no political scientist, but he knew what little he'd been taught about war reparations and what happened when the losing side was handled badly.

"You have something to say, Human?"

"Um. As I understand it, humanity has just been declared sentient, or we're about to, therefore I have the right to speak. Right?"

"What can you have to say on the Rik's behalf?" the Merith asked.

"It's too much—and it's not enough," Sam said, trying to think his way through. "It's not enough for them to be demoted or revoked or even to die. They owe us. They owe us a... a blood debt." Sam glanced at the Spo emperor. "A true debt. The Hadron explosion killed millions of my species and nearly destroyed our planet. Demoting them does not pay the debt," Sam said.

"What then?" the Merith said. "If your people desire debt payment, you may attack the Rik without hindrance in the future. They have no status."

"You don't pay a blood debt with death," Sam said. "At least, we humans have not found that to be effective."

Sam paused. What did he want? The Merith was right that many humans would want the Rik to suffer for what they did. But all those humans weren't here right now. Sam was here, and he could make a choice.

"We have an old word... wergild. Payment that benefits the clan of the victim; it is not satisfied with the death of the killer."

"Then what?"

"I... suggest that the Rik maintain their status, on probation. So that they can be held responsible for their debt and as a sentient species begin to repay us. That fleet coming towards us now, for instance, would be extremely helpful in human hands. Our own space travel is not to the level of Spo or Rik craftsmanship." That was a gross understatement and flattery all in one. Sam smiled.

"Also, I understand the Rik are rather expert traders in culture. As part of their debt, they may be required to teach their expertise to us. A sort of... apprenticeship."

"You would trust them? You would let them on your planet?" the Merith said.

"I rather think that the Rik are already on our planet, whether I want them to or not," Sam said, gesturing at Tishing. "Punishing them wouldn't take away that threat, it would only make them more determined to destroy us.

"That makes me uncomfortable. Perhaps, if the Rik in turn were given apprenticeships—to some of our painters, moviemakers, chefs, people of that type—they would have a vested interest in helping us."

Shara inhaled sharply, and Sam grinned for a second, before smoothing his face over. He was onto something, he knew it. If he could leverage the Rik right... this could be humanity's gateway to the galaxy. The Merith looked grim at this idea, but Sam didn't care.

"As a carefully watched ally, the Rik have the opportunity to repay their debt and eventually, perhaps, to gain true status, and maybe even true culture. I believe this would be in everyone's best interest," Sam finished.

"This is a large request," the Merith said. "You are risking your own species, Sam."

Sam shuddered imperceptibly. It was the first time the Merith or any of the Council members had used his name. What was he doing? The Rik as allies? He must be nuts. But he knew the Earth needed help to get started in galactic culture, and who better than the Rik, who had no culture of their own and so knew how to market any other culture so well? And maybe, if they had the hope of human apprenticeships, there could be an actual alliance...

The Merith continued. "The Rik have already shown that they will kill and steal human bodies. There is that risk. Also, if they are allowed to grow, they may in the future try to claim Earth in war. If you choose this, you risk your entire planet. Is that your choice?"

Sam's vision doubled for a moment, and cleared. It was the interview all over again. Making choices for others. Taking risks for his family. Taking risks for the cadets, and his species in general. Only that time he'd been manipulated into it, and this time his eyes were wide open.

This was what the Spo trained him for. This was who he was, and he was willing to risk everything.

Sam wanted to look at Greg, as he had on that first day in the Crystal Cathedral when questioned by the media, but now he was strong enough to resist.

"I make this choice," Sam said. "The humans demand a wergild of the Rik. And all that that entails."

The Merith silenced everyone. "The humans have passed the sentience and sanity test. As one has taken voice for his species, the species is no longer a malignancy, but a culture in growth, in control.

"Let us vote," said the Crosspoint. "Because I'm getting hungry. I move that humanity be granted full sentiency status."

The vote was quick, and almost anticlimactic. Every one of the subcommittee voted yes.

Sam breathed deep, hardly able to grasp that this doom, which had been hanging over their heads for years, was finally past. Was this was what they wanted all along? How did the Merith phrase it—someone to 'take a voice" for their species? From the waiting room, he could hear yells and whoops and cheering from the other cadets.

Sam cleared his throat and rubbed his bald head. He would deal with the ramifications of his choice later, for now it was enough that the trial was nearly over.

Nat had tears in her eyes. She was looking at the time stamp on the video, which had a small smiley face next to it, but she smiled at him when he came back to her side.

The Merith continued. "As a sentient species of the Council, Humanity undertakes to sponsor the Rik in their probation. On the condition that the Rik pay wergild (he stumbled over the word) for their crimes."

"Let us vote."

Another vote, and the thing was done.

Sam knelt next to Nat and wrapped an arm around her. "It's going to be alright. It really is."

EPILOGUE

AKEMI ZOOMED through the space station, virtually of course, blending the view of each security camera in make-believe flight. She could almost feel the ship's atmo brushing past her cheeks. The Spo had installed her into their space station, and she had access to all systems.

She monitored four ships docking with the station and gave one of them a stern warning about adjusting the atmo in their airlock before pressurizing with the space station. She sealed their dock until they confirmed. The Tergre were funny little aliens. They seemed to regularly forget that not everyone (in fact, nobody but them) breathed a mixture of helium and selenium. It was a deadly combination and made humans squeak in rage before they died, which wasn't a pleasant or dignified way to go. And if somebody didn't watch the little buggers, they would open-dock their ship to the space station and let it all dump into her clean hallways.

Akemi finished her indoor flight and unslaved the cameras to continue their normal rotations. She could still see every viewpoint, if she focused on it, but there was no need. Instead, she began composing her next fashion blog.

Her blog followers didn't know she wasn't human anymore, because she wasn't allowed to reveal her AI existence. But since she didn't know more than a handful of them in person, nobody missed her yet.

Today's fashion post would be about the new cadet uniforms designed by Shara (specifically made less itchy, by Sam's request). In the past, Akemi generally followed Japanese fashion, like the fantastic 19th century retro look, but now she had new worlds to explore. Literally. She was the computerized hub of the Spo space station, and lots of species were starting to visit Earth. Some were curious, lots were greedy, and some were dangerous, but they all wore interesting clothes. Well, except for the weird Crosspoint, who dressed in fluorescent body paint.

Akemi finished up her blog with some pictures of the cadets in their new, 'spacy' attire.

The space station was a safe place for Akemi, or her brain, since it wasn't built for space jump. She'd suggested to Sam that she be moved aboard, and the Spo had been surprisingly happy to oblige. Akemi guessed that, despite publishing a statement condemning the Rik scientists who killed her, they were still terribly excited by the potential of the human brain in a spaceship.

Akemi answered a few blog comments while sending another message to Nat and Sam. She had become Sam's personal secretary/translator for all his alien communication. When Earth's trial went public, many species seemed to assume that Sam was sort of a king. It was causing more than a few disgruntled conversations in high places, which amused Akemi to no end. Now the ambassador from Merith wanted to visit Earth, and he insisted on seeing Sam.

Sam thought the royalty misunderstanding was funny too, until an alien prince sent him twenty slaves of a species they'd never heard of before. As far as Akemi knew, the 'slaves' were being temporarily housed on a small island in Indonesia. They seemed to enjoy the warmth and even the Spo didn't know how to communicate with them or if they were sentient.

Nat and Sam were in huge demand, both on Earth and abroad, but Nat still made time to come to the space station regularly, to 'visit' Akemi.

There were huge celebrations on Earth, in the week after the trial was aired, but already the good will was beginning to fade and Sam and Nat were busy. Akemi gave a virtual shrug, making the Spo captain jump as the lights in the engine room dimmed. Just for fun, she'd linked some of the station's non-vital systems to the peripheral nervous system of her brain. It was hysterical when she got the hiccups.

Regardless, with the ambassador's message passed on, Akemi had more work to do. That morning she'd downloaded the newest footage from the documentary that Shara and a couple of her Rik friends were putting together. Sam had hooked them up with a Hollywood producer named Apple who didn't seem to mind (or even notice) that she was working with aliens. The culture of Earth was in high demand, as the newest species on the Council, and Apple's video (with the help of the Rik) would showcase the culture of Earth from a trade perspective. It would be a digital catalog, Apple explained, and who didn't love a good catalog? Akemi already had requests from eight species to see the video when it was finished.

Akemi settled in to watch, and the only thing she missed was a bucket of popcorn.

And while she watched, Akemi also sorted through a list of alien names and faces. Any Rik who had refused to surrender were being searched out and arrested. There were quite a few Rik in human bodies scattered through the galaxy, and if they didn't voluntarily come in, human and Spo forces were allowed to arrest them. Akemi focused on one face. He looked vaguely familiar to her. One of the Rik on Mars maybe? She made a mental note to check and went back to watching the catalog.

Such fun.

The End.

AUTHOR'S NOTE

Thank you for reading along! I think of *Exiles* as my first 'ambitious' novel, so it has a special place for me. Two questions I often get about this book:

Q: *Where did you get the idea for Exiles?*

I originally wanted to make a sci-fi retelling of the story of Daniel in the Bible. *Exiles* obviously became its own story as I continued, but the main components I borrowed from the book of Daniel were: the invasion by an 'alien' people, Sam's selection and training by the invaders (including a few references to how he ate differently than the other cadets), the lion's den situation, and his rise to influence.

Q: *Are your other Alien Cadet novels based off Bible stories?*

Yes! I was also inspired by Esther and Joseph, two other exiles from their homes. And towards the end of the series, I also drew elements from Acts (Paul the apostle on the road to Damascus).

I hope you will continue to enjoy the further adventures of Akemi, Sam, Nat, and the others... They still have a long way to go!

Cornelia Clark

SNEAK PEAK

Dreamers, Book 2 in the Alien Cadets

Sam got comfortable in the chair next to Nat, waiting for the interview to start.

The studio lights were bright and warm on his face, something he was becoming all too familiar with ever since the trial. He was now accustomed to the smell of stage makeup, hot bulbs, and coffee.

He was used to the back-and-forth of live interviews, and the pandemonium that went on just out of sight, beyond the camera lenses.

But this interview was different. He and Nat were on the Spo space station, and he could see the blue curve of Earth in the port-hole. New Zealand and the edge of Australia were drifting away from him.

The hosts for this interview were not Hollywood types either, but rather a team of Tergre aliens. They were expressive little creatures that topped out around four feet. They had long anteater noses and soft fur in varying shades of brown, cream, and sometimes green.

Compared to the insectoid Spo, they were downright adorable, and they gave off a strangely familiar scent, rather like wet grass and wet dog.

Usually microphones and cameras swung around him like Spo scavenger birds, and cords snaked across the floor in makeshift river systems, but the Tergre system was more streamlined. They had a number of cameras, but they were small drones, hovering and moving on their own.

The two Tergre were on stools that put them at the same height as Sam. The paler one rubbed its tan fur and wiggled its anteater nose. It made noises that were the Tergre equivalent of vocal warm-ups, a kind of alien tongue-twister. The other one was a darker brown, with a green tint around its eyes. Sam wondered if the fur grew green, or they had some kind of algae or fungi growing in there like a sloth.

One of the cameras flew close to Nat's face as she cleaned her glasses, and she waved it away. "Too close, please," she said. "We don't want pictures taken up our noses."

One of the Tergre twizzled a small laugh. "And no wonder," he said.

He spoke in his language, actually, but Sam's glasses put a translation in the heads-up display. Nat and Sam both wore computerized glasses now with a display screen and a tiny camera embedded in the frames. They were connected to Akemi.

She was safely installed in the Spo space station where the biobank that housed what was left of her mind would be safe. She could communicate with the station computers, but she could also communicate through the glasses.

These Tergre love sensational journalism, so be careful. Akemi sent to Sam. *I'm watching some of their older feeds, and it's a mix of talk show TV and Gossip Girl.*

"Hm, good to know," Sam said.

With small barks and toots, the Tergre informed them that it was time to start. Two of the hovering cameras lit up while the others hung back.

"We are here with two of the newest species to the Galactic Council, the humans!" said the dark Tergre. "Don't let their flat, hairless faces fool you, they are smarter than they look. In one of the most watched trials in the last century, the humans turned the tables on the prosecutors."

"That's right," said the pale Tergre. "With stunning evidence, riveting cross-examination, and a twist ending, you'll never guess what they're doing next. Watch and pledge to find out the rest."

Nat spoke under her breath. "We've been reduced to click-bait journalism."

But very successful *click-bait journalism,* Akemi sent to them both.

"Now, this young human is Sam Locklear, a Spo cadet graduate and the new *ruler of Earth and humanity!*"

"Yikes, no," Sam said, "I'm only a representative, which is very different. We're in the process of forming a newly elected group, the Human Coalition Government. They will be in charge of Earth."

"They fired you from the position already? How ungrateful!" The Tergre looked toward a camera. "Answer our live poll! Should Sam Locklear be angry: yes or *absolutely* yes?"

"Er—I'm not angry," Sam protested. "This is a good thing."

"But, Sam Locklear, will the Coalition Government honor the Rik treaty? That is what the universe wants to know. Do those scum still have a sponsor?"

"I don't know that *scum* is the best word—"

Nat snorted softly; she was not a fan of the Rik. "It's not the worst word."

The Tergre laughed. "It is not! Here we have Natsuki Fujimara, another Spo cadet graduate and *mate* of Sam Locklear."

"Nope, she's not that either," Sam said quickly...

Read more in: *Dreamers,* Book 2 of the Alien Cadets!

ABOUT THE AUTHOR

Cornelia Clark is the science fiction and fantasy penname of author Corrie Garrett. In all her stories, from historical romance to speculative fiction, her characters always face impossible odds, build deep friendships, and find lasting love. She lives in the beautiful hills of West Virginia with her husband and four kids, and some of her favorite hobbies are reading, hiking, and poking her fluffy cat with her toes. Cautiously, of course.

www.ingramcontent.com/pod-product-compliance
Lightning Source LLC
Chambersburg PA
CBHW030648020726
47493CB00006B/1927